Where We Fall

Nicole Baker

Contents

Chapter One

Lexi

This damn coding is going to be the death of me. I've been sitting here for hours trying to determine the disconnect between the two systems. It's clearly a coding issue, but I've been at this for so long that my brain seems to have given up on me.

The dark sky illuminates my screen in my office, just another reminder that I should be at home, not sitting here alone trying to figure this out.

My eyes are starting to see double on the screen.

I push my chair away from the desk.

"Okay, Lexi," I say to myself. "When you start to go cross-eyed, you need a break."

I stand up, take off my glasses, and stretch my arms over my shoulders to work out the stiffness. Leaning my head to one side, I try to work out the kink in my neck. A loud sequence of cracks echoes through the room.

I need a massage. Endless hours spent behind a computer do a number on me.

My phone lights up on my desk. My friend Grace's name flashes across the screen.

"The kids must be in bed," I say after I answer.

She groans into the phone. "Girl, they took longer than usual tonight. Matt had to work late again so I was on my own. Layla came out of her room like twenty times when I was trying to put Addy to bed, which just got Addy more wound up."

"It's like they know it's just you at night, so they make it ten times harder."

I sympathize with her. Matt is an attorney and has many late nights in his office trying to find his angle to work for his cases.

Grace and I went to high school together. We've been friends ever since, even though she's in Chicago where we grew up, and I moved to Cleveland for work.

"Don't get me started. I tell Matt that all the time. He thinks I'm being paranoid. He doesn't think the girls are old enough to be that manipulative."

I laugh into the phone. "He doesn't know how young that starts. Or he just doesn't want to think of his sweet little angels being anything but perfect."

"He's screwed when they become teenagers."

"Completely," I agree.

"What are you up to tonight?" she asks.

Now it's my turn to groan because I know what's coming.

"Alexandra Miller," my best friend scolds. "Tell me you're not at the office at ten o'clock at night."

"Fine. I'm not at the office."

"Liar," she responds to my sarcasm.

"Well, I need to get these two interfaces talking correctly so our orders can continue to run smoothly. It's actually an emergency this time."

"Uh, huh. That's what you always say. When was the last time you went out and had fun...or went on a date?"

I roll my eyes as I sit back down in my computer chair. "Let's not have this conversation again. I've already told you I'm focused on my career."

"I wonder why," she mumbles.

"I heard that."

"Yeah, well, maybe I wanted you to hear it. You're twenty-eight, you don't have forever to find someone. I just don't want you to wake up one day and realize your time to have kids has come and gone. You know, men aren't the enemy. Despite what your mom says."

My head falls back in my chair. Sometimes I feel like I'm being pulled in two different directions by two of the most important people in my life.

Grace is always trying to get me to settle down and start a family. Which I get, she's found someone and is happy, but it might not be in the cards for everybody.

On the other hand, my mother constantly reminds me that you can't trust anybody but yourself. Her words play in my head when I'm working my ass off to continue to rise up in my career.

My dad left us when I was five. He left for some twenty-something year old, deciding he no longer needed to take care of the first family he started.

"My mom has good intentions and has some valid points."

"But she was always miserable. That should have been a sign that you may not want to listen to everything she tells you. I love your mom, but I just don't want you to resent her later in life when you realize she led you down the wrong road because of her jaded view on love."

I feel a headache begin to form as I listen to her words, knowing she also has a point.

"I know. I'm gonna work on having a more balanced life. I promise," I tell her, half serious, half full of shit and just wanting to shut her up.

"I don't believe you."

"Let's talk about something else. I need to get back to work soon, and I want to focus on something happy. Like how Addy and Layla are doing. Does Layla like preschool?"

While Grace chats about the girls, I do my best to focus and listen even as my brain goes back to what she said earlier.

I never meant to get to this point in my life where I've never had a serious relationship. It just kind of...happened. I was so focused on my grades in college.

Sure, I went out with my friends. I even had a guy here and there spend a couple of nights in my sheets. Nothing about them lit me on fire, made me feel like I had to have them. They just died out on their own.

I look over at my framed college diploma hanging on the wall of my office, seeing my reflection through the glass. Hair up in a ponytail, not the sexy ponytails some women pull off, glasses, no makeup—nothing special.

I guess I've been able to blend into the scenery since I graduated. No one notices me.

That's because you dress so that nobody will *notice you.*

Ugh, I shouldn't care about this. It's like my mom said: if you dress like half the women today do, you're going to attract the wrong type of men. Men like my father.

But does that mean I should be dressing like a six-ty-year-old? Baggy blouse, slacks that don't hug any part of my body, colorless face.

"She drew a picture of cookies with a glass of wine on the side." I hear as I bring myself back to the conversation.

"Wait...what? A glass of wine next to cookies?" I ask with a laugh.

"Oh my god, it's so damn humiliating. She told her teacher it's her mommy's favorite drink."

I fall forward laughing as I rest my hand on my desk.

"That is the funniest thing I've heard in a long freakin' time. I can't believe she said that. You can't get in like...trouble or anything with the school for that. Can you?"

"God, no. Her teacher gave me a look of understanding. It's still not my proudest moment as a mom."

"I think it's a moment of pure honesty. We need more of that today."

"Yeah, I don't know. My girls are too honest sometimes."

I smile as I think of what those girls have said over the years.

My computer screen goes dark, reminding me I have been away from my work for too long.

I sigh. "I wish I could keep talking, but I really should get back to work. Thanks for calling. I miss you."

"Miss you more. I'll talk to you soon."

"Bye, Grace."

I spend the next ninety minutes figuring out where the coding went wrong, then fixing it so that the two programs are able to communicate seamlessly with one another.

I close my laptop, take it off the docking station, and then put it in one of my office drawers before I lock it with a key from my keychain.

I routinely grab my purse, switch off the lights, and close my door. I walk past Marcus' office, one of the owners here at Giannelli Family Selections. He's the youngest of the four siblings, and just so happens to be down this part of the hallway by my office along with our Marketing Director, Savannah. Savannah is married to one of the siblings, Luke.

Luke, Mia, and Gabe are on the other side of the hallway.

It's just the six of us in the office. They travel worldwide to find wines that they recommend and sell to restaurants and stores across America.

I've been here for over a year now. It's been a great experience, and everybody is welcoming. Sometimes the guys are a bit intimidating for me. They are without a doubt the best-looking men I've ever been around.

Mia is sweet but has a fire to her when she's passionate about something. I appreciate her drive and ability to stand up for herself and what she believes in. I wish I were more like her. She isn't afraid to be sexy and successful.

As I drive back to my apartment, I reflect on my conversation with Grace. I don't know why her words are sticking with me for so long this time. I can typically brush them off quickly.

Maybe it's because I'm settled in my career now and haven't done anything to switch my focus to my love life.

Truth is, I wouldn't even know where to start.

I moved to Cleveland over a year ago but still haven't found a group of girlfriends to go out with. Even if I did, I don't want to meet a guy at a bar.

Aside from going to work or the gym, I usually don't go anywhere else. Instead, I choose to travel to Chicago to see Grace and my family, or I fly to New York to see my college friend, Zoe.

How do people near thirty find someone to date? It's not like I'm in school and going out with friends every weekend and the thought of trying online dating makes me cringe.

Call me crazy, but my life is spent on a computer as an IT Director. I don't want my love life found on there as well.

I also don't find anybody in my league remotely attractive. I could never get somebody who looks like my bosses, but lanky guys with bad haircuts don't do it for me. Maybe that's why I've remained single all these years.

I could never get the attention of the type of man that would turn my head.

I pull into my apartment complex; it's pushing midnight, and I'm starving.

I can't agonize over this anymore tonight. I'm too exhausted and worrying about something I have no control over is a waste of energy.

Right now, all I want to do is put on my sweats and eat something horribly high in calories. I skipped lunch and dinner, not walking away from the computer for longer than a restroom break.

I deserve a big bowl of pasta with some garlic bread and a glass of Chianti.

One thing that has improved since working for this company is my taste in wine. They've sent me home with so many expensive bottles of wine that I'll never have to buy my own for the rest of my life.

I haven't wanted to waste the bottles drinking them mindlessly, not understanding what it is that I have the privilege of drinking. So, I make sure to research each bottle, discover the region it came from and learn about the wine itself.

The next bottle on my list is this twenty-seventeen Chianti from a small farm in Italy.

Screw love, all I need are carbs, cozy clothes, and a bottle of wine.

Chapter Two

Marcus

I punch my counter as the coffee machine blinks a red light that means fucking nothing to me.

"Dammit! I don't know what that means. Just give me some *fucking* coffee!" I scream at the machine.

This day is gonna be shit, I can tell already.

I glance down at my watch. I have ten minutes to get to work on time. I throw my unused mug in the sink.

I guess I'll just get some coffee at the office.

I have a morning meeting with my siblings, so I drive a little more aggressively through traffic and pull into the parking lot with one minute to spare.

I'll drop my things off in the meeting room and tell them I need to grab a cup of coffee first. They'll just have to deal with it. I refuse to sit through that meeting without some caffeine pumping through me.

I walk through the impressive wooden doors of our office. Sometimes I still can't believe we made it this far. My siblings and I started a wine distribution company six years ago, and today, it's a multimillion-dollar business that keeps growing by the day.

If someone told me this would be my life ten years ago, I would've laughed in their face. Things don't always work out the way you think they will. I thought I'd be a professional athlete until I tore my rotator cuff, and my dreams of being a pitcher in the MLB were over.

I turn the corner and head into the meeting room where my siblings are seated along with our IT Director. I wasn't aware that she would be a part of this meeting. The four of us rarely need to meet with her together, it isn't an efficient use of our time. That's basically our entire company, aside from Savannah.

The room is quiet as I enter.

What the hell is going on?

"Hi, guys. Sorry, I'm a bit late. My coffee machine went haywire this morning. I finally had to give up and go without."

"Not a problem. If you want to take a seat, we have something we need to discuss," Gabe, my eldest brother says with a grim.

I sit in the chair across from him, my sister Mia next to me, Luke on the right of Gabe, and Lexi on the left of him. All of a sudden, the idea of asking to get a cup of coffee first seems like a bad idea.

"What's going on?" I question. "Is everything alright?"

I see my siblings exchange a look, one that doesn't bode well for me.

"We have a situation," Mia starts. Whenever they want to soften the blow of bad news, they make Mia do it. I adjust myself in my seat as I prepare myself for her words. "William Hansley is considering not renewing his contract with us at the end of the year."

Now that gets my attention. Mr. Hansley is our largest client. He makes up nearly ten percent of our annual revenue. Losing him would be a huge loss to the company.

"Are you serious? Why would he be considering not renewing? We bend over backwards to make sure he gets everything he wants."

"You," Luke replies.

"What about me?"

"He is considering not renewing because of you."

"Me! What the hell did I do?"

Mia sighs. "Apparently on one of your trips to Chicago, you slept with his daughter's best friend. I think he said her name was Maggie." She shakes her head as if it's beside the point. "Either way, you never called her back even though you promised you would. He said he doesn't like to do business with people who don't share the same values as he does. He thinks your...lifestyle can tarnish his reputation if anyone finds out he does business with someone like you.

My body releases fire into my veins. Who does this man think he is? Thinking he has me figured out by a one-chance encounter with his daughter's friend.

"Is he for real? It's 2023; we do business with all kinds of people with different views and opinions. Why does my sex life matter to him? And for the record, I *never* told her I would call her. I don't make promises I don't intend on keeping."

"You know how some of these men are. Their values are old school and they worry about their image," Gabe says.

"Whatever. It's not an excuse to act like I'm some scumbag he can't fathom doing business with."

"I agree. He's being a bit ridiculous," Gabe continues. "But you do also tend to get into trouble on your business trips. I've had to warn you plenty of times to keep it in your pants on your many trips to Italy."

I don't understand what the big deal is. I'm thirty and single. So, I have some occasional fun on business trips. They're acting like it's all the time, like I'm some man whore, and I'm absolutely not.

"You're exaggerating, and it's kind of pissing me off. I've taken like fifty trips to Italy, and I've slept with two women when I was there."

"Well, then I guess it's your choice of women because those two women were clients' daughters. You're lucky they know how to keep their mouths shut."

"Look," Mia cuts us off. "Let's not get sidetracked here. What we need is a solution. Mr. Hansley's annual fundraiser is in two weeks, and we need to make him see that it's just a misunderstanding of character.

I raise my eyebrow at my sister, unsure where she's going with this.

Luke leans in to speak. "Marcus, you need to show up at that fundraiser with a date. You need to play up how happy and in love you are with her. Maybe if he believes you've seen the error of your ways, he'll stay on with us," he explains. "I'm sorry man, it's the only way we could think to turn this around."

I lean forward, mirroring Luke, and rest my elbows on the table, not sure if I heard him correctly.

"I'm sorry. Are you telling me that instead of standing up for your brother, instead of being honest with this man and telling him that I'm not the guy he thinks I am, you're going to make me grovel and pretend I'm in love with someone?"

Gabe rubs the back of his neck. "Come on, man. Don't be like that. Of course, we tried to tell him, but he's a stubborn man. He won't listen. It's just for one evening. You know we can't afford to lose this account."

I rub my eyes with my fingers as my head begins to ache. Lack of caffeine and stress will do that to you.

"There's gotta be a better way. I shouldn't have to parade around with some stranger on my arm, pretending to feel things that I don't."

"Well," Mia says as her voice raises an octave. "She doesn't have to be a stranger."

Her eyes move from mine to Lexi's then back to me again.

It takes me a minute to understand what she's suggesting. When it hits me, a laugh escapes.

"You can't be serious. You don't want me to go with, *Lexi*?"

Lexi's eyes widen like *she* just realized what Mia's suggesting.

"Wait, what? I don't think that's such a good idea," Lexi protests.

"You didn't even *ask* her before bringing her into this meeting?" My mouth drops.

I look over at Lexi and realize she is every bit in the dark as I am. I fall back into my chair, rubbing my hand over my face.

"It seems like our best option," Gabe says sternly. He's the oldest in this room, and whenever he steps in, everybody listens. I know I'm screwed. I'm going to end up saying yes to this whole ordeal if Gabe is on board. "Trust me, man. I hate this just as much as you do. I wouldn't dare to even think of asking the two of you if I hadn't thought it over a million times. I just think it's the best way to settle his nerves for a little while. I really don't think it will be that hard. Lexi, you were already scheduled to attend the event anyway, since it's your hometown and all. It will be no different, except when you talk to the guy, pretend you're in love. It's not like the two of you have to spend the entire evening with each other."

I guess he does have a point. The evening won't be much different.

I steal a glance over at Lexi.

Shit, there's no way William's going to believe it. She's not the type of girl I'd ever go for.

Don't get me wrong, she's sweet and a huge asset to our team, I just don't think of her in that way.

It's like she's actively trying to be invisible, undesirable to the opposite sex. Her clothes always seem two sizes too big. Her hair is always effortlessly up, but not in a sexy way. More like in a *I didn't have time to do anything with it so this was my only option* way. I've never seen her wear makeup, or color at all for that matter, and her glasses are always sliding down her nose.

She starts to squirm under my eyes. I don't think she would be very comfortable pretending to be in love with me either.

"Well, what do you say?" Gabe says, bringing my attention back to him.

I exhale. "Fine. I'll do it."

"And Lexi, we're so sorry. We were going to ask you at our meeting yesterday, but you got tied up with working on the software reconfiguration and had to cancel. What do you say?" Mia's shoulders lift.

Lexi pushes up her glasses, looks at me for a brief second, and then back to Mia.

"I'll do it. If it'll help the company. I don't want you guys to lose your largest client."

"Perfect. Thank you so much for doing this. Both of you." Mia looks between the two of us.

I nod my head and stand up abruptly. I need a cup of coffee and some ibuprofen, stat.

I'm sure I'm overreacting to this news, but it feels so typical of my life. Just another person in this world who doesn't understand me or labels me as whatever they see fit.

I've heard it my whole life.

Marcus, the funny one, the idiot, the screw-up, the troublemaker. I'm normally pretty good at laughing it off, but I just can't do it this time. It generally doesn't crossover into business, unless it's a subtle joke from a sibling.

This is a client, and he thinks he has me figured out because I slept with someone and didn't call them.

And what about Maggie? She slept with me after only knowing me for a couple of hours. Why am I the prick in this situation?

After I grab my coffee, I head into my office and close the door. I need a second to myself.

And poor Lexi, getting dragged into this mess. I feel bad for her. She's too sweet and innocent to feel pressured into doing this to save my ass. Not to mention, I'm not sure she won't have the slightest clue how to pretend to be in love.

Come to think of it, neither will I. We're both in way over our heads.

I just hope that William doesn't want to talk our ears off. Maybe we can get away with a quick conversation where I introduce Lexi as my girlfriend, but he'll see right through us if we're with him for too long. Either way, I'm going to have to put a game plan together to figure out how to make this impossible fake relationship look real.

Chapter Three

Lexi

"You're kidding me, right?" Zoe asks over the phone.

"No, freakin' joke. I'm supposed to pretend to be his girl-friend. You should've seen the look on his face when he found out it was me he had to pretend to be head over heels in love with. It was pure disgust," I say as I recall our meeting this morning.

Zoe was my roommate in college and has remained a close friend of mine, even though she lives in New York City now. I call her about everything.

Ugh, just thinking about Marcus' reaction makes me cringe.

"Now you're just being ridiculous. Disgust is an awfully strong word. You're beautiful, even if you don't know it."

I sigh. "You know that's not true."

"I don't wanna hear it. I've seen you in your birthday suit; you've got a killer body. You just don't show it off enough."

"Well, either way, he clearly wasn't thrilled with the idea of having *me* on his arm at the event."

"Is he hot?"

"Zoe!"

"What? That's a perfectly legitimate question."

A small laugh escapes me. "Fine. Yes, he's ridiculously attractive. Completely out of my league, though, so don't even go there."

I know my friends love me and will always shower me with compliments, but sometimes I prefer honesty. And the cold, hard truth is that Marcus would never go for a woman like me. I'm okay with that. From what I can tell, he's a serial player with no intention of changing anytime soon.

I do, however, think that the client is being utterly absurd just because he found out one of the owners slept with *one* chick and didn't call her back.

I'm with Marcus on this one. Why is *he* the bad guy here? She willingly slept with him after only knowing him for a couple of hours. If she had expectations for a man she knew nothing about, that's on her. I would never sleep with a man that soon in the first place.

Now Marcus has to grovel to this guy like he did something wrong.

And it's always these older, rich men like William Hansley who cheat on their wives behind closed doors but pretend to be superior. They withhold judgment on themselves, and instead, place it on everyone else around them.

If it sounds like I'm bitter, it's my mother's fault. After my dad left, the amount of remarks I've heard about the evilness of men could fill an entire book.

"I'm not even going to address that comment. Nobody is out of your league. Where is this event? Pleeease say New York!"

"I wish! It's Chicago. But it's good, cuz I'll get to visit my mom."

"Oh, yeah. How's she doing?"

A knot forms in the pit of my stomach. "She's alright, I guess. Has good days and bad days. I'm just trying to enjoy the good days and not focus on the bad ones."

"I'm sorry. I hate that she can't remember things sometimes. It must be so tough."

"It is," I say as my eyes get misty. "She's only sixty-five. I just didn't expect to lose her this early. Not that she's gone. Although, sometimes, it feels like she is."

As much as my mother has filled me with bitterness and resentment, I still love her. She raised me on her own. She showered me with love and affection. She's only trying to protect me. I know there's good intentions behind all her craziness.

It hurts like hell to see her withering away at such a young age. I know sixty-five isn't thirty, but it isn't eighty either. I thought we would have more time. Young-Onset Dementia is an evil disease that slowly takes its victims away from their loved ones.

"Just tell me if you need anything. If you're tied up at work, I could always fly to Chicago to visit her."

This is why Zoe is so amazing. She is so selfless, always offering her time and resources to help someone she cares about. She's one of the best, and I'm lucky enough to have met her.

"Thanks. That means a lot. Let's hope it never comes to that. Work has been really good so far about letting me work remotely if I need to get back home for a couple of days."

"So, the boss man is hot and a good guy. Hmmm."

I roll my eyes as I walk to my kitchen to get a glass of water before bed. This girl needs to focus on her own love life and let me worry about my own.

"On that note, I'm going to bed."

She laughs. "I love how worked up you get. I'll talk to you soon."

"Sounds good. Goodnight."

"Night, girl."

I can't help but smile as I walk down the hallway and into my bathroom.

I take off my glasses and wash my face. I have always made an effort to keep a good skincare routine.

As I look in the mirror, I try to see what my friends see. I'm wearing black pajama pants and a white t-shirt. Nothing sexy at all. I notice the shine of my skin. I guess I do have good skin. I don't need to wear much foundation, and my eyelashes are naturally long. I'm sure if I used makeup, I could make some of my features pop. I've also been told I have nice lips.

I wonder what it would be like to be the object of someone like Marcus' desires. My body tingles just thinking about it.

For someone who always puts their career before men, I find myself reaching for my vibrator in my nightstand regularly. I have a big appetite for enjoying a good release; I just like to do it on my own.

What would it be like to have someone like Marcus give me a release? I bet he's someone who knows exactly what to do to drive a girl crazy.

I somehow managed to finish the rest of the week without seeing or talking to anybody in the office.

Correction. I avoided everybody like it was the damn plague, then spent the weekend hiding away from reality in my apartment. I think I ate my feelings away with cheesecake and pasta. Well, I tried to eat away my feelings. Come Sunday morning, I felt like complete junk, so I went outside for a long run and then forced myself to do fifty burpees.

It's now Monday morning, and we leave this Friday for the event on Saturday.

I'm seriously starting to doubt that we can pull this off.

I look at my screen for what feels like the hundredth time without progressing in my current task. I can't seem to focus.

A knock at my door pulls me from my thoughts.

Crap! I guess I can only hide from everybody for so long.

"Come in!" I shout.

The door opens quickly, and Marcus struts in wearing his expensive blue suit with his crisp white shirt and brown leather shoes. He is incredibly handsome.

This is the first time we've had to be one-on-one since the meeting. I have no idea how to act. I can feel the blood pumping in over time through my body, making me feel clammy and hot.

He smiles like he doesn't have a care in the world, then takes a seat in front of my desk.

"Hey there, Lexi," he says casually. "I've been meaning to get with you ever since our meeting. I guess our schedules haven't synced up."

"Oh, yeah, I've been pretty busy. Trying to get as much of this project done before we leave."

Liar! You're just too chicken shit to face him.

"I hear you. There's always work to be done. We appreciate you coming to the event on Saturday. I realize it's not paid time, but you're a large part of our success, and why we're able to manage such a large quantity of orders. It will be nice for you to share in the fun of these events and indulge in the food and drinks."

His words make me blush. All he did was compliment my work within the company, and I'm blushing like he told me I was the most beautiful woman he's ever laid eyes on.

"It's really no problem. I'm honored that you value me enough to want me there. Plus, I get to see my mom."

"Oh, yeah. She's sick, isn't she? Alzheimer's?"

I nod my head. "Something like that."

"I'm sorry to hear that. I'm sure it must be tough. My Ma is like my best friend; I'd be lost without her. So I can only imagine. If you ever need anything, extra time off, or anything, please don't hesitate to let us know."

"That's very generous. Thank you. Mia has been great with understanding when I need to go back and forth during the week."

He cringes at my words. "Mia is like the Momma Bear of our group. I'm sorry if I ever came off as inconsiderate. I assure you, Mia asks us first before she approves your requests. It's always a unanimous yes. If there's anything we Giannelli's understand, it's the need to put family first."

"It's made working far from home incredibly easy. I appreciate it."

Silence falls upon the room, and an elephant creeps in. Which one of us is going to address that in five days, we have to pretend like we are in love?

"So, uh," he starts as he pulls at the back of his neck, "I've been thinking about this arrangement we have coming up." My stomach feels like it's on a rollercoaster ride, waiting for the next loop. "First, I wanna thank you for agreeing to this. I hate that my actions have caused trouble for the company. I hope we didn't put you in a weird spot. It's not like my siblings to ask such a thing of anyone. That must show how desperately we need to hang on to this account."

"I'm happy to help. And just for the record, I think it's ridiculous that this man thinks he knows you based on one night."

He seems surprised by my words and then shrugs his shoulders. "I'm used to being the bad guy. It's a role I've come to accept."

It feels like there's more to the story. I wonder why he feels that way about himself. I wouldn't have ever called him the bad guy. He certainly has more personality than his siblings. He's always smiling and joking around.

Now is definitely not the time to ask him to elaborate on that, if ever. It's not like we're friends or anything.

"Well, whether you're used to it or not doesn't make it right."

He smiles. "I knew I liked you, Lexi."

An easy laugh escapes. He's starting to make me feel at ease about this whole thing. Maybe it won't be so bad.

"Anyway," he continues. "I...was thinking...maybe we do lunch this week and get our story straight. Just in case we get asked any questions about our...*relationship*."

He clearly struggled to get that word out, even knowing that it's not real. An odd sense of disappointment washes over me.

"Yeah, that sounds smart. We don't want to be caught red-handed. That would be humiliating, and almost guarantee you to lose your client." I look down at my calendar for the week. "I can do lunch tomorrow or Thursday."

"I think tomorrow is good. And while we're out...maybe...we can..." he's stuttering over his words. "Fuck, okay. I'm just gonna say it. I really want to make this thing between us look believable. Maybe we can go dress shopping together. There's also a salon nearby if you want to check it out with me."

Oh my god! He's trying like hell to say it as nicely as he can. I can feel my face begin to heat up.

"Oh, umm, yeah. Sure. We can do that," I try to say as casually as I can.

"I'm sorry, Lexi. This is horribly uncomfortable, I know. I'm just trying to make sure we pull this off."

He looks mortified that he's having this conversation with me right now. I almost feel for the guy.

"No, I get it."

I look down at my hands, clutching the edge of my seat so hard that they're turning white.

He doesn't say anything for a while.

"Okay," he says loudly. I look up and see him sitting straighter in his seat. "We're not gonna let this be awkward. We're gonna have fun. You get to go dress shopping, and some other clothes in case they ask us to dinner over the weekend. It's all on the company's dime. I'll drink champagne while you model for me. It'll be like our own little Pretty Woman experience."

"Except I'm not a prostitute," I say with a small smile.

He laughs. "Yeah, sorry. No prostitution in our version. So, what do you say? Lunch and a shopping spree on me tomorrow?"

I nod. "Sounds good."

"Good. I'll make a reservation for lunch tomorrow."

He pats my desk with a lopsided grin on his face, then walks out of my office.

I'm not sure what the hell just happened. I think I just agreed to a makeover from my boss. Shit, what the hell did I get myself into?

Chapter Four

Marcus

"Order whatever you want," I tell Lexi as we sit down at the restaurant. "It's on me."

She gives me a shy nod and thanks me.

Yesterday was quite possibly the worst day of my life. I hated having to suggest a makeover. But I also know that the stakes are high, and we can't risk it with this client. It still didn't make the look of embarrassment that flashed across her face any less painful to see.

I wanted to back out of it and tell her I was joking, but a joke about a makeover seemed ten times crueler.

It's not like she has nothing appealing about her. I can tell underneath the glasses there's a pretty face. I'm not an idiot. But she needs to look like someone who is confident enough to be on my arm. I think if she felt like she looked the part, she might come out of her shell a bit.

We need to look comfortable together.

"Alright," I clap my hands together, "tell me something about yourself."

She takes a sip of her iced tea then puts it down and leans forward on her elbows.

"That's such a broad question. Like what?"

I match her posture and lean forward myself.

"Anything. What were you like in high school? Was computer class your favorite?" I joke.

She smiles at me. I never noticed how pretty her smile was. Maybe it's because I've never paid attention. Her lips are nice and plump.

"No, I was into volleyball in high school."

"Volleyball, huh? I remember going to the training room before and after football practice just to watch the volleyball players through the window of the gym. Spandex was my kryptonite."

Lexi lets out a small but uninhibited laugh. I decide I like making her laugh. It feels like an accomplishment coming from her.

"Why does that sound so in character for you?" she jokes.

"Hey." I smile as I hold my hands up. "I never promised to be a perfect gentleman. But seriously, how can they expect to put high school girls in those shorts and *not* have the boys go crazy?"

"True. It was unfortunately something we dealt with at our high school. So, you played football?"

"I did. But my true passion was baseball. I was a pitcher."

"Ah. I can see you being a baseball player. You have the build for that."

Huh, I wonder if that's her telling me she's noticed my body. I don't want to make her feel uncomfortable though, so I keep my mouth shut.

"It was my world for the longest time. I played in college until I got injured. My plan was to make it to the MLB, but fate had other plans."

She looks at me, holding my eyes with such sincerity that I almost need to look away.

"I'm really sorry that happened to you."

"It's nothing." I shrug.

"It's not nothing. You had a dream, and it got taken away from you. Why would you say it's nothing?"

Why am I acting like it's nothing?

"I don't know. I guess I think I'm supposed to say that. My alternative turned out to be pretty great. I'm living a life most people could only dream of."

"Still doesn't mean you should shrug it off like it didn't affect you."

Our food shows up while we are talking. I realize either the chef is working magic back there, or I was so into our conversation that I haven't realized how much time has passed.

I take a bite of my parmesan garlic fry.

"It definitely affected me. I fell into a pretty deep depression for about a year. Drank my entire senior year of school, almost didn't graduate."

"Well, I'd say you landed on your feet."

"I'd say so. What about you? When did you know IT was your world?"

She thinks about her answer as she chews. I can't help but watch her.

"My sophomore year in college. I was going down the direction of Finance, like most people do when they have no clue what they want to do. I happened upon an IT course for business and loved it. I realized I was good at it too."

"You are good at it. I'm constantly amazed at how your brain works. You have so much patience. The way you can sit there for hours looking at a bunch of jumbled up letters and numbers, I'd go crazy."

She covers her mouth as she laughs. "I like your description of my job. A bunch of jumbled letters and numbers."

"Thanks." I smile. "Feel free to steal it and use it on your resume. Not that I want you updating your resume."

Shit, that's not what I meant.

"Don't freak out over there. I knew what you meant."

She smiles so genuinely at me. It feels like we've already taken a step towards being more comfortable with each other.

The rest of the meal passes by quickly. By the time I've paid, I realize we never got around to planning our story for Saturday. I guess we will while we shop.

We park at the mall near the restaurant and start to head inside. I have a personal shopper waiting for us at the department store. I want to make sure Lexi has the help that she needs and feels comfortable.

Once I give the woman at the nearest counter my name, we are escorted to a private changing area. There's a large couch with a mirror that takes up one of the walls. There's a curtain across from the couch, presumably the changing room.

"Mr. Giannelli?" an older woman, maybe fifty, says as she walks into the back room.

I put my hand out. "You can call me Marcus."

She takes my hand and offers me a warm smile. "Marcus. You can call me Trudy."

"Trudy. This is Lexi."

"Lexi. I hear we have some gowns we need to find for you as well as some other odds and ends that can accommodate a couple of different occasions."

Lexi's cheeks turn a light shade of pink. I do my best to fight off a smirk.

Trudy starts to lead Lexi out of the room to begin selecting gowns to try on.

I'm about to take a seat on the couch when Lexi stops and looks at me.

"You're not coming with us?" she asks, sounding slightly disappointed.

I stop myself from sitting and stand up straight.

"Do you want me to?"

She nods her head.

I smile. "Well, let's get this party started then."

She bites the inside of her cheek, but I know she wanted to smile. I laugh behind her, loving her reactions. Making her laugh is going to become my new goal in life.

Then I see her shake her head in front of me as she continues to follow Trudy, and I laugh even harder.

"Okay, so what are we thinking? Long or short?" Trudy stops and turns to us.

Lexi turns to me to answer the question.

"In the past, most women were in long dresses."

"Okay. What size are you, dear?"

Lexi begins to fidget with her hands behind her back.

"Umm, I'm a four."

Trudy seems to do a double take at Lexi, like she doesn't believe her.

"Well, let's start over here. We will pull together some classic black dresses then maybe some statement pieces. How about this one?"

She pulls at the fabric of a black dress that has thicker straps at the shoulders. It seems plain in my opinion, but I also don't know how comfortable Lexi would be in something that showed off more of her body.

"I think we can pull it as an option," I say. "What do you think?"

Lexi shrugs. "It looks nice."

I realize quickly that Lexi isn't going to open up and give her opinion easily. As we walk through the dress section, I pull things and hand them to Trudy. There's a wide range of options. Surely, one of the dresses will work.

Once we get back to the changing area, I take a seat on the couch.

"Alright. Let's get this fashion show started," I say with a smile on my face then proceed to sing the Pretty Woman song.

Trudy giggles while Lexi glares at me and rolls her eyes.

Okay. Make that two reactions I like to pull from Lexi. Laughter and annoyance. She's always so buttoned up at work. It's nice to get a different reaction from her.

"Let's start with the simple black one," I hear Trudy tell Lexi.

Since there's nothing else to do while she's changing, I pull out my phone and try to get caught up on my emails. I scroll through the emails I'm copied on to see if I need to respond or delete it. A cluttered inbox gives me massive anxiety. It's one thing I always make sure I keep up with, even on the weekends or vacation.

I hear the curtain yank open as Trudy walks back into the dressing room like she has a sixth sense.

"Well, that's nice," Trudy says.

I look over at Lexi. I'm surprised to see her delicate arms and small waist emphasized in the dress. In the time she's worked for us, I don't believe she's wore anything but oversized long-sleeved blouses.

The dress flows out from her high waist, not showing off any other part of her body. It goes all the way up to her neck and wraps around it. It looks good, but not sexy.

Trudy stands there and studies it further.

"What do you think?" she asks Lexi.

Lexi looks down at herself. "I don't know. It's okay. It feels a bit..." she struggles for the words.

"Boring," Trudy finishes for her. "You're clearly hiding quite the body underneath those clothes. Let's try something a little more exciting."

Trudy follows her into the dressing room and pulls the curtain back, eyeing me with a strange smile on her face.

Weird, but whatever. I go back to my emails when Trudy steps out from behind the curtain first.

"This one is much better," she says. Trudy turns back to Lexi. "Get out here, honey. You look stunning."

Lexi walks out slowly, and I momentarily forget to breathe. She is standing in a light pink dress that hugs *every* part of her body while dipping in a small V-shape in the front. Her breasts are large, but not too big, and are complemented perfectly with her tiny little waist.

Shit, how the hell did I not know she had a body like that?

She's not wearing her glasses and her hair is down. It's longer than I expected, falling in waves down to her breasts.

She shifts from one foot to the other, looking a bit uncomfortable.

I try to speak but need to clear my throat first. "It looks really good, Lexi."

"You think so? It's not too snug?" she asks as she looks at herself in the mirror.

I shake my head. Fuck no, it's not too much anything. It's damn perfect.

"Oh, you haven't seen the back yet." Trudy interrupts our eye contact. "Turn around."

Lexi turns around so we can take a look. The second I get a glimpse, I feel my dick twitch in my pants.

Fuck! I can't believe I'm reacting like this to...Lexi. Maybe my body is getting confused because it knows we have to pretend.

But damn, her dress dips all the way down to the top of her ass. Her back is sexy as hell. Perfectly feminine and elegant. Her muscles are defined and show just how in shape she is. There's a beauty mark just under her right shoulder blade. An image flashes in my brain of me kissing that mark as I make my way down her back.

"Are you okay?" Lexi asks as she looks over her shoulder.

"Huh?" I ask hoarsely.

"You look weird," she tells me.

"I'm fine." I shake my head and sit up straight to try and get some semblance of control back. "It's a great dress. I think you should get it."

I look over at Trudy who has a knowing look on her face. I don't know what that's about.

"You think so?" Lexi asks.

"I do. You look beautiful, Lexi," I tell her.

Her cheeks blush, and I try not to smile. Clearly, she isn't used to hearing those words. She would hear them every damn day if she dressed like this.

"I agree. This dress is *the* dress," Trudy chimes in.

Lexi smiles. "Okay. Well, that was easy."

"Now we need to find you some regular clothes. Marcus has instructed me to find business clothes, casual clothes like jeans, and laid-back workout attire."

"Are you sure about that?" Lexi looks to me.

I shrug. "You never know what we will be thrown into this weekend. It's best to be prepared. I'm gonna step out and make a few calls. You ladies enjoy yourselves."

I walk out of the room and make my way toward the doors to the parking lot. I need a breath of fresh air. This day is not going how I had planned, and it's throwing me a bit. Finding out my employee has a killer body that can make my dick react was nowhere on my agenda.

"It's fine," I tell myself.

I'm around pretty women all the time and can contain myself. This is no different. There is *nothing* different about Lexi.

Chapter Five

Lexi

This feels weird—so weird!

Finding a dress was easier than I thought. Sure, it was different to feel so exposed, but then Marcus looked at me like he *truly* appreciated what he saw. He even called me beautiful.

I never would've thought I could garner a reaction like that from a man like him. It made me feel slightly empowered. Even now as we walk from his car to the salon, I'm in a new set of slacks and a silk, cream shirt. Trudy practically forced me to wear it out of the store.

The rest of the clothes will be delivered to my place tomorrow.

Marcus is walking behind me but is oddly quiet.

"I was thinking about work and the new..." I turn around and see him trailing his eyes from my ass to my face. "Were you just looking at my ass?"

I can't see his full reaction behind his sunglasses.

"No!" he says a little too defensively.

I smile at him, and he matches it with his own shit-eating smirk.

"Just get in the damn salon, Lexi."

He holds the door open for me. My fun and playful mood vanishes, instantly feeling insecure. All the women who work there have perfect hair and makeup, making me feel like an ugly stray dog.

I stop in my tracks as my stomach starts to do flip-flops. I'm more nervous about this than I was about trying on clothes. That part suddenly seems easy.

Then I feel a warm, comforting hand on my back. "You're not climbing back into your shell now, are you?" Marcus whispers in my ear.

"I've never felt comfortable in salons," I admit to him.

Why did I just say that?

It makes me look so pathetic in front of someone like him. Someone who has probably never felt ugly or inadequate.

"Whatever words you're speaking to yourself right now," he continues. "They aren't true. Come on, this is supposed to be fun."

He takes my hand and leads me to the front desk.

"Hi, Lisa," he says enthusiastically.

At first, I think he knows everyone here by name, but I realize she's wearing a name tag.

She looks him up and down, not subtly might I add, then flutters her eyes and smiles.

"Hi. How can I help you today?" she says to him.

Ugh, gross. Part of me wants to wave my hands in the air and scream at her, "Ummm, what if he was my boyfriend...or husband? Have you no shame?"

Instead, I just stand here and watch her ogle him.

She looks like his type. Long blonde hair. A real live Barbie.

"We have a one o'clock appointment with Stacy," he tells her, not giving her any real attention.

He looks back at me and winks. I feel my cheeks blush and I touch them to see if they feel warm.

Crap! I think he noticed. He's smirking at me right now.

We are led to a chair in the back of the room. A petite redhead is smiling behind the chair as I approach.

"Hi, you must be Lexi. My name is Stacy." She motions for me to sit down. She looks at me through the mirror on the wall, Marcus standing off to the right with his arms crossed over his chest. "What are we going for today?"

Before I can panic, having no idea what to ask for, Marcus steps in.

"We have an event on Saturday. I figured you could take this already beautiful woman here and make her *feel* beautiful so she can walk in feeling confident. Nothing crazy or drastic. Just a little something to add to her natural look."

I want to punch him. I glare at him through the mirror. It was not necessary to lay it on so thick with comments of my "beauty."

"Oh, that'll be easy. I'll go mix up some colors. I'm gonna add some highlights to your hair. You have a nice dirty blonde color; some lighter highlights will make it pop and add some texture."

She walks away, leaving me with Marcus.

"I wasn't lying before," he says. "You're beautiful."

I'm starting to worry about how well he seems to read my thoughts.

"Just leave me alone. Go flirt with the front desk lady or something," I blurt out.

He laughs as he walks away. Ugh, he is a mixture of infuriating and sweet. The combination is confusing.

Two hours later, Stacy is blow-drying my hair after she cut in some layers. My ass hurts from sitting in this chair for so long, and even Stacy, who appears to be a chatterbox, is running out of things to talk about with me.

The blow dryer is giving us a break from forced conversation. I've never loved a blow dryer so damn much as I do at this moment.

Just when I think she's done, she pulls out a curling iron. I want to get a glimpse of how it looks, but she has me facing away from the mirror.

"Don't worry. We're almost done. It looks so good on you. Anna is waiting for you over in makeup," she says then gets to work with the curling iron.

I didn't realize that I was getting my makeup done. Although, that part I'm a little bit excited about. I've always been curious—thinking about all the colors of lipstick there are for me to explore.

I remember specifically watching my friend's mom always putting on a new shade of lipstick and wishing I was her.

Before I know it, Stacy places the iron back in its holder.

"Okay. I think you should wait to see the final product when your makeup is done," she squeals with excitement. "You look so gorgeous. Come on, follow me. No cheating and looking in a mirror on the way. Here, take my hand. Keep your head down, I'll lead you over there."

I can't help but laugh at her giddiness, but I give her my hand and follow her ridiculous instructions to keep my head down. She leads me to another section of the salon.

"Here, take a seat in this chair," she says. "Anna, she's ready. We're not letting her see herself until you're done. And don't you dare show her a mirror until you bring me back. I want to see her reaction."

After Stacy walks away, Anna and I start talking about makeup. There are so many different options between powder and liquid, color variety, skincare. By the time we're done, I've learned more than I did with the eighteen years I lived with my mom.

Anna moves on to applying my makeup. It's oddly relaxing to close my eyes and let her gently do her work. I almost fell asleep a couple of times.

"Okay, we're done," Anna breaks me from my trance. "Let me go get Stacy before you move. She'll kill me if I don't."

I smile, knowing that I've only just met Stacy, but it definitely sounds like her. She's got quite the personality on her, but I kinda love it. If I like my hair, I might continue coming to her. I like how she didn't force conversation if there were lulls. It was a comfortable silence.

Only seconds later, they are both walking back to me. Stacy's face lights up when she sees me.

"You're stunning! Seriously, Lexi. Oh my god, I wish I had your bone structure," Stacy says.

At this point, I feel like they're being a bit dramatic, and they do this to every client. If I had to pretend every client was so beautiful that I couldn't contain myself, I would never come to work. I'm not much for being anything but genuine.

"Okay, we're going to walk you over to this tall mirror in the corner of the room. Close your eyes again," Anna says, then puts her hand out for me to grab.

I follow her lead with my eyes closed until her hands stop me from walking any further.

"Okay, open them up girl," Stacy squeals.

I'm about to tell her she doesn't have to pretend with me when I open my eyes and catch a glimpse of a woman I've never seen before. I look closer into the mirror, wondering if it's a picture rather than a reflection of myself.

I mean, I know it's me. It looks like me, but at the same time—it doesn't.

The highlights draw my attention to my hair first. Stacy made my boring old color fun and edgy. The cut frames my face and has more body than I've ever been able to attain. But it's the makeup that gets me. It's so much more subtle than I was expecting—everything was done very naturally, but my face has never looked so good. My cheekbones pop, and my eyes are vibrant.

I don't think it's something I've noticed until now, but I must've looked like tired and old before. It's not until you see the alternative that the difference really hits you.

My favorite part of the whole thing has to be my lips. Painted red, the one feature that is not subtle, and I freaking *love* it. I've always been curious about lipstick, worrying that I'd look like a clown if I put it on, but it's so fun.

I won't be afraid to use such bold and daring colors from now on.

Couple these changes with my new outfit, and I'm officially blown away. I feel amazing.

Tears begin to prick my eyes as I the woman looking back at me makes me proud for the first time in a while. I'm not saying that I hated myself before, but I never prioritized my appearance. At the end of the day, it feels like all of this was for me and nobody else.

"Are you crying?" Stacy looks concerned. "Are you okay? Do you hate it?"

"No," I whisper as I shake my head. "I love it. Thank you."

"You're a natural beauty," she says.

"I'm just shocked to see myself like this," I admit to them.

"Like what?" Anna pushes me.

"I don't even know how to describe it. Not to get too personal, but my mom always told me looking like this attracted the wrong kind of guy. I got so accustomed to my minimal routine, that I didn't even realize what I was missing."

Stacy looks sad as I catch her eyes in the mirror. "Your mom's wrong."

"I know that now. This doesn't feel like it's for a guy, it feels like it's for me."

"It can be for both. There's nothing wrong with that," Anna adds.

She's right. She's *so* damn right.

"Well, come on. I think there's someone special up front who's dying to see you." Stacy gives me an eyebrow wag.

It takes me a minute to realize who she's talking about and what she's insinuating.

"Oh," I begin as we walk to the front. "He's not mine, or we aren't—he's my boss."

"We'll see about that," Stacy says mischievously.

When we get to the front, Marcus is sitting in one of the chairs looking preoccupied with his phone. I'm surprised he made it this entire time without losing his mind. Most men wouldn't be able to wait this long if it were their wife or girlfriend.

He looks up at us and then back down at his phone. I'm hit with a wave of disappointment. I was hoping for a bit more of a reaction from him.

Then it hits me, he didn't recognize me.

He's back to typing away at his phone like we aren't standing in front of him waiting for him to notice.

Stacy coughs while her shoe taps away on the hard floor. Marcus looks back up at us then does a double take at me.

His jaw falls open. His eyes drag slowly down my body from my feet up to my face then back down again.

I shift uncomfortably in place, waiting for someone to say something—anything. I'm not used to having attention on me, and Marcus being stunned into silence is unnerving. Lucky for me, he seems to recover with a small shake of his head.

"Damn!" he smiles as he stands up. "Is that my IT Director or a runway model?"

I roll my eyes. "Don't be dramatic."

He chuckles at himself, almost like I just imagined his reaction a moment ago.

Maybe I did.

"Let's go, Lexi. Let's see which one of my siblings falls out of their chair first when they see you."

"My money's on Luke," I tell him, granting me another deep laugh from him.

I like being the one to do that to him.

Marcus pays the front desk while Anna and Stacy say goodbye to me. Anna gives me the makeup she used on me as well as an entire bag of other eyeshadows and lipsticks. She assures me Marcus insisted he'll pay for whatever she thinks I should have.

Who knew agreeing to help the Giannelli's would result in so much free stuff? I want to feel guilty, but I can't, considering what I have to do on Saturday. I just hope I can pull it off.

Chapter Six

Marcus

I drain my second cup of coffee of the morning as I try my best to catch up on the work I didn't get done yesterday. Who knew it took so long to do hair and makeup?

The most concerning part of it all was realizing Lexi was the beauty standing in front of me. I recovered quickly—I hope.

How could I have been so blind to what was hiding underneath the baggy clothes and glasses?

But this is business, so I shook it off and moved to lighter territory. I've found a good joke or a foolish remark eases the tension in a room and I'm all about making everybody in the room feel at ease.

My siblings never meandered to our side of the hallway yesterday, so they never actually saw Lexi's new look.

Today is now Thursday and we leave for Chicago tomorrow. I have a mountain of work to get done to prepare for being out of the office early tomorrow. There never seems to be enough time in the day, but I love it. I thrive on being busy.

There's a light knock at my door.

I look up and see Lexi standing in front of me in one of the work outfits that her and Trudy must have picked out.

Fuck me, she looks good. This new Lexi is going to take some getting used to.

Honestly, I didn't think she'd wear the clothes or makeup until this weekend. I certainly don't want her to feel like this was some new requirement at work.

Dammit, now I feel bad about the whole thing. It's starting to nag at my conscious that maybe making her get a makeover was a dick move, but I don't know how to apologize.

It was an impulsive move on my part, and I didn't stop to consider how it would make her feel. But damn, the results are a little distracting.

She's wearing a tight, gray skirt with a black button-down shirt. The shirt is snug and neatly tucked in, showing off her breasts and trim waist. I'm surprised to see that she wore her hair down and her makeup is done pretty well. She's wearing lipstick again—accentuating her already full, luscious lips.

Yeah, I guess having an attractive co-worker is going to be the new norm for me, but I can take it. I'm attracted to plenty of women that I never develop feelings for.

"What're you doing here so early?" I ask as I glance down at my watch.

"I'm always here early," she says as she walks into my office.

"But you're always here late," I point out.

"True. It's the nature of the job. There's always some problem to fix in one of our systems that takes hours of research to figure out."

I never knew she worked so many hours.

I don't like it. She should've said something. That's not the kind of environment I want for my staff.

I make a mental note to look into adding to her department budget so she can hire staff underneath her.

I can't help but glance down at her skirt again.

"Are you going to be able to get that thing to budge enough to pee today?"

She starts to laugh. "I can't believe you said that. I was thinking the same thing when I was putting it on this morning."

My chest vibrates from laughter. "If you need help taking it off, you know who to call."

Another eye roll from her, which I enjoy immensely. "You're not my fake boyfriend yet."

"Ooh, so what are the rules when I am your fake boyfriend? Do I get to help you take off your clothes then?" I ask as I wag my eyebrows.

"Oh my gosh!" she laughs. "I see why we're in this mess in the first place."

I know it's a joke, all in good fun, but it's a sensitive topic for me. My smile falls from my face.

"I'm so sorry," she continues. "I didn't mean it like that."

"No, it's fine," I lie. "Anyway, I should get back to work. Mia is sending out all the details for the travel arrangements. Thanks again for doing this, Lexi. It means a lot to the company."

She nods her head, but I can tell she still feels bad for her comment. I'm in no mood to get into it right now, so I put my head down and get back to work.

Nearing lunchtime, I get a meeting invite from Mia for this afternoon. I swear, I can never get shit done because we're always having meetings. Reluctantly, I click accept without even reading what the damn thing is about. If I decline, Mia will storm in here and bust my ass anyways. It's not worth it.

I get as much work done as I can before my computer interrupts me with a fifteen-minute reminder for the meeting.

I walk into the conference room to find my siblings already there. Mia, Gabe, and Luke are sitting next to each other, so I take a seat across from them.

I'm about to say something when I see the three of them look like they've seen a ghost.

"Are you guys okay?" I ask, then hear something behind me.

Lexi is walking in, apparently part of today's meeting. Then it hits me, they haven't seen her new look yet.

I turn back around and try to hide the smirk on my face as I watch them fumble over themselves.

"Hi, sorry I'm late," Savannah, my sister-in-law, and Luke's wife, says as she walks in.

She's pregnant and has been dealing with some serious morning sickness and fatigue. My guess is she was either getting sick in the bathroom or was taking a nap in her office. It's been good entertainment to watch Luke freak out because he can't do anything to control the rollercoaster ride that pregnancy entails. Fatherhood is gonna be a big adjustment for him, but he's gonna kill it. He's great with our niece and nephew, Sienna and Joey, Gabe's kids.

Savannah looks over at Lexi, and she joins the room with big bug eyes.

"Holy shit," Savannah exclaims. "Lexi? Damn girl, you look hot!"

I chuckle in my seat. Savannah is the best. Since she isn't an owner of the company, she doesn't have to try and maintain any sort of image. She is free to be who she wants, and I love every part of it.

"Thanks, Savannah," Lexi smiles then surprises me when she pulls out the seat right next to me.

I look over at her and lift an eyebrow. "I don't think you've ever sat next to me before."

It looks like she's considering my words. "I guess so. Maybe it's because I know you a bit better and have realized there's not much to be intimated by. It's all a facade."

Luke chokes on his water, but his grin can't be contained.

"Touché." I nod at her.

I like this side of her. I don't know where it's been, but I hope we get to see more of it.

"So, Lexi and Marcus," Mia starts. "We wanted to get everybody in the same room so we could all be on the same page for this weekend. Have you guys talked about the game plan for Saturday? Like how long you've been dating, etc.?"

"We meant to do that yesterday, but the day got away from us," I say.

"Well, this incident happened three months ago. So, your relationship can't exceed that timeline," Gabe says.

I look over at Lexi, wanting to know what she would prefer.

"Do you have a preference?" I ask.

She puckers her lips as she contemplates. My dick stiffens a bit at the sight. I'm stunned that within twenty-four hours, this woman that I've been around for over a year can suddenly affect me like this.

"I guess the longer the better, right? If we're going to act so in love. Maybe you can say it's the reason you never called that woman. You can say we started working closely on a project when you returned. and things just sort of started changing between us."

"I like that," Mia chimes in. "It's a good reason not to have called the girl. You fell in love."

"Aw, it's so sweet," Savannah says as she puts her hand over her heart.

I look over at her. "Are you crying?" I ask as I watch her wipe the corner of her eye.

"Shut up! It's the hormones. Plus, it's super sweet, you falling in love like that."

"You do realize it's not real?" I ask.

"It's still cute!" she defends.

Luke shrugs his shoulders. Clearly, even he doesn't know what to say back to his wife. This pregnancy is making her crazy. How are me and Lexi *cute*?

I steal a glance at Lexi and her cheeks are red. Damn, this woman is going in and out with her boldness. It's like the mere mention of the two of us together for real is making her blush.

I want to lean in and say something to lighten the mood, but I'm also very aware that there are shifting emotions between the two of us. I need to tread carefully. The last thing I need is for this whole thing to blow up in my face.

"What else can we do to help you two out?" Gabe asks.

"I don't know. Maybe don't let us be alone with him. It will help if there's someone there to steer the conversation away if we get into a sticky situation and can't answer his questions," I tell the group.

"I do have to warn you guys that I am not the greatest liar," Lexi says. "I think it's best that I do minimal talking."

"Really? You're not a good liar?" I ask playfully. "I would have never guessed that."

Lexi sighs then looks at the group. "Are we sure this client will believe I'm in love with this guy?"

"Hey, I'm quite the charmer."

She folds her arms and looks at me. "Until you open your mouth."

I think she might actually be serious until a tiny smile spreads across her face. My eyebrows curve down.

"Good one," I say, rolling my eyes.

She chuckles at me. When I look back at the rest of the group, they are watching us curiously. I don't know if Lexi and I will be able to pull this off. There's a strange feeling in my stomach, like a warning of what's to come.

Chapter Seven

Lexi

I'm on my way to the airport, not one that I've been to before because apparently, we're flying in a private jet to Chicago.

The palms of my hands are damp as I try to rub them off on my jeans for the tenth time this afternoon. It took a good hour-long phone call with Grace last night for her to talk me up and convince me that I can handle this. It's not so much the pretending anymore that's starting to worry me, it's the weird feelings that being around Marcus is starting to evoke.

I'm normally so calm and cool around the men that I date. It's probably because I'm never that into them. They've been just attractive enough for me to have a slight interest, but I've always felt in control of my feelings with them.

But with Marcus, heat engulfs my body when he looks at me like he wants me. It's a short and fleeting look. Almost as if he catches himself, he turns it off.

I'm worried that when this is all over, these weird feelings for him are not going to go away. That would be a disaster because I love my job.

Grace said if I sense any interest on his side, I'd be a fool not to go for it. I sent her a picture of me the other day and she about lost it. She told me this is my chance to grab life by the balls and make it my bitch—her exact words.

I get what she's saying, but she's underestimating how handsome Marcus is, and how out of my league he is.

Plus, he's my boss. Well, technically Mia hired me, but still.

Either way, it's completely ridiculous. Even if I did catch him looking at me with a sense of interest or curiosity, he'd still never go for someone like me. I may have snooped on his social media page the other night. Over the years, the women on his arm were stunning. I can't compete.

The driver drops me off at the front door of the building. As we're unloading my suitcase, a warm hand finds my lower back.

"I'll get it," a deep voice, that I know to be Marcus, whispers in my ear.

Shivers break out all over my body.

Crap! This isn't good.

"Thanks," I reply, voice hoarse.

I turn around and find him in a long-sleeved gray shirt and jeans. He has a dark baseball cap on and is sporting a warm smile.

"Not a problem." He lifts the handle to my suitcase and starts to roll it in one hand while he rolls his in the other hand.

I follow him into the building where the rest of the group is waiting. It's surreal being at a private airport. Just outside the doors is the tarmac where several different-sized planes are parked.

Gabe and his wife, Alexis, are standing with Mia as they laugh about something. I've only met Alexis a couple of times, but she seems kind. I believe she stays home with their kids right now. Luke and Savannah are sitting in the seats while Savannah rests her head on his shoulder. By the looks of it, Savannah isn't feeling all too well again.

Both couples are adorable together. Luke and Gabe are surprisingly attentive to their wives for being such rich and handsome men.

That's my mom talking through me right there. Somehow, I'm trained to think rich and handsome equals mean and disinterested.

When I look at Marcus, his eyes are on me. He acts like he got caught doing something wrong when he looks away quickly.

I'm not accustomed to this kind of thing happening to me a lot, but I think he was checking me out. Grace's words ring in my ear, but I ignore them. He's probably just still surprised to see me dressing like this. I'm reading into it.

I went for a pair of skinny jeans, which feels like spandex, and a long-sleeve white shirt. It's simple but feels cute. I also packed the cream sweater that Trudy picked for me in case it's a bit chilly on the plane.

It's September here in Ohio, so the temperature is always questionable.

"I think that's us," Marcus says as a pilot and a younger woman begin to approach the doors from the tarmac.

I've literally been inside the building for all of ten seconds, and we are already being approached by the pilot? I figured we would have some time to kill here as we waited.

I guess the rich don't wait.

We follow the pilot and are on the jet and seated within minutes.

"What can I get you to drink?" Marcus asks before I'm settled in.

"Oh, um, what are the options?"

He smiles at me. "Anything you want. Alcohol, pop, sparkling water."

"Ooh, are you my server today?" I smile with excitement.

"More like your perfect boyfriend here to make your dreams come true," he says with a wink.

Damn, if only he knew.

"I'll take a white wine spritzer, please," I tell him. "Unless that's too complicated for my boyfriend."

"Nothing's too complicated for me. You should know that by now, sugar lips."

He walks away, my stomach flipping.

Get a hold of yourself, Lexi.

Who cares if him giving me a nickname like that makes me feel special? It's all just a joke—an act.

He sits across from me so we face each other, then hands me my drink.

It looks like he poured himself a whiskey on the rocks.

"No wine for you? I'm surprised," I tell him.

"I enjoy some whiskey here and there."

The plane starts to taxi out to the runway and we're instructed to put on our seatbelts. I look out the window as I watch the entire process of takeoff, enjoying the new feeling of being in a private jet.

"So, Lexi, tell me more about yourself," Alexis, who's seated across the aisle from me, says.

I take a sip of my drink which is surprisingly very well made. Of course, the man knows how to make the perfect drink.

"What do you want to know?"

"How'd you get into IT?" she asks.

It's not an interesting story in my mind. I switched majors in college when I discovered how much I enjoyed my information systems class.

Alexis tells me about her degree in finance and her career over the years. I didn't realize she was so smart. These Giannelli men seem to be attracted to a woman with beauty and brains.

They are all so intimidating, yet so nice.

I get so lost in conversation with her, that I'm surprised when the captain comes on to let us know that we need to buckle up for landing. Although, we were only coasting in the air for about thirty minutes.

When we get to the hotel, Marcus still insists on taking my suitcase. Gabe checks us all in and hands me a keycard to my room. It looks like I'm on the twentieth floor. Marcus walks with me to the elevator and hops on while the others decide where they want to eat.

I've already told them I was going to check in and then go visit my mom, so I'm surprised Marcus is following me to my room.

"How far is your mom's from here?" he asks, leaning against the opposite wall of the elevator as we go up.

"It's thirty minutes outside of the city. She's in an assisted living facility."

He seems surprised. "I didn't realize it had gotten to that level yet."

"She actually has an early onset case of dementia. She can't live alone."

"Does your dad help out too?"

The elevator doors open, and we walk out.

"He's not in the picture. Left when I was young."

He stops in front of my door and turns to me. "I didn't know any of this. I'm sorry you have to take this on by yourself."

I shrug. "I'm used to it."

"Doesn't make it any easier, I'm sure."

I don't know why, but I can't meet his eyes. I don't want to see the sympathy in them. Just more confusing feelings that I don't need in the mix right now. Being kind and understanding of my family life is another layer of him I don't need to know.

I hold up my keycard and open my door.

"Well, thanks for everything. This week, the plane, helping me to my room."

"Don't forget, you're the one helping us out. Thank *you*, Lex."

I nod my head and close the door.

Instead of dwelling on anything, I freshen up and take a car to the assisted living center. I'm familiar with most of the front desk staff, but tonight there's a man I've never seen before.

"Hello, there," he says as I approach. "How may I help you?"

"Hi. I'm here to visit my mother. Elaine Miller."

He glances down at the daily itinerary.

"Not a problem. Looks like she just had dinner. She should be back in her room. If you would just sign in over here, please."

I sign the sheet, like I've done a hundred times before, then thank the man and head towards my mother's room. When I get to her door, I peek inside. She's sitting in her rocking chair as she watches the television across the room. A rerun of I Love Lucy is playing.

I knock on the door.

She looks up at me with a blank stare, but at least it's not one of confusion. I feel hopeful that tonight will be a good visit.

"Hi, Ma," I say. "How are you?"

I grab the seat by the door and move it closer to her. She looks older than when I saw her last. Her sixty-five is looking more like seventy-five to me. It hurts my heart just thinking about losing her early. She was diagnosed at sixty. We managed pretty well for the first three years, not seeing too much of a difference. But she has been on a steep decline in the last two years, and I worry that it isn't going to slow down until it takes her away from me.

I don't want her to see me cry, so I do what I always do when I see her and want to break down, I suck it up.

"It was apple pie day for dessert."

I smile at her. "You love apple pie. Did they give you vanilla ice cream with it?"

"Well, of course. They know better than to give me warm apple pie with no ice cream."

That's true. One thing that has come with her dementia is the ability to tell anybody off that she pleases. The staff tells me to laugh it off as often as possible. They say it's the easiest way to get through it.

"How are things going? Are you getting your exercise in?"

She waves her hand at me. "Exercise is for the birds. What do I need to exercise for? I'm not goin' anywhere."

"It's about keeping your body fit. You need to make sure your ticker keeps ticking."

"My ticker ticks without any nonsense exercise."

I sigh. Alright, it's not worth fighting over, that's what we pay the staff to do. When I'm here, I just want to enjoy our time together.

"So, I've got a big charity event to go to tomorrow. You should see the dress I've got, it's by far the fanciest one I've ever owned."

Her eyes meet mine and look me up and down. "I always told my daughter, don't dress for the rich or handsome, they'll just end up crushing your spirit."

I stop in my tracks, not sure what exactly is happening. Did she just say my daughter?

"Mom, it's me, Lexi," I say emphatically.

"Lexi?" her eyes focus closer on me. "No, my Lexi doesn't look like that. She would never wear pants that tight or a shirt cut that low. And look at your hair? No...no...not my Lexi."

She gets up and starts to pace back and forth.

"Who are you? Why would you pretend to be my Lexi? Who sent you?" she says in a scathing voice.

"Mom, it's me." I try to inch closer to her, but she backs up with deliberate speed.

"No! Stay away from me."

We have gotten to the point where she doesn't remember to turn the oven off, doesn't remember recent events, gets paranoid or confused, even has had slight personality changes...but she's never flat-out not recognized me. I mean, I know I have highlights in my hair, but I didn't put on makeup aside from some mascara. I can't look *that* different.

I never thought about how changing my appearance could cause such confusion for her. It makes me feel so guilty. *What the hell was I thinking?*

"What's happening in here?" a nurse rushes in.

I look over at her with moisture pulling in my eyes.

"She..." I start but my voice cracks. "She doesn't recognize me."

Her face instantly softens with sympathy.

"Elaine. Who is this lovely woman here that has come to visit you?" she starts toward Mom, who seems more at ease with her in the room.

It's like a knife to my heart. This woman in front of me, who used to brush my hair at night before bed, who would stand in the kitchen for hours letting me bake with her, is looking at me like I'm the enemy.

"I don't know. But she's trying to tell me she's my Lexi. She isn't, and I don't like it. Tell me who sent her."

My body is now shaking as I stand here, paralyzed in fear.

The nurse turns to me. "Can I see you for a second outside?"

I nod my head. "Sure."

"Now, Elaine. I'm going to go talk to this sweet young lady for a minute. I'll be back in to check on you."

Just outside of her bedroom, the nurse stops me.

"She's never done this before," I say as tears now begin to fall down my cheeks.

I look down at my outfit, thinking about how I felt when I put it on this morning. The smile that took over my face, the confidence I've felt throughout the day. Now, all I see is my father leaving us, my mother crying herself to sleep.

"I know my hair is different. I put highlights in, and my clothes aren't my usual, but I thought..."

"Now, honey, don't go blaming yourself. You didn't come in with a new face. Those are minor changes. This is the disease, it's nothing you did."

"But it's the first time I've changed these things and the first time she hasn't recognized me."

"I don't think that it..." she begins, but my mother is calling from the other room. "Look, she's agitated and confused tonight. As tough as this might be to hear, I think it's best if you leave tonight. Try another day."

"What? You want me to leave?"

"This disease is hard to navigate. When they are in this kind of mood, this confused...it's best to eliminate the source of distress."

"Which is me," my voice trembles.

If it's best for my mom, I know I need to do it. As much as it hurts.

"Okay. I'll go. Can you just...call me with an update? So I know she's calmed down."

"Absolutely. You go take care of yourself tonight."

With that, she goes back into the room, and I'm left standing on the outside like a stranger.

Chapter Eight

Marcus

Trips with my siblings are no longer the same. What was used to be the four of us going out all the time, enjoying fancy dinners, has now become lonely nights in the hotel room.

Gabe and Alexis are enjoying their time away from kids to "reunite" as Alexis so eloquently put it. Luke and Savannah are spending the night in since Savannah can barely keep her eyes open past dinner time, and Mia said she's tired and just wants to read a book.

So, here I am, eating room service in my pajamas on a Friday night. Can't say it's that awful, it's cozy, just a tad bit lonely.

An image of Lexi flashes in my head.

There's a connecting door to our rooms. She's going to be sleeping just a handful of feet away from me. For some reason, it makes me feel something strange. I can't quite name it, but I know it's something that I shouldn't be feeling for her.

I hear a door open and slam shut. It sounds like Lexi's door, but that can't be right. She didn't leave too long ago. Surely, she would still be with her mom right now.

Then I hear it, it's an unmistakable sound. The sound of her crying.

I jump from my bed and rush over to our connected door. Without hesitation, I knock.

No answer. I still hear the cries, just softer now.

I try again. "Lexi, I can hear you in there. Are you okay?"

"I'm alright."

Lies. She is still crying. I can't stand it, I don't like hearing her so upset without doing something about it.

"Lexi, open up. Please."

I'm not used to begging, but I don't care how I come across right now.

The door slowly opens, and I see a completely wrecked-looking Lexi in front of me.

"Are you okay? What happened?"

She looks over at the lamp on the TV stand as she shrugs her shoulders. "I'm fine."

I put my hand under her chin and force her to look at me. "Let's try that again. Come on, tell me. I want to help."

Tears still run down her cheeks as they hit my hand.

"My mom," she whispers.

"What about your mom? Is she okay? Did something happen to her?"

Oh gosh, please tell me her mother is safe. I don't know how to comfort someone who lost their mom. I'd probably cry along with her, just thinking of losing my mom makes my heart break for her.

"She didn't recognize me."

I can't help but notice her beauty, even through her pain. Her long lashes complimented her green eyes.

"I'm so sorry. That's awful."

She nods her head in agreement. "I thought maybe it was from my new look."

Guilt hits me hard, making my chest physically ache. Did I cause this?

"Shit, Lexi, I'm so sorry. I never should've suggested you change your appearance. I wasn't thinking. This is all my fault."

She shakes her head as tears continue to fall, but she doesn't disagree with me. I can't help it, I pull her into my arms. I feel her tears on my chest which brings attention to the fact that I'm not wearing a shirt. Just my pajama pants.

I don't care, I move her further into my arms as I wrap her up tighter. I'm not sure if it's helping, but after a couple of minutes, she begins to settle.

When she pulls away, she must notice the tears on my chest. She makes a move to wipe them off me. Her hand caresses my chest, running through the little amount of scattered hair there. My abs flex in response to her touch.

"I'm sorry. I didn't mean to cry all over you," she says with more composure now.

"It's no problem."

She looks up at me and we just stare at each other for a minute then her stomach makes a noise. Her cheeks get a touch of pink on them.

"Did you eat dinner?" I ask her.

She shakes her head. "I never got the chance to."

I grab her hand and bring her further into my room.

"Come on," I tell her.

"What are you doing?"

"I'm ordering you some dinner." I reach for the room service menu and hand it to her. "Here. Order anything on it. We'll charge it to my room."

"I don't want to put you out. I can order something from my room."

There's no way I'm letting her sit in her room by herself, eating alone. This has absolutely nothing with the fact that I like her company. This is purely being a good person. At least, that's what I'm telling myself.

"I'd rather you stay here. It doesn't feel right to leave you alone. I was about to watch a movie and order dessert myself."

She bites on her bottom lip as I watch her survey the room, considering my offer.

"Okay." She looks at me as she agrees. "But you have to put a shirt on. It's distracting."

I smile. "Deal."

"First let me go change. It's not fair that you're the only one in pajamas."

While she goes to change, I slip on a gray t-shirt. I sit down on the bed, realizing there's only one bed in here. Whatever, it's a king-sized bed, and it's not like we're sleeping in it together.

After all, this isn't a romance novel.

She comes in wearing black pajama pants with a DePaul University gray t-shirt. I'm guessing that's where she went to college. Her hair is up and she's wearing her glasses. She looks kind of adorable.

I don't understand. This is back to the Lexi from last week. Hair up, baggy clothes, and glasses with no makeup—and yet, I find her to be breathtaking. It's like since I've seen her beauty, I can't unsee it.

She looks a bit nervous.

I smile. "Shirt is on. Are you happy now?" I wink.

That seems to loosen her up. She smiles as she walks towards the bed.

"Thank you. I like your pajama pants, by the way," she says with a light chuckle.

"What's so funny about my pants?"

"I don't know. I guess I just didn't peg you as a flannel pajama kinda guy."

"I'll have you know, there's never a reason to discontinue wearing flannel pajamas."

"Even becoming a millionaire?" she raises an eyebrow.

I chuckle. "Especially after becoming a millionaire."

I grab the phone from the nightstand.

"Do you know what you want yet?" I ask.

"Yes, the burger with a strawberry milkshake."

"Got it." I pick up the phone and put in her order as well as a cheesecake for myself.

While we wait for our food, I click through the options on the television. We settle for a new comedy release, something to keep the mood light.

We begin the movie and wait for our room service. I pause the movie when I hear a knock at the door. Once we're all set up on the bed with our food, I hit play again. There's a comfortable silence between the two of us.

We make comments here and there while watching, laughing, and interacting like this entire evening is normal between the two of us.

"This burger is so good," she says as she sits cross-legged on my bed. "Don't judge me, but I'm going to dunk my fries in the shake."

In all the times that I've spent in bed with a beautiful woman, and there have been many, it was never watching a movie while she ate however she pleased in front of me.

"I couldn't possibly judge that. I've dipped many Wendy's fries into my Frosty before."

She laughs uninhibitedly then grabs a fry and dunks it.

I've already finished my cheesecake, but she's making those fries look too damn good not to steal some. I reach over her shoulder, grab a few, and dip them before shoving them into my mouth.

She turns around, wide-eyed, then nudges me with her hand.

"Excuse you! I never said I was willing to share."

I laugh with my mouth full. "You can't just eat fries and a shake like that and not share. Plus, I ordered it. The least you could do is share."

Her eyebrows turn down. "Fine. You could have a couple more, but I get most of them."

"Deal."

I go for more, reaching over her shoulder. I feel her eyes on me. When I look up, my face is just above her shoulder, our lips only inches apart. Something shifts in the air between us.

My entire body feels like it breaks out in goosebumps. My eyes zero in on those luscious lips of hers.

Never in my life have I wanted to taste a set of lips before. Her tongue drags along her bottom lip. My dick becomes stiff at the sight, which is about when I realize what I'm about to do. I'm about to kiss her.

I pull my attention from her lips, turning back to the fries then dunk them in the shake. I lean back and eat them, trying my best to play it off like I wasn't affected. All I can do is hope she doesn't see through what she is doing to me.

This weekend isn't supposed to be real. But none of what I'm feeling is fake, and that's dangerous.

She finishes the food on her plate and puts it on the night-stand. We both seem to settle back into the movie.

Maybe the moment wasn't anything more than being in close proximity to someone of the opposite sex while on a bed. Like our bodies got temporarily confused.

The thought eases my worries. That makes more sense than me feeling differently for Lexi after knowing her for over a year.

Now that we are finished with our food, I reach over to the wall and hit the lights so we can continue the movie.

I don't know if it's the week catching up with me or what, but my eyes begin to feel heavy. My head sinks into the pillow as I feel my body begin to relax.

A bright light wakes me. I look around the room feeling confused until I remember where I'm at.

The hotel.

I think the television woke me up, I don't normally fall asleep with it on. I grab the remote in the middle of the bed, but before I turn it off, I see a body in bed with me.

Lexi. She's curled into a ball on the other side of the bed. She must've fallen asleep during the movie like I did.

I'm too fucking tired to deal with it. I click off the television and go back to sleep.

The next time I wake up, I feel refreshed and warm. *Why am I so warm?*

I'm holding somebody in my arms. Questions begin to flood my brain.

Who is this?

Did I go out last night?

Wait...shit. I realize the woman in my arms is Lexi.

I open my eyes to confirm that Lexi is indeed the woman who I'm currently spooning with.

How did we get into this position? My legs are intertwined with hers, and one of my arms is snaked around her tiny waist. The first thing I notice is how perfectly she fits in my arms. The next is how nice she smells. My head leans in closer to her neck to get better access to her scent.

I look at the clock on her nightstand. It's only four.

Instead of doing what I absolutely should, I wrap her tighter into my arms and close my eyes. Fuck it. It's already happened, might as well just deal with it in the morning. They don't call me the younger, irresponsible brother for nothing.

Chapter Nine

Lexi

What the hell do I do? I just woke up in my boss's arms.

I must've fallen asleep during the movie last night. The emotions of the day had been intense and wiped me out. Somehow, we ended up in this position. I feel so small in the warmth of his arms. Every inch of us is connected, even my ass and his...wait a minute. Holy shit, he's hard right now.

The realization makes my body temperature spike. My body involuntarily wiggles against him, garnering a low groan from him.

Why the hell did I do that? I just rubbed my ass all over my boss's hard dick.

My body freezes, waiting to see if he's awake. Oh, gosh, I can't bear to face him. *What if he looks at me like I'm crazy? Like I initiated this and he wanted nothing to do with it?*

After a minute of stillness, I crawl out of his arms as stealthily as possible.

I turn back around to make sure he isn't awake. When I see his sleeping face, my heart flutters. He looks so sweet while he sleeps.

Nope, don't do this to yourself, Lexi. Get in your room immediately!

Once I'm in my room alone, door closed, I let out the breath that I was holding. The clock shows me it's only six. I've got all day to myself, and I could use more sleep. I climb into my bed and wrap the comforter around me. This time when I close my eyes, I dream of being back in his arms.

A knock at the door wakes me from my sleep. The clock says ten. I slept for four more hours.

I look through the peephole to see Alexis and Savannah. Thank God it's not Marcus. I can't deal with that before I get some coffee. I need my wits about me to not blurt out something stupid, like *let's do that shit again tonight.*

I open the door and am greeted with two huge smiles.

"Oh, good, we aren't the only two who took advantage of the opportunity to sleep in," Alexis says.

"I didn't mean to sleep this late," I admit.

"No judgment here," Savannah says. "I just spent the morning alternating between throwing up and sleeping."

I give her a sympathetic look. I hate that this pregnancy is so hard for her. You wouldn't know it by looking at her. She's handling it like a champ.

"Anyway, we have an appointment in two hours for our hair and makeup. We thought the three of us could get some food before we all go," Alexis says.

"Oh, I'd love to join you for lunch before your appointment."

"Your appointment too," Savannah corrects me. "We made the appointment for the four of us, Mia included. Mia and the guys are meeting with another client for lunch, but she'll catch up with us later. Don't worry, all of it's on the company card."

"Oh, wow. Okay. Ummm, I'll meet you guys downstairs in twenty?" I suggest.

"You got it," Savannah says.

I close the door and look around the hotel room. Okay, well at least I don't have to worry about doing my hair or makeup for tonight. I was worried about that.

I'm able to get myself together faster than I thought and meet the girls downstairs a little early.

Alexis holds up a cup of coffee for me when I approach her. "You're my favorite person right now," I tell her as I take the cup.

"What the hell?" Savannah says jokingly. "I'm right here."

I'm surprised how easy it is to be around them. As we walk the streets of Chicago to the restaurant, we laugh and talk about nothing in particular.

We arrive at the restaurant and sit down. Not long after we put in our orders the questions start.

"So, tell me about this makeover. Was it for a certain someone?" Savannah asks, sounding intrigued.

I tuck a non-existent stray hair behind my ear. "Oh, umm, not really. It was just for this event."

They look at each other, then me. "Was Marcus behind this?" Alexis asks.

I shift uncomfortably in my seat. I don't want to get him in trouble, as they seem to be headed in that direction. But I also don't want to be caught in a lie.

"Ugh, I'm gonna kill him," Savannah says, the answer evident in my silence.

"No, no, please don't. It was honestly good for me. I don't want to go into too much detail, but I grew up with only my mother. She wasn't a big fan of dressing for anybody, so I never put in any effort. My friends have been begging me to do something like this. They were both ecstatic with the results."

Alexis sighs. "It still wasn't any of his business."

I shrug. "Maybe...maybe not. I was all on board for it, until..."

Memories of last night flash in my mind. I got a phone call from the assisted living center last night after I fell asleep. They left me a message letting me know that she had settled down and all was forgotten. Although I'm grateful they remembered to call, I'm still feeling confused about this new me, and wondering if it was selfish of me to do without considering my mom.

"Until what?" Alexis looks concerned.

Instead of overthinking it, I fill them in on everything. Mostly, the guilt I'm left with from last night.

Neither speaks for a minute as they are taking in my words. I like how thoughtful and considerate they are.

"Are you happy with how you look? Honestly?" Savannah asks.

I think about the feeling I have every time I look in the mirror at the new me. The level of pleasure and satisfaction it gives me. The newfound level of confidence.

"I am. I'm actually very happy with it."

"You have to live your life for yourself, Lexi. Nobody else," she says.

I nod my head. "I know. It's just really hard to see her get so upset. It was easy to just place the blame on myself."

"She'll get used to it. It's not like you made any major changes. But despite her reaction, you can't put your life on hold or hide who you really want to be to make her happy," Alexis says.

"It's sometimes hard to separate the disease from my mom. Like, I wonder if she would be okay with it if I did this before her disease."

"I'm sure all of your questions and fears are normal things that every loved one goes through when their parent has dementia. But again, you have to prioritize your own happiness first," Savannah tells me.

I nod my head. "You're right. Thanks for listening. Sometimes it's easy to get in my own head and just tell myself what I'm doing is wrong."

"No problem. Don't hesitate to come talk to me anytime you need to clear your mind. I'm always here," Savannah adds.

It's nice to feel like I'm finally making some close friends since I moved to Cleveland a year ago.

The rest of the lunch we talk about much lighter subjects, like Alexis's kids and Savannah's pregnancy. It's still stuck in the back of my mind that I need to figure out what I'm going to do when I see my mom tomorrow morning before we fly back. I don't recall what clothes I packed, but I might need to run to the store to find something baggy. As pathetic as that sounds, I don't know if I'm ready to stand up to my mother, or if I'll ever be.

An hour later, I'm sitting in a chair with my hairstylist, showing her a picture of the style of my dress. When she asked me how I'd like my hair for tonight, my blank *deer-in-headlights* stare was enough for her to know I'm in uncharted territory.

"Oh, that's very pretty. It's simple, letting the cut of the dress do all the talking. I think we do the same with your hair. I suggest we do a low bun. I'll leave the hair on the sides a little loose and have some fall free to give a softer, more romantic look."

"I trust your judgement," I tell her.

While she does my hair, I'm let to sit here to relive last night. I wonder if Marcus is panicking. Is he going to bring it up or are we not going to talk about it?

He hasn't texted me at all today. I'm kind of disappointed. But then again, I was the one who ran out of the room this morning. What else can I expect?

I'm lost in thought when I realize she's telling me to head to makeup. My hair looks incredible, nothing I would've ever been able to create on my own.

I thank her and follow her directions to my makeup artist. This time with makeup, I feel more confident in what I want. I tell her I want everything to be simple and elegant except for my lipstick. I want a big pop of color on my lips.

We settle on a dark beige color that will pop off my light pink dress.

By the time the four of us are done, we only have forty minutes to get back to the hotel and change. While we walk back, Mia pulls me to her side.

"Thank you so much for doing this, Lexi."

"It's really not a problem. I was gonna be here anyway."

"But it's not a traditional ask for an IT Director."

I laugh. "Definitely my first request of the kind. Honestly, you guys have been so good to me. I *want* to do this for you. I just hope we can pull it off."

"Well, whatever comes of it, it's not your fault."

I think about how Marcus would feel if they did lose the client, and even though I should keep my mouth shut, I can't.

"You know, if the client did pull out because of it, I don't think that's really Marcus's fault."

She looks up at me curiously. "No?"

"I mean, I just think you can't sleep with someone you don't know and have any expectations. It just seems unfair that he gets labeled as a bad guy for her poor decisions or misguided expectations."

"Hmm. I suppose there's some truth to that."

I feel good about sticking up for Marcus. Mia appears to have taken my words to heart, and nothing bad happened.

Is this part of the new and improved Lexi? Another wave of satisfaction rolls through me at the realization that I'm finally starting to find myself. If only my mom could understand it. If only she would accept me for me.

But she's sick, and I can't hold anything over someone who's sick.

When we get to the hotel, we nearly sprint to our rooms to get ready. I'm supposed to meet them in the lobby in twenty minutes. It sounds like a lot, but I have some boob tape that I need to contend with.

I will say, my breasts have held up nicely over the years, but I'm not about to go out without some kind of support.

I get into my room and kick out of my clothes, being extra careful not to ruin my hair or makeup.

My dress is hanging up in the closet. I rip open the plastic cover and pull it off the hanger. After I step into it, I let it rest on my waist while I get to work on the tape.

Ten minutes later, there's scattered pieces of tape that I've ripped off my breasts and thrown on the ground. Oh, did I mention that I didn't realize that there are nipple covers in the box? Have you ever tried tearing tape directly off your nipples? I don't recommend it. The amount of curse words that I've screamed in the last six hundred seconds is probably more than I've spoken in the last year combined.

With two minutes to spare, I finally get the damn tape in place. I pull my dress up and tie it around my neck then slip into my heels.

I pull out the gold jewelry that Trudy picked out. I've gotta give it to her, she really thought about everything.

When I look in the mirror, I'm struck by how different I look. I've never looked like this before. It makes me feel oddly brave. I can do this. I can be the woman who belongs on Marcus's arm.

I grab my clutch, throw in my lipstick then spritz a last-minute spray of my perfume.

Okay, here we go. It's time to go pretend to be in love with the man who had his arms wrapped around me all night, who makes me feel things I've never felt before. What could go wrong?

Chapter Ten

Marcus

"How're you feeling about tonight?" Mia asks me as we wait for everybody else in the lobby.

I pull at the cuff of my sleeve. "I think we'll be okay. I'm not too worried about it."

In reality, I'm kind of nervous to see her again. We haven't talked since our little snuggling escapade last night. I don't know why she ran off this morning, but I'm hoping she just didn't want to disturb my sleep.

I don't want any awkwardness between us. Especially after what she went through last night. I can't imagine what it would feel like for your own mother not to recognize you. I've never wanted to steal someone's pain away from them as much as I did in that moment.

Mia gives me a strange look.

"What?" I ask defensively.

"Nothing. Lexi and I had an interesting talk on the way back to the hotel."

My eyes keep wandering towards the elevators, waiting to see when she will appear.

"Oh, yeah?" I respond, slightly distracted.

A set of elevator doors slide open, and I catch a glimpse of a familiar pink dress. My heart rate accelerates as she walks out.

When I get a full view of her, I lose my breath. It's a disturbing reaction to someone I'm supposed to be pretending with tonight.

But I can't deny how stunning she looks. She's almost hard to look at, yet hard to look away from. If Mia is talking right now, I can't hear her.

I can't hear anything but the beating of my own heart, and I can't do anything but stare in awe like a complete fool.

Lexi stops in front of me with a warm smile.

"Fuck, Lexi," I whisper. "You look...absolutely stunning."

Her blush appears but she wears it with pride this time. "You look pretty handsome yourself."

"Doesn't she look amazing!" Alexis says, giving me the same knowing look I got from Mia just minutes ago.

I look around the lobby. "When did you guys get here?" I ask as I notice Gabe, Luke, and Savannah.

"Uh, we came down with Lexi. You didn't notice us?" Alexis asks.

I cough. "Uh, no, I guess I didn't."

"Limo is here," Gabe says, distracting Alexis from our conversation.

I let everybody else head for the door while I pull Lexi back.

"Are you ready for this?" I ask her.

"A little nervous. I don't want to screw it up for you guys."

"That's not gonna happen. Just follow my lead. And I wasn't exaggerating when I said you look stunning." My eyes fall back down to her body as I admire her curves. I can't help but laugh when I see her blush. "I love how you get so affected by my compliments."

She smiles then bites her lip, like she's trying to stop herself. "I guess I'm not used to getting them from you. It's a bit of an adjustment."

"All of this is a bit of an adjustment. Like you running off this morning before we could talk about what happened."

There, I said it. It's out in the open.

Her eyes open wide in surprise. "I'm so sorry. I completely panicked."

She hides her face in her hands, and I have to laugh again. I grab her hands and pull them away from her face, forcing her to look at me.

"I think we just need to laugh it off. We're grown adults in our thirties. I think we can engage in some heavy cuddling without looking too far into it. Deal?"

This gets her to loosen up. "So, it was a one-night-snuggle? Does that mean you're not going to call me? Isn't that what got you into this whole mess?"

My head falls back as I let out a loud laugh. I wrap my arm around her shoulder and lead us outside before we piss off the others.

"Dammit! I keep doing that. Snuggling with chicks and then not calling them."

Gone are the nerves I was feeling about the evening. Lexi and I can do this. She's so fun and easy to be around, it'll be like hanging out with my best friend on my arm all night. When we get to the limo, they are already inside waiting for us. I hold my hand out for Lexi to climb in then follow in after her.

Alexis already has the bottle of champagne opened and is pouring everybody a glass.

"Sorry, Savannah. I'll drink your glass for you," Alexis says with a wink. "I believe that was your line when I was pregnant."

After she pours, I grab two glasses and hand one to Lexi. Ignoring everybody else, I clink my glass against hers.

"To a successful night with my one and only love," I say.

"Cheers, darling," she replies.

We both smile at each other while we bring our glasses to our mouths.

"There's gonna be food there, right?" Lexi whispers. "Because I'm really hungry."

"It's a stuffy place with stuffy people. There will be finger foods. I always end up getting something else to eat after I leave these things. But it should be enough to hold you over."

She crunches her nose. "Ugh, fine."

"Do you know that you scrunch your nose a lot?" I ask with a tap to her nose.

"Do I?" Her eyebrows raise. "Huh, no one has ever told me that."

"It's cute," I tell her.

She looks at me thoughtfully then takes a sip of champagne. I'm not sure what is going through her head, and I don't know what I'm doing, flirting with her like this.

The limo comes to a stop outside of the event. When the door opens, I get out first and then help Lexi next. I like the feel of her hand in mine. It's soft and small compared to mine.

While we walk inside, I put my arm around her small waist and rest my hand on her hip. Her body tenses for a second at the contact then seems to ease into my touch. My hand here reminds me of holding her last night. It gives me an odd desire to pull her in closer to me, but I resist.

We take the escalator up to the third floor to the event. There's a silent auction set up along the perimeter of the room.

"I always like to scan the auction items first," I whisper into Lexi's ear. "What do you say?"

She looks up at me. "Are we spending your money?"

I smile. "Of course. I'll even let you keep it if we win something."

"I'm in. Let's go."

We begin to walk along the tables looking at the displayed items. At first, there's nothing catching our eyes.

"Oh, look," she pulls me forward. "Tickets to the 2024 Super Bowl!"

Damn, she isn't a cheap date. I'm not sure she realizes what people are likely bidding to win these tickets.

"I have a question first. Are you a Chicago sports fan?"

Her eyebrows turn up. "Umm, of course, I am. Let me guess, you're a Cleveland sports fan?"

"Obviously. And hold the jokes or judgment or no bidding."

Her lips pucker up like she's doing her best to hold them in. I like seeing her squirm.

What would she look like squirming as I fuck her with my tongue?

I momentarily freeze as the images start to flood my brain. Fuck, I need to get them out, but I can't. I accidentally gave my brain ideas, and now it's running with them. I do my best to ignore the images.

"Fine. What do you think people are bidding for these?" she asks as she inspects the box holding the bids.

"I don't know. Average Super Bowl ticket costs are like eight grand a piece." I glance down at the description on the card, getting a whiff of her familiar scent from last night. "These seats are pretty good. Lower level, thirty-yard line. This is for charity, so I'd say people are betting around twenty to thirty for them."

"Thousand? Twenty to thirty thousand?" Her voice slightly rises.

I happen to look over at Gabe and Mia across the room. They're talking to William and his wife, Kathryn. When I see their heads turn towards us, I quickly look back down at Lexi. I guess it's showtime.

I wrap my arm around her waist again, grabbing her hip, giving it a solid squeeze.

"It's Super Bowl tickets, Lex."

She doesn't seem to bat an eye at my hand on her body. It annoys me. Is she not feeling what I'm feeling right now?

"Still, that's an awful lot of money. Let's just keep walking."

I grab her hand and interlace our fingers as she starts to look at the other items. This seems to get her attention. She looks down at our joined hands and then back up at me.

"Are we being watched?" she whispers.

I wink at her then move my hand to her neck as my lips graze her ear. "Why? Is this making you feel...uncomfortable?"

Her body shutters under my touch as I drag my hand down the length of her back until my fingers brush along the lower part of her back, just above her ass. I look down at my hand and take in the eyeful of her perfect ass in this dress.

I let out a barely audible groan. The view shows off her long slender back in this dress.

When our eyes finally meet, she looks like she's drunk on my touch. Her eyes are heavy and her breathing is labored.

I'm so lost in her, that I don't notice our company.

"Marcus," Gabe says, giving a stern smile when I look at him.

I give him a curt nod then turn to William.

"Hi, William. Pleasure to see you. Thank you for inviting us, it's quite an amazing event," I say as I extend my hand. He shakes it and looks over at Lexi then back at me. "Allow me to introduce my girlfriend to you. This is Lexi."

I bring her to my side, smiling with pride. Who wouldn't with a woman like her in their arms?

Lexi shakes William's hand.

"Nice to meet you, Lexi. This is my wife, Kathryn." While the ladies are shaking hands, he looks back at me. "I must say, I'm surprised to hear that things are getting pretty serious between the two of you."

Lexi looks up at me with a smile that to the public, might seem genuine, but I know to be fake. I lean down and kiss her on the forehead.

"Not serious enough. She keeps trying to slow things down, but what can I say? When you know, you know."

Kathryn is smiling at us like we're the sweetest thing she's ever seen. "You two make a beautiful couple. Your love is unmistakable. I could see it from across the room."

"It's a bit soon," William cuts in. "Just a couple of months ago you were here in Chicago. I hope you were single then."

Lexi clutches my hand. She's got a lot of strength in that tiny hand of hers. I look down and see the anger in her eyes.

I know, the man's got some nerve to try and bring it up right here, in front of my *girlfriend* and everybody else in the room. But we aren't here to make a scene, we are here to put on a show for the man standing in front of us, insulting me *and* Lexi.

"Well, Lexi and I have worked together for a year now. It started as admiration for her work ethic and dedication to her family. When I got back from Chicago a couple of months ago, we had to work more closely together. That one-on-one time, getting to know her, seeing how sweet and fun she is. Well, that was all it took for me to fall head-over-heels."

I know I'm supposed to be saying these words to William, but I find myself staring into Lexi's eyes as I say them.

"I see," Williams says.

Lexi breaks our connection and turns to William. "Marcus is amazing. He can somehow make anyone in a room with him feel welcome and accepted. He's thoughtful and he's honest. I know all about his past. There's nothing he doesn't tell me, and I appreciate that quality in him. Our time together has been incredible. I've never been happier."

"Well, I'm glad he found somebody to settle down with. It's important to show the world you aren't afraid of commitment."

"It's also important to make sure you don't rush it, or worse, force yourself to settle down with the wrong person just for the sake of appearances," Lexi says with a challenging tone.

What the hell have I done to deserve her loyalty? Not a damn thing, but here she is...giving it.

"Leave them alone, William. They're obviously in love." Kathryn swats at her husband's arm. "We're going to let you two get back to the auction. That is, after all, the reason we are all here."

We say our goodbyes then William and Kathryn walk away.

As soon as they're gone, the muscles in my body begin to soften as I feel my shoulders droop down.

"How do you think that went? I'm so sorry for what I said to him. Do you think he felt like it was out of line?" Lexi asks sounding panicked.

"You were perfect."

I kiss her temple. Shit, that wasn't even for appearances, it just came naturally to me.

We walk down the rest of the tables, settling on some bids for a spa basket and some aged bourbon and whiskey.

"Okay, I need to eat something," she says after we put in our last bid.

I laugh. "Come on, this way."

I lead her to the finger foods where she promptly fills up her plate with two of everything. I follow her lead, doing the same. One, because I'm hungry. Two, because I don't want her feeling bad about eating more than me. I'm pretty sure women are sensitive about that shit.

"How'd it go?" Mia asks as she joins us with her own plate of food.

Lexi shrugs her shoulders. "No offense, but the guy is a total dick. But I think it went fine."

Mia looks surprised by Lexi's words. I throw a stuffed mushroom in my mouth and smile, feeling proud of Lexi's bold statement.

"What did he say?" Mia asks.

"He basically asked for the dates of our relationship to make sure it didn't coincide with when Marcus was here with that other girl. What kind of prick does that to people he doesn't even know? He also made it seem like people who aren't married and settled down early are commitment phobic. The nerve of him."

I scoot in closer to Lexi, and bring my hand to her back, trying to ignore the reaction of my body.

"Don't worry, my beautiful girlfriend here stood up for me."

"Oh?" Mia asks surprised.

"No, no. It wasn't like that." Lexi begins to panic. "I was polite. It just bothered me so much that he was being so rude to Marcus. In the end, I think he believed us. His wife sure does."

Mia laughs. "Don't worry Lexi That guy has some nerve putting us in this position in the first place. I hate that we have to bend over backwards to kiss his ass. I don't blame you for being pissed. Speaking as a single adult approaching thirty myself, I take offense to his comment too."

After we finish our food, we wander over to the bar where I order some wine. Somewhere along the way, we lost Mia. Gabe and Luke are off networking. I'm normally taking advantage of these events, but tonight I don't seem to care. I'm enjoying my time with Lexi.

Chapter Eleven

Lexi

I feel his hand snake around my waist again—I've lost count of how many times.

I'm not sure if he's playing up the act or if it's real. It feels real. My body responds every damn time. When his hand drags up and down the length of my back. my body feels like an inferno.

Something about the way he does it so absentmindedly makes it feel real. What hasn't helped are the two glasses of wine that I've had. It's lowered my inhibitions. Now, all I want to do is touch him back. I want to feel those muscles that were wrapped around me this morning.

"Care to dance?" he whispers.

I look out at the dance floor and see several couples swaying slowly in front of the band while they play Sinatra.

"Sure."

He grabs my hand and leads me out onto the dance floor. He twirls me in a circle before pulling me towards him. I laugh as I spin, feeling lighter and happier than ever before. His eyes sparkle as he smiles at me. I love the small lines that form around the corner of his eyes, looking so handsome and sophisticated.

He pulls me closer and everything changes. Our smiles fade, the moment shifts, and it feels like nothing will ever be the same.

My body is connected to his, I can feel everything. Every hard muscle, every breath he takes, I feel it.

I'm so lost in the moment, I don't even realize I haven't made any move to touch him back until he grabs my arms and wraps them around his neck. Then his hands move to my ribs as they slowly move down my body, settling on my lower back.

His eyes never leave mine while his hands explore my body.

How is he able to garner this much of a reaction just by dancing with me? I've never felt like this before. This level of desire isn't something I thought was real.

My heels give me a bit of height, so our lips aren't that far apart. I can feel his breath on my mouth. The smell of wine and mint is intoxicating.

He leads us around the dance floor, clearly no stranger to the art of dancing.

He breaks the silence. "We seem to have an audience."

I don't even look, I don't care who is watching us.

When he notices my attention never leaves him, his eyes turn dark.

"If you would've told me last week..." he starts but closes his eyes and shakes his head.

"What?" I whisper.

"You keep surprising me." He leans in a bit closer.

I feel myself lean into him. It's impossible not to.

Then next thing I know, his lips are on mine. It's a gentle kiss, but it lights my body on fire. I feel him start to pull away, and I panic. I want more.

I rise on my toes and deepen the kiss. My tongue mixing with his.

He groans into my mouth. For a second, he doesn't kiss me back, and I think I've made a terrible mistake.

I try to pull back slowly, but he stops me. Then he takes control as his lips press firmly into mine. His hands move up and grab my face. His tongue is invasive as it plays with mine. The kiss is like a drug. I feel my entire body lose control and submit to the feeling. I don't know how long we kiss. Time ceases to exist. All I'm aware of is the feeling of his wet lips moving along mine.

Eventually, he pulls away, but only slightly, our faces only a breath apart.

I don't know what just happened. Was that a real kiss or did he do it because people were watching? We never talked about kissing as part of the deal, but it makes sense. My brain is spinning right now with questions.

He looks past my shoulder.

"Hi, guys," Savannah appears by our side with a serious looking Luke while they dance. "Nice work. After that kiss, there's no way William's doubting anything. It looked pretty damn real."

I laugh nervously as my body freezes. Then I feel his hand on my hip, giving it a couple squeezes like he's trying to reassure me that he's got this.

"I saw you guys looking at us while talking to him. I figured it was the end of the evening, we needed to seal the deal, right?" he says with a wink.

I know I'm supposed to feel relieved. He took the heat off us. But are his words true or is he just covering for us?

After we finish our dance, Luke calls it a night since Savannah is getting tired. Which leads to everybody deciding to head back to the hotel.

Marcus holds my hand the entire time he says his goodbyes. When we are all walking out to the limo, I look down at our locked hands and wonder if this is it. Will this be the last time I get to enjoy a touch like this from him? After this, him and I will no longer be playing the part.

I don't know if I'll be able to handle things going back to the way they were. Friendly hellos and nods around the office, but no laughs or touches. I feel like tonight was my time to do something different, be someone different, and it's slipping away.

Still reeling from the kiss, I climb into the limo and somehow end up on the far end with the girls.

The guys on the other end are laughing and joking about something.

"Nice work tonight guys," Alexis says as she looks to Marcus and me. "Not sure if he would've totally bought it if it weren't for Kathryn being there. She wouldn't stop saying how cute you two are together."

"Do you think it worked?" I ask the gang, hopeful.

Gabe shrugs his shoulders. "Time will tell. But I think as far as what we were going for tonight, it worked. He couldn't really complain about image when each of the men here had a beautiful woman they were in love with on their arm."

"What kind of shit is that?" Mia interrupts. "He doesn't care what I do? Why? Because I'm a woman? Frickin' double standards."

I giggle next to her. I completely agree with her. It's a double standard and an archaic way of doing business.

The ride to the hotel goes by in a flash. I'm the last one to climb out of the limo. I grab the hand that helps me out expecting it to be the driver instead I'm surprised to see Marcus.

"Thanks," I tell him.

"Not a problem."

He lets go of my hand this time as we walk side by side through the doors.

The other five must've already taken an elevator up because they are nowhere in sight. Marcus and I step onto the first elevator that arrives and ride it up in silence. I'm not sure how to act around him now that this is all over. I stare down at the dark tiles in the elevator, unsure where to look.

But as the silence grows in the elevator, so does the tension. I steal a glance at him and notice that he's looking at me like he was right before he kissed me.

His eyes rake over my body, and his appreciation for what he sees is evident. He pushes off the wall and starts towards me, but before he can take another step, the elevator doors open.

The moment seems to have passed and he turns away to walk toward our rooms.

We stop outside of our doors together, silence filling the air around us.

"Thanks again for everything, Lex."

"You're welcome."

He seems torn about something. I want to tell him to come into my room. To kiss me again. To keep making me feels these things that I've never felt before. The words are almost out of my mouth, and I feel like he's waiting for them, but at the last second, I chicken out.

"Goodnight," he whispers.

I don't know how to invite someone like him in without the fear of rejection stopping me.

"Goodnight," I reply and walk into my room.

Dammit! This is not what I want. Why can't I just tell him what it is that I want?

My phone begins to vibrate. For a second, I think he's calling me. I fumble through my purse until I pull it out to see Grace's name on the screen.

"Hello," I answer as I push off the door.

I kick off my heels and walk further into the room.

"You sound out of breath. What're you doing?"

I stop in front of the mirror and look at my flushed cheeks.

"Do I? I'm just getting in from the event."

A knot is sitting in my stomach at the missed opportunity.

"You sound weird. What's going on?" she asks.

I swear, she knows me too well. I don't have to say anything for her to know that there's something different in my voice.

"You'll never believe what happened tonight."

I rehash the events of the night to her going over the details of the kiss, all the way to how we ended things at our doors a moment ago.

"What? Girl, you need to go for it. Come on! He obviously wants you."

"Are you crazy? I can't just go for it. He's my boss for one, and he's..."

"What? Out of your league? Girl, you sent me a picture before you left, you look hot. Tonight is your chance to do something for yourself, for once in your life!"

I want to do that. Everything in me wants to knock on his door and make him see what I think is there between us. I want him to see me as more than just boring, old Lexi. But I just don't know how to do that.

"What do I do?" I ask. "How do I make him see me differently?"

"You need to make him go crazy. You want him to be dying to touch you again."

My breath accelerates just thinking of doing that to him. What would it be like to know that he's dying to touch me again, to have me?

"Tell me what to do."

"You knock on his door and take control. Make him lose his damn mind then end it abruptly, walking out and leaving the ball in his court."

How do I make him lose his mind? The only way I've ever come close to doing that to a man is to...

I gosh, do I have it in me to do that? I think about losing this opportunity, about letting the night pass me by.

I have to do it.

"Okay," I breathe. "I have to do this. Don't I?"

"Yes! Call me when you get home tomorrow. Make tonight your bitch."

I smile as I put the phone down. I look at myself in the mirror, and I see the woman I've always wanted to be. If not tonight, when? I fix my hair, trying to put some extra body into it. I look at my lips, noticing my lipstick has faded, so I dig into my purse and pull out my stick to reapply.

After one final deep breath and last glance in the mirror, I walk over to our joined doors and knock.

When he opens it, he's standing there with his pants un-buckled and shirt hanging open. It makes my body come to life. He is so damn sexy. All my fears disappear and I step forward to take what I want.

My hand reaches out to feel the strength of his chest. I slowly begin to graze my fingers down his chest. His mus-cles tense as I make my way down to his abs.

"What are you doing?" he whispers.

When my fingers reach the top of his pants, I grab the material and tug him towards me. With both hands, I unclasp his pants and slowly drag down the zipper.

"I think you can figure it out. Stop me if you don't want this," I say then push his pants to the floor.

His throat bobs as I watch him swallow, but he doesn't say anything. I fall to my knees, and he gasps when he realizes what I'm going to do. I reach up to the waistband of his boxer briefs and pull them down to meet his pants on the floor. He steps out of them as he stands in front of me in only his crisp white shirt.

My hand reaches up and wraps around his thick length. Of course, he's got the perfect dick too. He is blessed with the perfect *everything*.

I love the way he closes his eyes as I grip him tighter and give his dick a tug.

"Lexi," he whispers.

I open my mouth and lean forward running my tongue in a circle around his tip. He exhales loudly as I do it a couple more times then close my lips around him and rest my tongue flat on the underside of his dick.

"Fuck!" he growls. "Those damn lips. Look at them, plump and stained from your lipstick. They look incredible wrapped around my dick."

Moisture pools between my legs. I've never had a man talk to me like that before. It makes me feel powerful and *sexy*.

I've never felt sexy before. It's exhilarating and gives me the strength to continue.

With one hand wrapped around the base of his length, I get to work. Sucking hard and fast as my saliva begins to build, running down my chin.

"Holy. Fucking. Shit." He grabs my hair and squeezes. "Where the hell did you learn to do this? I've never seen anything hotter in my damn life. You better not stop."

I suck even harder, and he lets out a low scream then fucks my mouth for a few pumps before giving me back control. With each bob, I feel it get messier and messier until I'm slurping and making sounds I've never made. It's by the far the dirtiest blowjob I've ever given, and I'm loving every second of it.

"Your lipstick," he starts but loses his breath as he looks back down at me. "Fuck, it's everywhere and it's everything." I run my tongue everywhere I can, and when I create more suction, he gasps. "Oh, fuck, just like that, Lex."

I keep the suction and increase my pace.

"Fuck, yes. I'm gonna come so fucking hard baby."

And he does. He explodes in my mouth with thick bursts of his salty cum. And I gulp it down like it's the only thing I've ever wanted to have in my mouth.

I pop off him and swallow, wiping my mouth with the back of my hand.

He continues to stare down at me with dark eyes, but before he can say anything, I stand up and walk back into my room, closing the door behind me.

I go into the bathroom and turn the light on. My hair is wild from his hands and my mouth is a mess. Lipstick is stained all around my skin like I'm the fucking joker. It's evidence of just how crazy I got. I smile at myself in the mirror.

For once, I put aside all my fears and went for something that I wanted.

Chapter Twelve

Marcus

Sunday nights at my parents' house are always the refresher that I need if I've had a tough day or something's on my mind. We landed a couple of hours ago, and my brain has yet to slow down. It's flooded with images from last night.

The sexiest slideshow of Lexi's mouth wrapped around my dick. Her lipstick smearing all over it with each slide of her mouth. Each time I imagine it, I picture a different shade of lipstick. I want her to paint the fucking rainbow on my dick with those colors.

Never in my life have I been so utterly lost for words than last night after she popped off my dick and retreated into her room.

I paced back and forth for what felt like an hour, trying to figure out what to do, what to say.

Did I want to ask her what the hell that was for? We work together, we shouldn't be doing that. Or did I want to throw her on the bed and return the favor?

I'm so damn confused. Well, my brain is confused. My dick knows exactly what he wants.

Luckily, I pull into my parents' driveway, and my nerves begin to settle. I know I'll get to go inside and distract myself, even if only for a little while.

I open the front door and am hit with the familiar aroma of her sauce.

"Uncle Marc," Sienna, my oldest niece, comes running into my arms.

I wrap them around her and lift her up. "Ahhh, SiSi. I missed you."

She giggles. "I see you all the time."

"It's not enough," I say dramatically as I walk into the family room with her dangling off my neck.

I put her down and kneel on the ground to give my nephew Joey a big kiss on his soft, chubby cheek.

"Train," he says as he points to his toys in front of him.

"Wow, cool trains!" I reply as I lie down on my side and start moving a train around the track. "Choo, choo."

He giggles. "More. More."

"Hi, Ma. Hi, Pa," I shout as I hear them talking from the kitchen.

Pa strolls into the room with a beer in his hand then takes a seat next to Gabe. Alexis must be in the kitchen with Ma.

"Hi, son."

"Hey, Pa. How's it going?"

"Nothing worth complaining about."

My Pa was a masonry. He worked hard all his life and earned each penny with the sweat on his body. He never complained once. I've always looked up to him. I know he has a little back trouble from all the manual labor, but he never says anything.

To this day, he won't take any money from any of us. He's a proud man. Too proud if you ask me. His children make a lot of money and could set him and Ma up with a great lifestyle now that they're retired. But we've all learned to keep our mouths shut about it.

"Where are Savannah and Luke?" I ask as I notice they aren't here yet.

"Savannah's pretty beat from the trip. They're going to stay home tonight," Gabe tells me.

"Makes sense. She was up later than usual last night."

Ma calls all of us into the kitchen for dinner. Mia and Alexis are helping her bring the plates to the center of the table when we walk in.

"There he is," Mia says with a smile. "Good to see you finally arrived."

"I've been here for a while loser," I say as I tousle her hair.

She backs away emphatically. "Hey, what did I say about the hair?"

I laugh. "Get over yourself, Mia. Just because you now pay a grand for your haircuts, doesn't mean I'm gonna stop messing with you."

Ma gasps. "Mia! You pay a thousand dollars for your hair?"

Mia scowls at me as she takes a bite of her meatball. "No, Ma, I don't. I just lied to Marcus. It was an attempt to get him to stop doing that. An obviously failed attempt."

Sitting down with them is already becoming my much-needed escape.

Joey starts to eat his spaghetti and meatballs with his hands. I watch in fascination as he gets every other bite into his mouth.

I chuckle when the next piece falls. He clearly decided he didn't have the patience for utensils tonight. Alexa introduced him to a fork and spoon earlier, so I'm used to seeing him eat pretty well.

"Is nobody gonna tell Joey to eat with his fork?" I step in when his face is covered in sauce.

Alexis sighs. "He's refusing to use them lately. I don't know what phase he's in, but I can't wait until it's over. He's always a complete mess after he eats now."

By the end of dinner, Joey is covered from head to toe in pasta sauce, wearing half of the noodles he had on his highchair tray.

I snap a picture and can't resist making it my home screen on my phone. That'll definitely be something to make me smile every time I use it.

Ma takes him out of his highchair and insists on giving him a bath before they go home. Mia gets up and asks to join, always the helpful aunt.

By the end of the evening, I'm feeling better. I don't know what will come with me and Lexi. I do know we need to talk about what happened, but I can handle it. Can't I?

I'm walking back from the breakroom with a fresh cup of coffee. I haven't seen Lexi yet, but I'm sure we can work this entire thing out. The more I thought about it last night, the more I realized that this entire thing is a bad idea.

There's clearly an attraction there, but it's probably for the best that we don't act on it any further. I made the mistake with the kiss and led her on. I just hope she understands and agrees with me.

I take a sip of coffee as I approach my office. Just as I'm about to walk in, Lexi walks out of her office.

When she sees me, her face lights up.

"Hey Marcus," she says as she walks past me.

I can't get any words out quickly enough, but my head automatically turns and follows her as she walks away. Her ass is swaying in her tight skirt. And she has lipstick on again. Red this time.

I want to know what that damn red looks like all over my dick. I bet it would stain my skin for days. My dick twitches in my pants just thinking about it.

Fuck! This isn't good.

I walk into my office and slam the mug on my desk. Hot coffee spills over onto my desk, but I just fall into my chair and lean my head back. I've literally seen her for three seconds and I'm already hard.

When I hear heels clicking on the floor, getting louder with every step, I lift my head. She appears again, walking past my room with a smile and wink this time.

Who the hell is this woman?

Lexi has somehow turned into the boldest, sexiest woman I've ever met, and I've turned into a stuttering mess of a man.

The roles have never been reversed on me like this before. I'm completely out of my element.

A knock on the door breaks me from my own personal crisis.

"I have the Peterson contract that you wanted to look over before it went out," Luke says as he holds up a folder.

"Sounds good. Just leave it on my desk. I'll get to it before lunch."

Luke tosses it on the corner of my desk then takes a seat.

"You alright? You seem a bit on edge."

I crane my neck to the left to try and work out some of the tension.

"I'm fine. I guess the whole thing with William made me a bit more tense than I realized."

"Lexi did a good job. She really pulled through for us."

"Yeah," I reply stiffly. "Lexi was amazing."

As thankful as I am for her helping, what I really would've appreciated was my brother's support. They never once told me that we shouldn't be in this position, that I'm not at fault here. Nor did it ever occur to them to not go through this charade and just stick up to William.

I know he's a major part of our business, but do we want to set a precedent that he can walk all over us?

I don't know. Even if we did go through with it, even if we did need to please the guy, some moral support that it's bullshit and that I'm a good guy would've gone a long way with me.

"Speaking of Lexi, she's working on that new configuration to have all of our orders go through an approval process. She needs one of us to go through the testing with her to make sure we are all squared away and like the final result. I figured you could jump on that."

"Yeah, sure. Just tell her to send me a meeting invite."

One-on-one time with Lexi is the last thing that I need, but what can I say?

"Got it. I'll let her know. Catch ya later."

He walks out of the office, leaving me to wonder what I did to deserve this continuous stream of bad luck. In the span of a year, I've only needed to work solo with Lexi maybe two times. Now, two days after she blew my mind and my dick, I'm told I need to be in a room alone with her.

Chapter Thirteen

Lexi

He doesn't know how to act around me. This morning I walked by him and winked, trying to play it cool, and I was surprised that he didn't say anything to me. It almost made me laugh to see his jaw-dropping stare. I feel like a whole new woman after Saturday night.

Even seeing my mom went a lot better on Sunday morning. She was in better spirits. I had a sweatshirt packed in case I got cold in the hotel, so I put that on. With baggier clothes and my hair up in a messy bun, I was once again the daughter she recognized. The reality of what I might have to do from now on with her made me a little sad. I wish she wasn't so triggered by a woman looking beautiful. My father leaving her for someone younger really messed her up.

It would've been nice if she could have gone to therapy and worked through those issues.

When I called Zoe last night to tell her what happened, it took an hour to convince her I wasn't lying. I still think a part of her feels I'm trying to pull one over on her. It's not just a little bit out of character for me, it's light-years away.

Instead of getting the space that he might feel like he wants or needs, based on how much he avoided my presence all morning, we're going to be working closely again. He's due in my office any minute to go over the first phase of testing. I'm oddly excited to see him, and not that nervous. It's more of an anticipation.

I finally get to have some time with him again. You would think that I would be insecure about him avoiding me, but his look of appreciation this morning was unmistakable.

A soft knock at my door startles me from my thoughts.

"Hi." I smile when I see Marcus standing there. "Come on in."

"Hi, Lexi," he says with a faint smile. The first words he's spoken to me since my mouth swallowed his cum. "Where do you want me?"

Images of him pushing me down on the desk and taking me from behind begin to flood my brain. I'm not normally the dirty-thinking type, but Marcus is bringing a new side out of me. A side I want to explore.

"Um, I thought we could just pull up a chair behind my desk. I wanted to start with running through the program with you."

He nods his head and brings a chair right next to mine. When he takes a seat, his scent drifts through the air. My body responds to it, thinking about what he smelled like when I was touching his naked chest.

"I meant to tell you that I talked to the team about getting you some help around here. Mia will talk about it with you in further detail, but it's safe to say you can begin looking into hiring someone to work underneath you."

I look over my left shoulder at him. "Wow. Thank you. That'll be really helpful actually."

His eyes fall to my lips then drag slowly up to my eyes. "Don't mention it," he says with a strained voice.

I can't believe he did that. He's full of surprises.

"Well, I guess we should get started." I turn my computer screen towards him, and he leans his body closer. "This is the overall new design of the order form. I gave everything a drop-down menu so people couldn't type anything they wanted and we'd have to manually verify the details with them. It should take some confusion out of it."

"It's a good design. Nice and clean. Not overcrowded."

"Thanks. I tried to keep it simple. The first thing I want to make sure is that when I fill out this test form, it goes to your email for approval."

He pulls his laptop out of his briefcase and opens it up. "Got it. Let me just get into my email."

Once he has his laptop resting on the corner of my desk, I continue. "So, the customer will start here by using this drop-down to identify their customer number. If they are a new customer, they will have to reach out to us to provide them with one. This will ensure that we don't have customers not yet through our onboarding process putting in orders."

I continue down the form, pointing out the parts that are going to make it automated, and how it connects to the other systems. He follows along, asking detailed questions and providing great feedback. That's one thing that I've noticed while working with him. He may get a rep for being the ladies' man or the fun-loving goofy one, but when it comes time to work, he puts in effort and is intelligent.

"Alright, let's go ahead and submit this one and see if it comes up in your email," I tell him.

Once I click submit, we give it a couple seconds before his email dings with a new notification.

I hold my breath, hoping his approval will do what it needs to on my end. This part can be a nightmare to find the issue, and I don't feel like working late tonight. My constant overtime could be a thing of the past once I hire someone else. He will never know how much it means to me that he made that happen.

"Ok, I just approved it," he says.

We both go back to my screen as I work my way through the logs to find the test submission so we can see if it says approved or not. As he leans over my shoulder again, he feels closer this time. I can feel the heat of his body. I strain my eyes to the left to try and see where he is, and I'm hit with a look of pure torture on his face.

"Are you okay?" I ask him.

I catch his eyes glance back down to my lips, and I wonder what he's thinking. All I know is that it's starting to feel really fucking hot in here, and I don't think it has anything to do with the temperature of the room. It is this man sitting next to me, looking at me like he's about to do something I've wanted him to do again since Saturday night—kiss me.

He takes me by surprise when his forehead hits my shoulder, and he groans. "No, Lexi. I'm not fucking okay."

I'm not sure what to say. This is not what I was expecting.

"I can't stop thinking about Saturday night. I'm so fucked up over it. I don't know what to say or what to do. I don't know how to stop picturing it. I don't even know if you want to forget about everything and go back to the way we were. You walking out after threw me for a loop. Fuck, I don't want to forget it happened, but I'm trying to let you take the lead here. I don't want to do anything that will make you uncomfortable."

My heart beats erratically. I can't believe the words that I'm hearing. I think of what to say back. I want to just turn around and kiss him, but I'm still processing everything. I don't know if he takes my silence as discomfort, but he lifts his head off my shoulder. Leaving his things behind, he rushes to the door.

Luckily, my brain reacts fast enough to stop him before he leaves. I don't want him to feel confused by what I want. I want to make it crystal clear.

Now is my chance. Take it.

"Wait. Don't go."

He turns around and stares at me. No words are spoken, he just waits. He watches me as I get up and slowly walk over to him.

"What is it?" he asks me.

I stop in front of him and look up into his eyes. "Don't you want to return the favor?"

His eyes grow big as his head turns to the side. "What do you mean, Lexi?"

"I mean," I begin as my hand comes out to touch his chest, "you never got the chance to return the favor on Saturday night."

Without breaking contact with my eyes, he reaches for the door and closes it.

"Are you telling me you want me to taste your pussy right now, Lexi?" he growls as he takes a step toward me.

Holy Shit! When he says those words out loud, it makes this entire thing sound so dirty. I'm not used to someone who is this bold. I can feel myself already wet and needy.

"Yes," I breathe.

"Thank fuck," he breathes.

His hand lands on the back of my head as he pulls me in for a searing kiss. Unlike our public kiss, this one is fast and hungry. He isn't holding anything back as he pushes me backward. It feels so good to let him take control. Both of his hands are on my cheeks while his tongue comes out and plays with mine.

"I've been going crazy trying to hold myself back from you," he whispers into my mouth then comes back down for another kiss that makes my knees weak.

"Don't. Please don't hold back."

A wicked smile takes over his face. He reaches behind me and drags the zipper of my skirt all the way down. The sound echoes throughout my office, making the moment feel intense. He drags the skirt down until it hits the floor. I step out of it without being asked to, knowing exactly what we both want.

"Sit on your desk, Lex."

I scoot myself onto the desk and push myself back further with my hands. The desire in his eyes is almost nerve-wracking. It makes this moment feel so much more extreme.

"Good girl. Now put those high heels up on the edge of the desk and show me your beautiful pussy."

I gasp. It sounds so wrong, but my body obeys him. My body wants more of his dirty words.

When I get my feet in position, I'm completely exposed to him. He makes a deep guttural noise as he stares down at me.

"You're perfect. Fuck. Look at how much you want this. You're dripping with excitement."

He starts to unbuckle his belt then pulls himself out, giving his length a long stroke. The view is incredible.

But it doesn't last for long because he reaches for my knees and bends them down to the edge of the desk. Then his fingers start to trace small circles from my knees down my thighs. One hand trails along the top of my pelvis while I wait impatiently.

My breathing is out of control.

"I dreamt about this last night," he admits. "I woke up with the biggest hard-on of my life."

His thumb grazes my clit and a I let out a small whimper.

"It was nothing close to the real thing," he says, then drags his fingers down my pussy.

When he brings them back up to my clit, they are coated with my arousal. He starts to rub small but firm circles then pushes them into me. The invasion is surprising, but welcome.

"Yes," I let out as he begins to curl his fingers inside of me.

He smiles. "Do you like my fingers fucking you like this?"

I nod adamantly.

"Do you want me to taste you, Lex?"

I nod again, this time he chuckles. But it doesn't last long. He becomes serious as he leans down closer and closer. While his fingers continue working inside of me, his tongue draws a torturously slow circle around my clit. He moans when he brings his tongue back into his mouth.

"You taste sweeter than anything I've ever had on my tongue."

He goes in for another swirl, this time with added pressure. With each swirl and flick, I begin to lose control. I know I need to keep quiet, but it's becoming more difficult. He flattens his tongue, moans into me, and then shakes his head back and forth. The pleasure from his mouth and his fingers combined set me off. I throw my head to the side as I clamp my hand over my mouth to silence my screams.

He works me until I'm completely spent, and all of my shudders and twitches are gone. When he stands up and wipes his mouth with the back of his hand, I notice his dick still hanging out and hard as ever.

I suddenly feel like I'm gonna die if I don't get him in my mouth.

I push myself off the desk and get on my knees in front of him.

"Fuck, yes," he says as he threads his fingers through my hair.

I wrap my lips around him and immediately start sucking hard and fast. He hisses as I grab his ass and push him closer into me.

"Dammit, I knew those red lips would look fucking perfect around my dick."

He pushes in and out of my mouth as his eyes remain locked on our connection. I moan when he says those dirty words to me.

"You like that?" he says. "Do you like knowing that I pictured all the different shades of color you could have on your lips while you sucked my cock? About what they would look like smeared all over me?"

I nod my head, agreeing that I love knowing his intimate admission. It makes me want to buy all the shades of lipstick in the world and test each one on him.

As I lick and suck him like he's a damn popsicle on the hottest day of the year, he begins to lose control. He cusses under his breath and tells me how perfect I am. It's an endless stream of compliments out of his mouth. I'm not sure he knows how much he talks during oral sex.

It's kind of adorable.

When he finally gets to the point of no return, he lets me know he's gonna come. Once again, I suck him harder and faster, letting him know I want it down my throat.

I love watching him come. His eyebrows scrunch forward, making him look like he's concentrating really hard. His lips go tight and his throat sounds strained.

With each pump of cum, he cusses until he is completely empty.

I pop off him and swallow the salty taste of him, mimicking his wipe of the mouth with the back of my hand.

I stand up and we both just stare at each other for a minute as we catch our breath. Then he takes me by surprise by putting his hands on my cheeks and rubbing gentle circles with his thumbs. He leans down and kisses me softly and slowly.

"That was the best meeting I've ever had in my life," he says when he pulls back.

I laugh with relief, loving that he knows how to make the moment feel fun and not so serious.

Chapter Fourteen

Marcus

It's Thursday already. Three days since we fooled around in her office. Every single day that she walks into the office, my heart races. She doesn't nag me, hang around waiting for me, or push me in any way. At first, I thought it was a relief, giving me time to figure out what I wanted to come of this.

Now, I'm not exactly a fan. Why is it so easy for her to stay away? I feel like the needy one, and it's driving me crazy.

I want to spend some time with her, but I want it outside the office. I just don't know how to approach her with the subject.

I'm sitting at my desk with my door open when I see her walk by without even looking in. Fed up, I decide I need to grow a pair and ask her out. That's how this goes, right? The man asks the woman out. I've never done anything like this before, but I've never dated a woman like her before.

I knock lightly on her door, and she looks up from her desk and smiles.

"Hey you," she says. "Come on in."

She's so easy and makes this all seem too natural. There's no pretense or games. If she's happy to see me, she shows it. I love that.

"You're looking beautiful today," I tell her as I walk in.

I come around her desk and lean against it, folding my arms across my chest.

"Thank you. What can I do for you?" she asks as she crosses her legs.

Her skirt slides even higher, revealing more of her luscious thighs. I do my best to focus on what I came in here for.

"Are you free tonight?" I ask.

"I am." She seems amused as she answers.

I clear my throat, feeling tense about asking her and getting rejected. When did I become such a loser?

"Would you...uh...like to come over to my place tonight?"

She smiles. "You want me to come over to your place?"

"That's what I'm asking."

"What are we gonna do?" she asks, still smiling at me.

I laugh. "Do you need an itinerary?"

"Sorry," she says with a laugh. "I think I'm just a bit nervous."

Relief comes over me. I'm glad I'm not the only one nervous about all this.

"Well, I think we should just start with dinner. I would cook, but won't have much time after work. I can order some takeout for us."

"That sounds perfect. You can text me your address."

"Great. See you tonight, Lex." I wink at her, then head back to my office.

***

One thing I'm thankful for is my cleaning tendencies. It makes this last-minute invite to Lexi a little less stressful since I don't have to run around my house trying to make it presentable.

The knock on my door urges me to look around one last time to make sure everything's in order. On the way to the front door, I check myself in the mirror. I changed into jeans and a white T-shirt to keep things casual.

I open the door and see her standing there in jeans and a green cotton T-shirt; only hers is fitted and shows off those beautiful tits of hers.

I smile and grab her hand, then pull her inside. Her laughs echo through my foyer and make my chest feel tight.

"Come here," I say as I pull her close and slam my lips down on hers.

It starts playful and light. But kissing her is like a drug; it doesn't take long before I'm addicted and craving more.

Her tongue meets mine eagerly, and we both release a moan. My hands reach for her ass, and I pull her into me. I'm already getting hard, and she's been here for thirty seconds. I feel like a teenager again.

I pull away and offer one last small kiss.

"Sorry." My breathing is erratic. "I was planning to be good...at least for a little while. Would you like to come in?"

She smiles. "I would love to."

"Let me show you around."

I give her a tour of my house, quickly moving from room to room. I'm in a rush to get my hands on her again. But as we make it to the end of the long hallway on the first floor, I realize I'm excited to show her this last room.

"So, this is my favorite room in the entire house," I tell her as we stand outside the closed door.

"Oh, God. It's not like a sex room or something. Is it?"

I laugh. "No, it's not a sex room. How creepy would that be?"

I open it up and turn on the light.

She gasps as she enters, her jaw hitting the floor, making me feel proud.

It's a two-story room, twenty-foot walls with built-in bookcases that go all the way up to the top. There's a twenty-foot ladder attached to the shelves, enabling it to slide along the wall.

It has dark hardwood floors and a huge bay window with cushions on the built-in bench. There's also a chaise lounge chair in the corner with a blanket draped over the back. The corner on the opposite side of the room has a dark leather chair where I like to sit and read in the morning with my coffee.

Lexi turns her head back to me. "This is incredible. Was this here when you moved in?"

"No. But when I walked in here, it was the first thing I envisioned, and I had to have it. I spend a lot of my free time here. I love to read. It's a huge stress reliever for me."

"Wow. I wouldn't have pegged you as a big reader."

I know it's an innocent comment, but it hits me in an already sensitive spot. I know people don't consider me the type of guy you take seriously. I usually just laugh it off, never taking it too seriously. But I care about what Lexi thinks of me.

"It's one of my favorite things to do with my free time."

"Mine too."

She walks along the bookshelves as her fingers glide along the spines of the books. Watching her, I realize she looks like she belongs in this room. I can picture her with me in the morning, both of us enjoying our coffee in silence as we dive into our books. It's the strangest feeling, but it makes my heart skip a beat.

I have never pictured something so domestic before. I don't know what she's doing to me, but I'm open to seeing where this goes.

The delivery guy knocks on the door.

"Food?" she turns to me and asks.

"Yep."

We start to walk out of the room, but I notice her look of disappointment. I laugh and wrap my arm around her. "We can come back to the room later."

She sighs. "You've ruined me for life. Now, I'll be picturing this when I read at my house. I will resent you forever. We won't be able to get past it. I'll have to quit."

"Wow. That's quite the overactive imagination you've got there."

"It's from all the reading I do," she jokes.

We reach the front door, and Lexi helps me carry the food into the kitchen.

"It smells amazing," she says as we place the containers on the island.

"Have you ever had DiStefano's before?" I ask.

"I haven't."

"Well, you are in for a treat. I didn't know what you liked, so I ordered a bit of everything."

She scans the containers as I open them.

"You ordered enough to feed me for a month."

I shrug. "I'll bring the leftovers in to work tomorrow. We can all enjoy some lunch on me."

"What should I try?"

"Well, I'm partial to the cavatelli. The Italian sausage and peppers or the chicken cutlets are also amazing."

She goes for the chicken cutlet with a bit of cavatelli on the side. I do the same, and we sit at my table, where I have a bottle of wine and two glasses waiting for us. I open the bottle and pour us each a glass.

"Thank you. What are we drinking tonight?"

"A Chianti from one of my favorite vineyards in Tuscany. It's a rare bottle," I tell her.

"Wow. I feel honored you're willing to share with me."

I look at her, wondering if she understands what she's doing to me. I would share my best bottle of wine with her. She's somebody that should be treated like the treasure that she is. I was an idiot not to recognize it for an entire year. It's not every day that something like this happens to me, that somebody makes me feel like this. I've never felt this way, and I'm chasing these feelings.

"Don't sell yourself short. You're worth much more than a nice bottle of wine."

She looks up at me, then glances down at her plate. "Thank you."

"Now eat up. You don't want to let this food get cold."

"Geez. Bossy much?" She smiles and then takes a bite of her food.

I picture what it would be like to boss her around. My body gets stiff just thinking about it. "You haven't met my bossy side yet. Trust me, you'll know when you do."

Her mouth stops mid-chew. She knows what I'm talking about. And fuck if I don't love the innocent look on her face. Is she picturing it right now like I am?

She gathers herself and starts to chew again.

"Damn, this is really good," she says.

I smile. "I know. I grew up eating this food."

"So, you're from around here?" she asks.

I nod. "I'm from a little neighborhood close by called Little Italy. My parents still live there."

"Oh, I've been there. There's a bakery there that I love, Corbo's."

"It's a great bakery. Grew up eating their stuff, too."

"What's your favorite trip to Italy?"

Wow. That's quite the question. I've never been asked it before, either. It takes me a second to consider it.

"There was one trip where I just spent the weekend driving around Tuscany with no destination in mind. I went from town to town, trying the wine and cheese and enjoying the open country roads."

"Wow, that sounds incredible. I would love to go someday."

"I might just have to insist on needing an IT guru with me for my next business trip there."

"Oh, gosh," she laughs. "Like anybody would buy that."

I shrug. "Who cares what anybody else thinks?"

I mean it. If I want to take her with me on a trip, I will. She's a part of our company; she deserves to experience our other areas of business at least once.

After we finish our dinner, we head outside to sit on the patio furniture with our wine. It's a nice night. There's a little chill in the air, but that's expected when you're approaching October. But it gives me an excellent excuse to scoot close and put my arm around her.

She rests her head on my chest while we sit in silence. It feels so easy like we've done this a hundred times before.

"I never did ask you how your visit with your mom went on Sunday morning. I was a little distracted on the plane. You see, a coworker of mine had come into my hotel room the night before and sucked my dicked so good I couldn't work my brain for a solid twenty-four hours."

She starts to laugh into my chest. "She sounds like quite the catch."

"Oh, she is the ultimate catch." I lift my shoulder to give her a nudge. "How'd it go?"

She sighs. "It was better. I made a point not to wear make-up and put my hair up in a ponytail. That seemed to help. I also packed a baggy sweatshirt, so I put that on."

"Can I ask you a question?" I ask hesitantly.

"Why is she like that?" she asks for me.

"I'm sorry. I don't mean any disrespect. I know you're struggling with her illness."

"It's fine." She takes a deep breath. I pull her in tighter to me, an odd sense of wanting to protect her from any negative emotion. "My dad left us when I was five. It was for a younger woman. She took it really hard. Never got over it, actually. She began to look at young, beautiful women as the enemy. From that moment on, she drilled it into my head that I should never dress to impress. She thought it attracted the wrong kind of guy."

It all makes so much sense now. Why she dressed like that. Why she always tried to blend in with the background. I hate that she ever thought she shouldn't be who she wants to be.

"Another question. Be honest," I tell her. "Are you actually happy with your new clothes and everything, or do you feel like you have to do it now?"

I tense up as I wait for her answer, worrying that it'll make me feel like the biggest dick in the world.

"Calm down," she smiles and looks up at me. She gives me a quick kiss on the lips. "I love my new look. I know I had a hard time that night with everything that happened with my mom. There are still a lot of wounds to unpack there, and I don't know if I'll ever be able to show her the new me, but I don't regret it. I secretly wanted it to happen for years. I just never had the guts to go through with it. You helped me."

I relax slightly, relieved that I didn't force her into something that made her feel bad about herself.

"You know, I think the new you isn't this huge difference in appearance so much as more confidence. None of the changes were drastic. But it may have brought out a part of you that you were afraid to show. An assertive and sexy woman that was just waiting to break free."

She gazes up at me. "You think I'm sexy?"

"If you don't know that by now, I've done a shitty job at showing it."

I lean down and press my lips to hers. The kiss starts slow but builds quickly. I slip my tongue inside her mouth, and she meets it with delicate strokes. My body starts to get heated, making the kiss more urgent.

My hand reaches for her neck and slowly grazes down until it reaches her breast. I give it a light squeeze, which grants me a small moan from her mouth.

I pull away from her, completely drunk off her kiss...and needy with desire.

"Do you...want to..." I start slowly, hoping she gets the hint.

Her eager nod is enough for me to push off the couch and pull her up. Instead of dragging her to my bedroom, I decide I can't wait another second. My dick is straining in my pants, and I've suddenly lost all patience.

I bend my knees and wrap an arm just under her ass, then hoisted her up onto my shoulder. She screams until I've got her settled on my shoulder, then she laughs.

"What are you doing?" she says through her laughter as I begin to take long, quick steps.

"I'm not wasting any time. It's been a long week without getting to touch you, babe. And you don't make it easy with your sexy new work outfits either."

"Oh my gosh! Just don't drop me."

"Woman, I would never." We make it to my hallway, and I start to slow down. "If I drop you, I can't fuck you."

That makes her laugh even harder. We enter my bedroom, and I throw her down on my bed. Her laughter is contagious. I find myself doing the same as I climb on top of her. Never have I been about to have sex with a woman for the first time while simultaneously laughing together. It's an odd but welcome change.

It shows how comfortable we already are with each other.

But when I look down at her, the tops of her breasts spilling out of her top, my laughter dies. Our erratic breathing mixes, her face falling when she realizes the change in mood.

"Lexi," I whisper.

"Yes?"

"This is gonna change everything."

She nods her head in understanding. "I know. And I've never wanted it more in my life."

I slam my lips down onto hers. Knowing what we're about to do, it's already got me so damn worked up. I can't hold back any longer. I deepen the kiss as my lips move against hers urgently.

"You've had the upper hand so far, Lexi. Not this time. This time, I get to make you lose your mind."

I start to trail kisses down her neck, letting my tongue slide along her skin. She writhes beneath me, rubbing her soft body against mine. My body takes notice and starts to move along in sync with hers.

My mouth reaches the apex of her breasts, and I begin to pepper kisses along them. I yank down the right side of her T-shirt and bra, exposing her breast to me. I cover her nipple with my mouth, eagerly sucking and licking.

My dick is straining in my pants, begging to be free. But I want to enjoy exploring her body. I want full access to feast on her.

"Sit up," I tell her as I push back onto my knees.

She sits up.

"Lift your arms."

She follows my directions, and I pull her shirt over her head, then reach behind her and unsnap her bra.

"Lean back, baby." When she does, her tits bounce most deliciously. "Fuck, you have no idea what you do to me."

Before she can respond, I get back to work on worshipping her breasts. While I suck on one, I play with the other, alternating until we are both grinding on each other like two teenagers.

Then I start to trail kisses down her stomach. My mouth begins to water as I think about tasting her pussy again. I dip my tongue into her belly button, and she squirms while letting out a small giggle. I smile, loving each reaction I can get from her. She's so damn cute.

I unbutton her pants, and she lifts her hips.

"Are you anxious for my tongue, baby?"

She nods her head.

Her innocent response shows she may not be as brave and assertive in bed as I thought.

I pull her pants down her legs along with her panties and throw them on the ground. Pushing her knees apart, I lean down on one elbow. I have all the time in the world, and I plan on using it.

I bring my fingers up to her pussy and let them slowly slide around, back and forth, up and down, letting them get wet with each passing swipe. Then I sink one finger into her pussy and start to move it in and out at a leisurely pace. I'm in no hurry to pull this first orgasm from her. I want to take my time and revel in her pleasure.

"Oh, please," she begs.

I smile up at her. "Do you want to come?"

"Yesss."

I shake my head. "Not yet. Do you feel this?" I ask as I sink another finger inside of her. "This is what you've made me feel at work since we've been back. I'm in a constant state of arousal, and it's been pure torture."

Her breathing is labored as she watches my fingers work inside of her.

When I feel like I've teased her enough, I lean in and give her one long stroke of my tongue from her pussy up to her clit.

"Oh my God!" she screams.

"Mmmm," I moan into her. "I've been craving this since I tasted it the other day. It's even better than I remember."

I offer several more slow licks, taking my time enjoying her squirms. Then I start to flick her clit with fast movements, watching her start to say unintelligible things as she gets closer to exploding. I press my entire face into her pussy as I suck her clit into my mouth, moaning so she can feel the vibration.

She grabs the back of my head and holds my face there.

"If you stop, I'll kill you," she screams.

I smile while sucking and flicking my tongue, enjoying watching her lose all her inhibitions. It's intoxicating.

"Ahh, I'm coming," she shouts as she rides out her orgasm on my tongue.

I watch in complete wonder. It's the best visual I'll probably ever see in my life.

When she stops trembling and her body goes still, I give her my best shit-eating grin. She smiles back at me.

"You're really good at that," she says.

I crawl up her body and brace my hands next to her face, caging her in between me. Then I dip down and kiss her lips. I give her my tongue and let her slowly take the lead.

"Mmm," she moans. "I taste myself on you."

"I want your taste in my mouth every damn day."

I roll over on the bed and open my dresser door, then pull out a condom. I pull my shirt over my head and toss it on the floor. Then I work to unbuckle my belt and pull down my pants. My dick springs free, but before I can even work my jeans completely off my body, she leans in and takes my dick in her mouth.

"Mmm. I missed this taste in my mouth," she says, then continues to suck.

I hiss at the pleasure that she's able to draw from me. It's so damn good. My hand grabs a chunk of her hair, and I begin to thrust into her mouth.

"Fuck, where have you been all my life?" I ask as I continue.

She pops off me. "Right in front of you."

I look down at her. "All this time, right in front of my damn eyes."

I tear open the condom wrapper with my mouth and roll it down my shaft. I crawl on top of her and settle myself between her thighs, then steal a kiss before I line myself up.

Wanting to draw out the pleasure, I slide in only an inch. It's enough to make both of us gasp at the contact.

My forehead falls to hers. I close my eyes and then slide in another inch. Her hands claw at my back, adding to the moment's intensity. In one last movement, I push myself all the way in.

"Fuuuuuuck," I growl while she lets out a scream. "Holy. Shit."

I open my eyes and get lost in her stare as I slowly pull out and then push back in. The warmth of her feels different from anything I've ever felt before. I rest my weight on her and begin to grind in a circle every time I push back in so I can stimulate her clit.

Moving my hands to her hair, I grip it and begin to fuck her harder. Her jaw falls slack as I feel her walls tighten around me. She's getting close, thankfully, I'm not gonna last much longer.

"Your pussy, Lexi. Fuck, it's perfect." She does something, I don't know if it's intentional or not, but it grips me like a damn vice. "Oh, shit, baby. If you do that again, I'm gonna come."

I increase my speed and fuck her harder than I think I've ever fucked anyone. We are both a panting and whimpering mess as my movements start to get jerky and uncoordinated, both fighting to reach our goal. She meets me with each thrust until she screams out her orgasm.

The second I know she's coming, I let myself release inside of her.

"Fuck, yeah," I scream as I come.

I've never screamed during sex before. It felt like the only way to deal with the pleasure that came with her gripping my cock.

I fall on top of her, letting my lungs fight to get my breathing under control. I pull out and lie down next to her.

"Wow," I breathe.

"Yeah...wow."

Chapter Fifteen

Lexi

"Are you serious? Was it that good?" Zoe whispers through the phone.

I'm sitting at my desk, trying to be discreet but knowing she'll refuse to leave me alone if I don't give her some details.

"Why are you whispering?" I say softly. "You're not even at work yet."

She laughs. "Oh, yeah, sorry. Seriously. Tell me."

I sigh as I think about last night. "It was like...having sex for the first time because all the other times were nothing compared to it."

"Damn, girl. I'm so happy for you. When are you going to see him again?"

"We haven't talked about it. I mean, technically, I've already seen him this morning, but his brother was in his office."

"Well, if anyone deserves this, it's you."

"I'm not even going to argue with you on that. That's how happy I am."

"Good, you shouldn't argue because I'm right. Now, I'm gonna let you get back to work. Call me tonight when you leave so I can ask more questions."

I laugh. "I'll talk to you later."

I hang up the phone and do my best to focus on my to-do list instead of worrying about Marcus across the hall.

Last night was not what I had expected. I figured it would be good with him. I didn't know it would be so good it would crush all fantasies I've ever had. I always thought sex that good wasn't real. If I only knew.

My phone rings. I look at the screen and see that it's Marcus' extension.

My entire body tingles with excitement.

"Hello," I say with a sultry voice.

"Hey, Lex. Can I see you in my office for a minute?" he says casually.

"Oh, um, yeah. I'll be right there."

"Thanks."

I feel a bit embarrassed. Here I am thinking he's calling because he's thinking about me when it's actually business-related. I need to figure out how to separate this...whatever this is...with our professional relationship.

When I walk into his office, I'm fully prepared to be hit with some task or question regarding the new order forms.

I tap lightly on the door.

When I open it, he stands from his desk and takes calculated steps in my direction. I almost think he's angry with me. I begin to rack my brain for what it could be about. I don't think I could've done much from last night to now.

He grabs the door behind me and shuts it, then backs me up against it.

I'm about to ask what's wrong when he begins to chuckle.

I realized he was messing with me. I swat him in the chest. "What the hell? You had me freakin' out."

He continues to laugh. "I'm sorry, babe. Just having a little fun."

Babe? It's one thing to be called that in the bedroom. In the light of day at work is an entirely different story. My heart accelerates from the term of endearment.

He grabs my face and kisses me.

"I just couldn't stand knowing you were only feet away from me. I needed something to hold me over," he whispers into my mouth.

Then his lips press against mine again, this time with a bit more purpose.

"You coming over again tonight?" he asks.

I smile. "I suppose I could do that."

"Good. Now, let's eat some lunch before I lose control and have my way with you right here. I brought those leftovers in."

He opens the door, and I follow him to the breakroom. We work together to pull out the containers and determine what we want.

"What the fuck? You brought in DiStefano's and didn't tell me?" Luke barks at Marcus when he walks into the room.

"Give me a break. I haven't even warmed mine up yet. I was gonna text you guys to let you know. There's plenty for everyone."

"Why does Lexi get some before me?" he complains.

I smile as I place the last meatball on my plate and then wink at him. Marcus starts to laugh.

"You guys fake date for like a day, and now she gets special treatment over me?"

I look over at Marcus, and he smiles as he places our plates into the microwaves on the counter. He doesn't seem worried by Luke's comment. I know it's too early to talk about it, but I wonder when we'll tell his siblings or if we'll ever get to that point.

"Did I hear there's DiStefano's for lunch?" Mia walks in with Gabe trailing behind her, Savannah not too far behind.

"I go first. You can't say no to the pregnant lady," Savannah shouts as she runs in front of everybody.

"Ugh, fine," Gabe grumbles. "You're lucky I like you, Savannah."

Marcus and I sit down at a table and begin to eat our warm food while they fight over who gets what.

It's odd what a weekend away with them can do. Suddenly, I feel like part of the group more than ever. It's like I'm part of their family. That's a scary thought. It's dangerous to get attached to the idea since Marcus is known to be a ladies' man. The odds of this going anywhere serious are pretty unlikely.

Only it feels so significant when we are together, like it's meant to be.

Stop thinking that shit, Lexi. Don't go falling in love too soon.

I do my best to shake off the worries floating around in my head. I just need to enjoy my time with him and see where it goes. After all, this was all supposed to be fun. I wasn't supposed to go falling in love, right?

***

"I love your freckles right here," he whispers while we lie naked in his bed.

His fingers skate over the scatter of freckles I have on my chest.

I smile as I watch him continue running his fingers over my skin like he's in awe at what he sees.

"Thank you. Do you know what I love?" I ask.

"What's that?"

I run my fingers down the ridges of his abs. "These things right here."

He laughs, which only makes them tighten up harder for me.

We lie there for a bit together, caressing each other and enjoying the time as we recover from another sweaty round of sex. The man's stamina is pretty incredible. I've never had so many orgasms before from intercourse alone.

"You know what I wanna do?" I lean up on my elbow. His eyebrows raise in question. "I wanna go back to your library. I never really got to see your collection of books."

He smiles and kisses my nose. "That's what you're thinking about while we lie here naked together?"

I shrug my shoulders. "I'm not ashamed. That room is amazing."

I climb out of his bed and grab his T-shirt that's lying on the floor. He throws on a pair of sweatpants, and we head down the hall together.

When he opens the door, he only turns on the lamp in the corner this time. The room glows in the soft light as the darkness outside makes the room feel warm and cozy.

It still takes my breath away to see the bookcases that reach the double-story room. It's so high that I wonder what books he likes to keep up at the top.

"Can I use the ladder?" I ask as I approach the bookcase.

"Sure. Just be careful."

He stands next to the ladder as I begin to climb up, just a couple of steps at first, as I scan the books around me. I seem to be in the sports section as I examine books on famous athletes. They're all in prime condition. He hasn't read any of them or takes care of them while he reads, careful not to crease any of the spines.

"I've read most of the books in that section if you're wondering."

"Get out of my head, weirdo. How'd you know that's what I was thinking about?"

His light laughter makes me smile. I look down at him, and he winks. Swoon! This man is like every fantasy I've ever had wrapped into one perfect package.

I focus my attention back on the books in front of me and decide to climb a couple more steps, ignoring his smug, but adorable, little attitude below me.

I hear him groan and catch a glance of him resting his head on his arm that's leaning on the ladder.

"What are you whining about down there?" I ask as I scan the books in front of me.

"Woman. You're not wearing any underwear."

"Yeah, I'm aware."

"Well, your pussy is glistening right now. It's distracting me. Is that from earlier, or are you turned on looking at my books right now?"

I giggle. "You'll never know."

"That's it," he says. I continue laughing, but the ladder begins to wiggle slightly. Marcus is climbing up behind me, eyes dark and serious.

"What're you doing?" I scream.

He keeps climbing until he is standing on the step right below me. We're now eye to eye, his arms holding onto the step above my head.

"You think you can flash that slick pussy at me and not expect me to be tempted?" he whispers on my lips, then just barely kisses them.

"But we're up high. What can you possibly do?"

As soon as the words are out of my mouth, I regret them. They're basically a damn challenge.

He smiles. His hand starts on my inner thigh but starts to slide north until he's just below my ass.

"I could do many things. You better hold on tight, baby."

One finger swipes through my folds. I try not to react, but my breaths are already coming faster. I feel his lips on my ear.

"You can pretend you don't love this, but your pussy says otherwise. I feel you getting wetter and wetter by the second."

Dammit, he's right! I'm so turned on right now. The feeling of being suspended in the air like this with no ability to do anything with my hands is intense, but it's hot.

I feel the second finger join his first, and then he pushes them inside of me.

"Ahh." I can't hold in the pleasure he's already creating within me.

He pulls his fingers out, then pushes back in and wiggles them. He does this repeatedly, hitting my favorite spot every time he wiggles them inside me.

"Please..." I beg.

"You want to come?"

I nod my head as my hands squeeze tightly around the wood. He pumps his fingers faster, the sounds echoing in the room proof of just how wet I am. I would be embarrassed if I weren't so turned on. What I don't expect is to feel his thumb rub along my pussy for a brief second, then disappear. I feel it hit my back entrance and start to rub in wet circles.

This is an area that I've never explored before. I'm so close that I don't even care that his thumb is there. It feels kind of good.

"You like that?" he asks as he fingers me and continues rubbing his circles at my ass.

"Yes. Fuck. Yes," I reply, so close, yet he's not letting me get there.

"You wanna feel something really good?"

I haven't even responded yet when he decides to show me. His fingers curl inside of me, hitting my spot repeatedly at the same time that he inserts his thumb. I go off like a rocket, screaming and quivering as the orgasm seems to get more powerful with each spasm.

It takes me a second to catch my breath. I look down at the ground, shocked that he was able to get me to forget how high I was...and that I managed to hold on the entire time.

"I'll get you back for this," I say on an exhale.

He smiles. "I look forward to it."

He starts to climb down the ladder.

"Where are you going?"

"I'm gonna let you get back to the books while I find something for us to snack on."

It takes me a minute after he leaves to get my composure back, but his time away allows me to enjoy the options I have at my fingertips. So many books, so many classics, it's incredible. After I find the one I know I want to read, I push and slide the ladder back and forth on the wheels. I officially feel like Belle in Beauty and the Beast.

Marcus returns to the room, holding a tray of cheese, meats, and crackers. The tray also has a bottle of red wine and two glasses.

I start to climb down the ladder with my book in hand.

"What did you pick?" he asks.

"Little Women. I'm surprised you have this in your collection."

He shrugs. "I don't discriminate."

He pours some wine and hands me a glass.

I walk over to the oversized chaise lounge chair and get comfortable. Marcus follows me, then scoots beside me, snuggling up to my side.

"What are you doing?" I ask, not that I mind, but I figured he'd find his own book.

"I've never read this book before. Read to me."

He rests his head on my chest, and my heart flutters. This is so much more intimate than anything we've ever done before. It feels like we've just crossed the line from having sex to something bigger.

I take a big gulp of wine before I open the book.

As I start to read out loud, he plays with the ends of my hair. This side of him is one I would've never guessed. I know Work Marcus and have heard of Ladies' Man Marcus. But this man, he is like a dream come true.

I'm not sure how much time has passed, but I've already read three chapters. He's been quiet for a while now. I look down and see his eyes closed and his breathing slow and even.

He's asleep. I look at his face while he rests on my chest, and I can't deny it anymore. The rate at which I'm falling for this man is alarming. I should get up and go home tonight to try and gain some control over these feelings. But he's too comfy and warm, and I don't want to leave him.

I put the book on the table next to me and rest my head on the back of the chair.

Before I know it, I'm drifting off to sleep with the most gorgeous man I've ever laid eyes on, asleep on my chest.

Chapter Sixteen

Marcus

I wake up to the familiar scent of Lexi. We're tangled in my sheets, my arm wrapped around her stomach.

Sometime last night, I woke up to find myself asleep in her arms. Instead of waking her and risking her leaving in the middle of the night, I carried her to my bed.

Having her here in my house just makes everything feel better. I like waking up to my arms wrapped around her. I also like seeing her in my shirt. It brings out the caveman in me.

It's the oddest thing. I never felt like this with the women I've been with in the past. Lexi is bringing out a side of me I didn't know existed. I've seen it in my brothers with their wives, and to be honest, I was always jealous of what they had.

She starts to wiggle around, stretching her arms out in front of her.

"Morning," I say as I lean up on my elbow.

"Mmmm...morning."

"How can you look so damn beautiful in the morning?" I ask.

I know it sounds like a line, but it's not. She looks like an angel lying in my white sheets.

"Oh, stop it. I know the kind of women you've been with. I'm nothing compared—" she starts, but I cover her mouth with my hand.

"Don't you dare say what you're going to say. If you ever belittle just how gorgeous you are, I will have to punish you. Do you understand me?"

She nods her head as I lift my hand off her mouth.

"Good. Now, let's get up and get some breakfast."

"Are we going out for breakfast?" she asks as she rolls out of my bed and glances down at herself.

"Nah. I want you all to myself. Don't you even dare think about changing out of my shirt."

She crosses her arms over her chest, trying to look tough. I try not to smile. I also try to ignore her hard nipples that are poking through my shirt.

"Fine. But you can't put a shirt on."

"I can't wear a shirt?"

"No. You've got to stay in those gray sweatpants for me."

"You've got yourself a deal, baby," I say with a wink. "Now, let's see what I have in my fridge."

I scan the contents of my fridge, trying to think of what I should make. I generally try to keep my place stocked with food. I try to eat in whenever I can, not wanting to be the typical bachelor who only gets takeout. I'm too old for that shit.

I forgot I cut up a bunch of veggies the other day to make omelets.

"How do you feel about an omelet?" I ask over my shoulder.

"I can go for an omelet. Do you need any help?"

"Nope. Veggies are already cut. It'll be easy. If you could just get us some coffee."

I point to the coffee bar that I have set up. "There should be plenty of options."

"What kind do you want?" she asks.

"I'll just take the medium roast."

I start to whistle while I cook when the front door opens, and I hear someone walking across the hardwood floor.

It's got to be one of my siblings. They're the only ones who invite themselves in.

Shit! I look over at Lexi, standing in only my shirt while she sips her coffee. I don't think she noticed the door open and close.

"Hey, brother. Was just stopping in to give you cannoli from—Oh, shit!" Mia shrieks, frozen in the kitchen with eyes wide as saucers. "Umm, hi, Lexi."

"Hi," Lexi stands still, not moving a muscle while she looks at me for help,

"I'm so sorry to barge in here," Mia says, looking between the two of us.

"You literally barge in all the time. No need to apologize for it now. I guess the secret's out."

I'm not sure it was something that was really a secret to begin with.

"I would say I'm shocked, and I kind of am, but I'm kind of not."

"Really?" I ask as I flip over the omelet in the pan.

Mia walks into the kitchen and places the dessert box on the counter. "Something about the kiss that night at the party. It just seemed unlikely that it was fake. There were other signs, like how you guys looked at each other and how Lexi defended your honor all weekend."

"Are you mad?" Lexi asks nervously.

I turn around and place the omelet on a plate, then hand it to Lexi. I take the other one, already done and probably a bit cold, and walk over to the table, waving for Lexi to join me.

"No, I'm not mad. I just..." Mia stops and seems to ponder her words. "Never mind. I just hope you two know what you're getting into. Office romances can get kinda messy."

I know what she really wants to say, *'Watch out, Lexi. He's a heartbreaker. He'll have you in tears by the end of the week.'*

I want to get mad, to defend myself, but I guess I haven't given her any reason to think anything else about me. It would still be nice if she trusted me.

It's not like I was going to sleep with Lexi just for the sake of getting laid.

"I think we can handle it. We're two consenting adults, and I trust Marcus," Lexi says to Mia, taking me by surprise.

I wonder what I've done to garner such trust from her. Either way, it's a refreshing feeling. And to hear she was defending my honor all weekend in Chicago floors me.

"Sorry, didn't mean to overstep or anything. I just care about you two." Mia seems a bit surprised by Lexi's words but not at all mad.

I know Mia has a ton of respect for Lexi. She's always talked so highly of her at work.

"We appreciate your concern, sis. I have a good feeling about this one. I might just keep her around if she behaves," I say smugly, then take a bite of my eggs.

Lexi laughs, and Mia rolls her eyes. "Really?" Mia says to Lexi. "You sure you don't want to set your bar a little higher?"

"I don't know. This is a delicious omelet. I might have to keep him around for his skills in the kitchen alone."

I wink at her. I have other skills I'm sure she wants to keep me around for, but I'm aware that it's my sister we're talking to right now.

"Well, I don't want to interrupt your morning. I was just stopping by to drop off the cannoli. I'll... see you guys tomorrow, I guess."

"See ya, sis."

"Bye, Mia," Lexi says.

Mia pops her head back into the kitchen. "Oh, Marcus." She eyes me critically. "Please don't make me keep this thing between you guys a secret from Luke and Gabe for too long."

I roll my eyes. "I think you can handle it. Don't be a baby."

"Ugh, fine!" she says, then storms off.

Lexi smiles at me.

"What?" I ask.

She shrugs her shoulders. "Nothing. It's just you two have a really cute relationship. All of you guys do, even Savannah and Alexis."

"Yeah, I guess I've never really thought much about it. We love each other, but can also drive one another crazy."

"It must be nice to have. I wish I had siblings growing up. It would be much easier to care for my mom if I had someone to do it all with."

I never considered how doing it without another sibling would feel. It must be lonely and kind of terrifying.

"You can lean on me whenever you need to," I say as I grab her hand.

"Thanks," she says softly, looking down at her plate.

"I'm serious, Lex. I want to be here for you. Anytime anything happens, you need me to fly out there with you, or you just need someone to talk to about it. I'm here."

She shakes her head back and forth as if she's annoyed.

"What's that for?" I ask.

"I'm just waiting to find a side of you that sucks. You keep getting better and better."

I smile. "Wanna go back to bed, and I'll get even better for you?"

Her head falls back with laughter. The sound of it makes my heart skip a beat.

"Can it get any better?" she finally says.

I drop my fork on my plate. "Challenge. Accepted."

I pull her up from her chair and slam my mouth down on hers. While our lips tangle together, I wrap my arms around her and move her to the kitchen island. Once her back hits the counter, I break the kiss and turn her around. I place my hand on her back and push her down until her chest hits the countertop.

"I'm gonna fuck you right here, so I can picture your sexy ass every time I walk in the kitchen."

With both hands, I grab the bottom of my T-shirt she's wearing and move it up her body. I place one hand on her back to keep her in place while the other hand works its way down. My hand circles her ass, one cheek at a time, then I grab a cheek and squeeze it.

"I'm gonna come on this ass one day," I tell her, then give it a slap.

She gasps at my words, which makes me smile. She is the perfect mixture of innocent and dirty. I move my fingers further down until they find her slick pussy. She is constantly dripping for me. My fingers slide in easily. I know she likes it when I shake them inside of her, moving against her walls.

I do this as my thumb rubs against her back entrance again.

She came so damn hard last night when my thumb played with her ass. I haven't asked her, but I could tell she hasn't done much ass-play before, just by her tense reaction to it last night. But she trusted me enough to let me show her what it could feel like.

I pull down my sweatpants and stroke my dick as she watches over her shoulder.

"Wait..." she whispers as my hand falls. "Do that again."

"Do what? Touch myself?"

Her head nods up and down. Fuck, I love being with her. She's so brave and honest with what she wants. No woman has ever requested I play with myself for her.

I bring my hand back to my dick and stroke it a couple times in a slow, deliberate manner. When I see a bit of precum start to leak out, I glide my thumb over my tip to pick it up and lift it to her mouth. She opens willingly and sucks my thumb into her mouth. My eyes grow dark just watching her.

I pull my thumb back and squat down, so I can have the perfect view of her pussy and her ass. Grabbing her cheeks again, I spread them apart.

"Fuck, Lex. You are so damn sexy."

My thumb grazes her clit, which is already drenched with her arousal sliding out of her pussy. I alternate rubbing her clit with each thumb, then drag both thumbs up until they reach her ass. Then I sink both into her back entrance together.

"Oh, shit! she screams.

"What does it feel like?" I ask.

I pull them out and slowly push them back in, creating a rhythm.

"It feels different. Full."

"Does it feel good?"

She moans as I continue.

"Amazing."

I smile up at her. With my thumbs still working her ass, I lean in and suck on her clit. Her hands slam against the counter as she continues to moan her appreciation. She's getting greedy for her orgasm as she starts to rub herself all over my face. I release my thumbs and cup her cheeks again to spread them open and give me the access I want.

"Fuck, fuck. I'm coming!" she screams.

Her pussy leaks juices all over my face, but I keep sucking her clit until I get every last spasm out of her.

When I know she's done, I stand up and lean down over her body.

"I'm going to go grab a condom. Don't move."

"Wait. I'm on birth control...and clean."

I've never not used a condom. It was never even a question in my mind, but this is Lexi, and I trust her.

"I'm clean, too," I whisper.

I can't wait another second. I line myself up at her entrance and thrust in until my dick is completely inside of her.

"Oh, fuck," I growl.

My forehead falls to her back as I brace my hands on the sides of the counter.

"You feel so damn good like this," I tell her.

I haven't even moved yet, and the sensation of being inside of her with nothing on is fucking incredible.

I brace myself on the counter and pull out slowly, inch by inch. My eyes stay trained on her pussy as I slam back in as hard as I can. She screams, and I do it again. I watch her reactions as I start to fuck her at an animalistic pace, making sweat fall from my forehead.

I lean my body on top of hers and reach my hands up until they find hers. Our hands squeeze each other's as I slam in and out, over and over. We're both sweating and moaning together as the sensations take over.

"Fuck me, fuck me," Lexi screams. "Fuck!"

"Ahhh, I could fuck this tight cunt of yours all day long," I growl into her ear.

I feel her walls start to tighten around me, and then she screams her release. I don't let up the entire time she comes, fucking her roughly into the cabinet below us. As soon as she is done, I pull out of her and jerk my cock while spurts of cum fall out onto her perfectly round ass.

I love watching her covered in my release. It's the sexiest image I've ever seen.

It takes a minute to get my breathing under control.

"I think we need a shower, babe," I tell her as I wipe my forehead, drenched in sweat.

She smiles. "I guess you're right. It can get better."

Chapter Seventeen

Lexi

He told me to wear something casual with his favorite red lipstick. He wants to take me on a date.

Honestly, I'm surprised by the casual request. For someone with that much money, I would have pegged him for a fancy dinner kind of guy. It's just another reason I love being with him. He doesn't show off his money or think he's superior to anyone because of it.

I just watched a video on how to do my hair. I wanted some fullness and soft curls like I had done at the salon. An hour later, the results aren't half bad. I don't know if it'll last, but who cares? At least I can be confident for the first ten minutes of the date.

Anyway, I'm already comfortable enough with him that I won't worry about something like my hair.

I walk over to my front door and grab a comfortable pair of flats, and my phone vibrates.

Marcus: Get your sexy ass down here.

I giggle as I swipe out of the screen. Never a dull moment with him. I'm not sure I've smiled this much before. It's easy with him.

My apartment is on the third floor, so it takes me a second to get down the stairs. When I get outside, he's leaning against his car.

He opens his arms for me, and I run into them. His breath against my ear makes my skin tingle.

"How is it possible that I've already missed you?" his deep voice vibrates in my ear.

"I mean, I did just see you at work yesterday," I tease.

I pull away and see the shock on his face. "Are you saying that you didn't miss me?"

I did. So damn much I wanted to show up at his place last night. But he had plans with some friends, and I didn't want to be clingy.

He tickles my sides. "Woman, tell me you missed me."

I laugh. "Ok. Fine. I missed you, too. I thought about you all night. Are you happy?"

"Very happy," he says, but then his smile starts to fade, and he turns serious. "I'm actually the happiest I've ever been."

His admission leaves me breathless. "Me too," I whisper back.

He opens my door, and I climb inside. It's intoxicating being in his car with him. There's something about being in a man's car at night, smelling their cologne in the air, seeing them take control. I home in on his large hand wrapped around the steering wheel, seeing the veins run up into his shirt sleeve.

It's distracting. I can feel how sensitive my clit is by how good it feels when my jeans rub up against it.

Lucky for me, he doesn't know what his presence is doing to me. He pulls into a VIP parking spot outside of a small restaurant.

"You ready for this?" he asks.

"Ready."

We walk into a dimly lit restaurant with an old-world feeling. The walls are all brick, probably original to the building. Unique metal light fixtures hang above each table along the walls. It smells *amazing*.

Holding my hand, he leads me to the back of the restaurant toward the kitchen.

A chef spots us and smiles. "Marcus. Come on in," he gestures.

I'm not sure what is happening, but Marcus walks us into the kitchen.

"Nicholas. Good to see you. Thanks for letting us do this."

"Don't mention it, man. We have you guys set up over here."

Nicholas walks us to a section of the kitchen along the wall with some counter space. It has two bowls with towels over them and a line of toppings. When he pulls the towels off the bowls, a ball of dough is sitting in each one.

It suddenly dawns on me Marcus set up for us to make our own pizzas. I want to kiss him with how sweet and thoughtful this all is. I've never done anything like it before.

"The trick with the dough," Nicholas starts as he grabs a third ball of dough to show us, "is not to overwork it. If you spend too long on it, it will lose its elasticity."

He throws it up in the air, showing off his skills.

"You don't expect me to be able to do that?" I ask.

He laughs. "Nah. I'm just being a showoff. You will be perfectly fine if you lay the dough on the counter and work it out with your hands. Just work fast. You will be surprised how quickly the dough can become overworked."

After a couple more minutes of instruction, he leaves us alone to make our pizzas.

"Alright, that sounded simple enough," Marcus says while he looks at his dough.

We take our dough from their bowls and work them on the counter. The texture is oddly satisfying. It feels like an ASMR activity.

I look over and see Marcus rest the dough on his hand as he makes a fist.

"Oh, God. Are you going to try to toss the dough?"

"It didn't look that hard."

He pushes the dough in the air with his fist. It isn't a huge toss, only spinning once in the air, then landing back on his fist. His next toss is a bit higher, then higher...until he gets several spins in the air, and it still lands on his fist.

"Oh, yeah, baby! Businessman by day, pizzaman by night," he says, then winks at me.

I laugh and then get back to my dough. "Don't distract me. I don't want to ruin my dough by taking too long. You heard your friend; we have to work fast."

"I'll share my pizza, baby. Don't you worry."

I choose to ignore him, or I'll never get my dough done. Once we both have semi-decent-looking dough circles, we look at all the topping options in front of us.

"What are you thinking?" he asks.

"I think I'm gonna go for a tomato and basil with olive oil and grated cheese."

"Damn, that sounds pretty good. I'm definitely trying some of yours."

"I'll allow it."

He leans and kisses my neck. "Gee, thanks."

I laugh. "What kind of pizza are you gonna make?"

He looks around at the options. "There's too many toppings. My stomach is getting greedy and wants it all."

His inner child seems to be appearing as he continues to stare at all the options in front of him, unable to make a decision.

I get to work on my pizza while he stands there looking confused.

"It's a pizza, babe. Just pick some toppings. Anything will be good."

I feel his eyes on me. "You've never called me babe before."

"No?" I stop and look at him. "I guess I haven't."

He smiles innocently. "I like it."

He leans in for a kiss, slowly gliding his tongue against mine. His mouth has this interesting ability to make me forget about everything but him. I let his tongue mix with mine until he pulls away.

I feel slightly wobbly and off-keel from it.

"I like you," he says. "A lot."

We both get back to our pizzas, both grinning foolishly.

When we're done with our toppings, Marcus settling for every meat option with marinara sauce, Nicholas comes over to help us get our pizzas into a real wood-burning oven.

"I have a booth set up for you two while your pizzas cook. Follow me."

Nicholas motions for us to follow him from the kitchen to the main dining area. He directs us to a booth by the window, which overlooks the city street. A candle flickers in the middle of the table next to a bottle of wine opened and ready for us.

"Enjoy your evening," he says, retreating to the kitchen, giving us space.

"This has been the best date ever," I tell Marcus as we sit down.

"We haven't even eaten yet, and this night gets the honor of best date. Not too bad."

"It was such a creative idea. That was so much fun. I've never been in the kitchen of a restaurant before, let alone made my own dinner there."

I rest my hands on the table. Marcus reaches across and grabs one of them.

"Everything I do with you is fun. I didn't realize it could all be this easy."

"I know. It's never been this easy for me either. Honestly? I keep waiting for you to show some side of you that is wildly unattractive."

He laughs. "I'm sure I have plenty of those, babe. Just wait. I'm still waiting for you to think I'm a total fuck up and walk away."

"Why would you say that?" I lean in, wondering why he thinks that's even a remote possibility.

He shrugs. "I don't know. It's been my motto since I was younger. I guess I'm used to people thinking that way about me."

"At the risk of intruding, I'm gonna say something." His eyebrow raises. I'm not sure if it's a good idea to talk about this with him, but I feel compelled to. "Why do you let your siblings get away with treating you like you are still that young, immature person?

He opens his mouth to speak but closes it. It seems like he's contemplating how to respond. I wonder if anyone has ever asked him this question.

"Honestly, it might be a habit. For the longest time, I was the young, immature one doing stupid shit. They were older and wiser. I guess somewhere in there, I grew up, but nobody seems to have realized it."

"Not even yourself?"

He sighs. "Not even me. You're the first person to really see me, Lexi. I mean, I do still have this adventurous, goofy side to me, but I'm not the man they think I am. I *have* grown up."

"Well, next time you feel like they are treating you like the boy you once were and not the man you *are*...you should speak up."

"How can someone as perfect as you see me as somebody worthy? I'm still trying to figure that out. You're a killer combination. Sexy, smart, kind, funny."

It's amazing how someone like him can be blind to what a catch he is.

"You helped me see who I really am. Not just brains but..." I struggle to get the words out because it feels odd to say.

"Beauty... you can say it. You *are* beautiful. You don't realize the heads you turn when we are in public."

"I wouldn't go that far," I reply. "Either way, we're helping each other see what we're blind to see in ourselves."

There's a moment of silence where we stare at each other like we're looking into each other's souls.

"Do you believe in fate?" he asks, surprising me with his question.

"I don't know. I think so. I think there is something bigger out there that can intervene or help orchestrate something that's meant to be."

"I think fate brought us together."

My heart skips a beat. He just says whatever he feels. It's incredible how he can do that without worrying about getting laughed at or his feelings stomped on.

"You do?" My voice cracks.

"Yeah. I think getting us in each other's lives clearly wasn't enough. I was too blind. Fate needed to create a scenario that opened my eyes to what was right in front of me."

I try to hold back the tears that want to spill over.

I blow out a breath and blink quickly to lock down my emotions. "You do realize that's like the most romantic thing anybody has ever said?"

"Is it?" He shrugs his shoulders like it's nothing. "I think it's true."

"Me too."

We smile at each other, and I wish we weren't so far apart. I want to kiss him, to feel his warmth next to me.

"Alright, here we go." Nicholas interrupts, carrying two trays with our pizza on them. "You two enjoy."

"Wow." I look down at our food. "They actually look pretty damn good."

"Right? We got some skills."

We both grab a piece and take a large bite, moaning simultaneously. I know there's not really much credit we can take for this. The dough was made, the toppings prepared, the pizza taken out for us. But it's still fun to pretend it was our own doing.

"I need to try some of yours," I tell him after I take another bite.

"Same." He gives us each a piece of each other's pizza.

The rest of the evening is spent laughing and enjoying our food and wine. When it's over, I'm shocked it's been three hours. The night just flew by.

We thank Nicholas for his hospitality and then head outside to the car.

"You wanna come back to my place?" he asks as he pulls out.

I look over at him. "Nowhere else I'd rather be."

He grabs my hand and holds it the entire drive to his house. I'm fairly certain at this point that I've already fallen in love with him. It keeps running through my head at the oddest times. I'm surprised it hasn't slipped out yet. I wonder if he feels the same.

Chapter Eighteen

Marcus

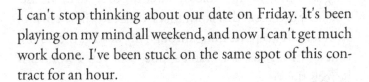

I can't stop thinking about our date on Friday. It's been playing on my mind all weekend, and now I can't get much work done. I've been stuck on the same spot of this contract for an hour.

It was more than just how much fun we had. It was how she made me feel. I've never had someone be so in tune with the deepest parts of me that they notice how I feel before I speak the words.

Her ability to see what bothers me with my siblings was staggering. In all fairness, I know my siblings love me like crazy. It's just a persona I've had that no longer exists, and they're struggling to see me as I am today. Part of us always looks at our siblings and still sees the younger version of them that we grew up with. But it definitely isn't fair to me if they hold onto that for the rest of my life. I didn't even think of speaking up for myself until she brought it up.

I hear Lexi walking toward her office and spot her figure as it passes.

"Hey," I call. "You just gonna walk right past me with no kiss?"

She smiles as she walks into my office.

"I'm trying to be professional while at work."

I lean back in my chair and cross my arms across my chest. "So, you're thinking about it as much as I am?"

Her shoulders fall in defeat. "Yes! It's ridiculous. I should be able to focus better than this."

"Well, let's solve this little dilemma. You come over here and kiss the shit out of me. We'll see if it's enough to satisfy us both until lunch."

She struts over to my desk and puts her hands on the armrests of my chair. When she leans forward, I get a glimpse of her breasts. I should've thought this through—I'm just getting more turned on.

Her mouth closes in on mine, and her lips start to move. When I said kiss the shit out of me, she got the memo. I groan into her mouth, feeling like everything else melts away. My hands cup her cheeks, and I deepen the kiss. I don't know how long we kissed, just that I lost all train of thought.

"Hey, Marcus. Was just wanting to see if you..." Gabe turns the corner and stops in place.

Lexi jumps off me and wipes her mouth. Judging by the look on Gabe's face, he didn't miss anything.

I stand up and grab the back of my neck. "Shit. Sorry. I, uh, we were just." I realize there's no way out of it. "I've been meaning to tell you."

His eyes turn down at me. I can see every muscle in his body is tense.

He's pissed.

"I'm so sorry, Gabe." Lexi sounds terrified. "It was so inappropriate for us to do that here."

I look at her, wondering why she thinks kissing here is inappropriate. Savannah and Luke work together and have been known to engage in PDA all over the office. I know for a fact that they've fucked in each other's offices as well. At one point, Alexis worked here, too, and Gabe was no saint when she was around.

"How long?" he asks.

Lexi and I look at each other. "Since the weekend in Chicago."

He nods his head. I'm guessing he assumed that much.

"Was there something I could help you with?" I ask, trying to move this along.

"Nevermind. I can ask another time."

He abruptly walks out of the office. Lexi's head falls into her hands.

"That was so humiliating," she cries.

"It wasn't ideal. I'm sure he just feels blindsided. He'll calm down."

"You think so? We shouldn't have been so cavalier. Kissing in the office without any concern about getting caught is irresponsible."

I close the distance between us and run my fingers along her soft cheeks. She leans into my touch, which makes my heart flutter in my chest.

"Don't worry about it, Lex. Trust me. Gabe and Luke have fucked their wives in their offices on more than one occasion. They're not innocent at all."

"Really?" she asks hopefully.

I lean in and kiss her forehead. I don't want her to feel an ounce of fear or guilt. I've never worried about someone else's feelings so much. She's changed me. I'm sure my siblings will think differently once they know that.

"Well," I start, "the good news is I'm no longer distracted by my need to touch you."

She laughs. "Yeah, that was definitely like a bucket of ice."

My eyes meet hers. "But just so you know, it'll likely not last long. Like right now, I'm already starting to picture you naked again."

"Oh my gosh!" She starts toward the door. "I'm going to get back to work before we end up in an even more compromising position."

"Good idea, babe. Take that sexy ass out of here."

She giggles on the way out of my office. I find myself smiling all the way back to my desk. I'm definitely falling for her. Shit, maybe I've already fallen. It's not as scary as I once thought it would be.

I guess when you trust the person, it *shouldn't* be scary.

I do my best to get back to work when a sudden knock on the door pulls me out of my thoughts. I glance down at the clock. Wow, I got lost in my work. It's been an hour.

"You free for lunch?" Gabe asks casually.

"Uh, I guess so."

I wanted to take Lexi out, but I suppose I owe it to him to have a discussion.

"Cool. Mia and Luke are gonna join us."

Great. A sibling's lunch an hour after he caught me making out with Lexi. I lock my computer screen and push off my desk.

"Where are we going?" I ask as I grab my jacket.

"Just down the street to Michael's."

Well, at least I'll get some good food out of this. Our office is in downtown Shaker Heights. It's a historical location with old buildings and great restaurants nearby. My favorite part of Shaker Heights is the trees. They are old and hang over the streets like a tunnel of greenery.

Once we are all seated at the restaurant and have placed our orders, an awkward silence falls upon the table. Hell if I'm gonna be the one to break it. I'll play the Michael Scott game of power and decline to speak first.

"Marcus. I'm guessing you know why I wanted all of us to get together," Gabe states directly.

He's always been the leader of the group, being the oldest. I know he takes a lot of the burden on him to make sure everybody is happy. Though, I'm thinking right now his worrying is for nothing,

"I have an idea," I reply.

"Mia informed me she already knew," he continues. "Surprised as I am, we all know she'll keep a secret for anyone. Luke, on the other hand, was as surprised as I was. As I am."

"That's because you two are idiots. After the kiss they shared at the event, anybody could see there was something there," Mia says bluntly. I fight to hide the smirk that wants to break free. "I'll admit I wasn't sure if either of them had admitted the obvious sparks that were flying, but in the end, it wasn't *that* surprising."

"Okay, we can argue about how obvious it was or not," Luke intervenes. "The real reason we're here is to talk about the fact that you decided to have sex with the one woman who I would likely consider off-limits, aside from our wives."

Well, that's unexpected. Off-limits?

"Why the fuck is she off-limits?" I growl out.

"Because she's our IT Director, Marcus," Gabe cuts in sternly. "What happens when you break her heart, and she can't stand to be near you anymore?"

"Why are you assuming I'll break her heart?"

Luke raises his eyebrows at me. "Come on, man. Be real. When have you *not* broken a girl's heart?"

"It's different this time," I say in a whisper.

"I just don't understand why it had to be her of all people in this city. She's innocent and sweet." Gabe looks at me, and I see disappointment in his eyes. It's a familiar look.

Maybe I deserve it. There is no guarantee that this thing between us will last. What if she does get her heart broken and leaves the company?

For the first time since I've been with Lexi, a bit of doubt creeps into my mind.

"I don't know what to say. Look, I'm sorry that you guys see it that way. I have no intention of breaking her heart. She's amazing. All I'm asking is that you guys give me a chance here. Let me see where this goes with her."

Not exactly the words I envisioned speaking on the way here. It's just so easy to get sucked into the world of doubt when I'm around them. Doubt that I'm not smart enough, mature enough...good enough.

"Come on, guys. Give him a chance. He's clearly trying to tell you this is different with her. I believe him," Mia says in my defense.

I can see the worry still etched on their faces, but they look at each other as they speak their older brother language.

"Alright," Luke says reluctantly. "Just promise me if it ends, it won't end in total disaster with Lexi leaving the company."

"Promise."

I don't intend for this to end with her leaving. I don't intend on it ending at all.

As our food is delivered, Lexi's words ring in my ears, telling me to stand up for myself. I should've told them to just believe in me, for once, and not expect the worst. I should have admitted how their constant doubts make me feel. I wish Lexi were here. It would make this whole thing so much easier to discuss. She helps me think straight and gives me confidence.

But fuck if I'm going to tell them that I'm falling in love with her before Lexi knows. So, I swallow my pride and eat my food.

The tension disappears somewhere in the middle of our lunch, and we're back to being best friends again. We joke and laugh. Gabe and I make fun of Luke for becoming the world's most annoying father-to-be.

He wants Savannah to just quit and stay at home now. He's constantly bothering her in her office, asking her how she's feeling.

She's a strong, independent woman though. I believe she just told him if he asks one more time, he'll lose his privilege of being in the delivery room.

Obviously, we all know it's an empty threat, but it's made him think twice about nagging her.

When we get back to the office, I go straight to see Lexi. She's deep in thought as she studies something on the screen. She bites her lip in concentration. It makes me think of how she bites her lip when she's turned on or when I'm fucking her and looking into her eyes.

She's wearing the sexiest shade of pink lipstick today. Fuck, I want that color smeared all over my cock.

And there it is; I'm slightly hard, and I've been in her presence for all of ten seconds.

She looks up and jumps back with a squeal.

"What the fuck, Marcus? You scared the crap out of me."

I chuckle at her reaction. "Sorry, babe. Just got back from lunch and wanted to come say hi."

She sits back in her chair as I round her desk. I sit on the edge of it as I cross one leg over the other.

"How did it go? Did you guys talk about us? Are they mad?"

I don't want to involve her in their concerns. She doesn't need to think my family has any reservations about us. I don't want her to feel hurt.

"We talked about us. They aren't mad, sweetie. Maybe a bit surprised, but not mad."

"Oh," she lets out a breath. "Thank God."

Her relief makes me angry that they still think I need to prove something to them. I should've told them how supportive I was the second I found out Gabe was sleeping with his nanny. And how I told Lucas to go for it with Savannah despite her being his student.

I have their backs no matter what. What's wrong with me that I don't deserve that same kind of loyalty?

"Yeah. Nothing to worry about. Hey, are you coming over tonight?" I ask to shift topics.

"I've been over almost every night since we've slept together. I'm surprised you're not sick of me yet."

I lean on the chair and crowd her space, bringing my lips only a breath away from hers. "Baby, no one's more surprised about that than I am. But you're the most addicting thing I've ever encountered."

"What if I told you I'll come over, but no sex?" she says with a challenge.

"No problem. I'm addicted to you, not your body." I lightly kiss her lips, then pull back.

When I stand up, I see her throat bob with a swallow.

I smile. "Did I just surprise you, Lexi?"

She nods her head. It appears my words have made her speechless. I like that.

"I'll see you tonight: sex, no sex. I don't care. Maybe pack some spare clothes to keep at my place. You'll be staying at my place a lot if I have anything to do with it."

I walk away and smile to myself. The idea of her leaving her things at my place makes me happy.

Chapter Nineteen

Lexi

I step out of his shower after desperately needing to clean myself off. He pulled out this time and came all over my body while saying the dirtiest things to me. It was enough to push me over the edge.

I've never come like that before. But I've also never had the hottest man in the world cum all over me while telling me how much he wants to fuck my ass.

You would think he would have had enough of me by now. When I walk into his room wearing my towel, he's lying in bed wearing only his boxer briefs. It's hard to tell if he's got a semi or it's just his big dick protruding out of them.

I reach into my bag that I packed to find something to wear to bed. I hear him groan behind me.

"Something wrong?" I ask as I turn around with a shirt in my hand.

"You're flashing me with your wet pussy and asking me if something is wrong?" he asks.

I may have bent a little bit more than necessary. What can I say? I like getting a rise out of him.

"I was just getting my shirt so we can go to bed," I say innocently.

He reaches into his boxers and pulls his dick out. It bobs in the air, getting harder by the second.

"What are we going to do about this?"

He starts to stroke himself. I don't know what it is about watching him touch himself that makes me so damn hot. I feel the moisture between my legs start to build. I squeeze my thighs together as I watch.

"I don't know. Does something need to be done?"

He growls. "Based on how hard you're squeezing those pretty little thighs together, I'd say there are two things that need to be done before we go to bed."

I know he's right, but I'm still frozen in place, lost in his strokes.

"Why don't you come over here and get a little taste? You clearly can't pull your eyes away from me," he suggests. My legs start to move toward him, saliva pooling in my mouth with how much I want to taste him. "Hold on. Is your lipstick in your purse right there?"

"Yes."

"Get it out. I want your lips the same shade of pink they were today when you suck my dick."

Some girls might find this demand demeaning. Honestly, if it were any other guy I've been with, I'd likely slap them and walk away. But there's something sexy as hell about it with Marcus.

When you trust the person, and dare I say *love* them, it's sexy when they tell you exactly what they want. Even sexier when they demand it.

I reach into my purse and pull out the lipstick. He strokes himself as his dark eyes watch me put it on slowly, trying to make him squirm while he waits.

When I'm done, I throw it on the nightstand and crawl to him on the bed. I kneel next to him and watch as his hand continues to move.

I reach my hand up to touch him. "May I?" I ask nicely.

"Fuck yeah, sweetheart. Let's see you get all messy for me again."

I smile. He has become obsessed with my blowjobs.

Who knew I'd be so good at it? I sure as hell didn't know.

I wrap my hand around his dick. He's so thick that I can't make my fingers touch. My body still struggles to accommodate his size, but he definitely has no trouble getting me off.

My hand glides up and down at a slow pace. I'm in no hurry, and sometimes, drawing it out makes it even hotter.

Especially when I look up and see his eyes, they give away just how torturously good this is for him.

As soon as my lips close around him, he groans in relief. I work my way up and down with my mouth, gliding my tongue along with it, knowing that's what he wants.

The first few strokes are slow and steady, clean. Then I start to let it get sloppy, the sounds getting wetter. I begin to see my lipstick stain his dick.

He looks downright ready to lose it.

"Look at those pretty lips getting all messy for me," he says as he puts a hand in my hair. "Let me see you work off that lipstick, baby."

I moan along his dick as I slip, slide, and suck harder. Faster than I've ever done before.

"Holy shit. Just like that. I'm gonna fucking come. Wait," he pulls me off him. "Not yet. Let me get a little taste of that pussy."

He pulls me forward until I'm sitting on his face. His mouth closes in over my clit without any hesitation. No slow lick to get me going. He is hungry for me, and I am happy to be the meal he feasts on.

He shakes his head back and forth forcefully, and I let out a moan of satisfaction. When I feel like I'm teetering on the edge, he pulls off me.

"Flip over baby. Suck my dick while I get you off."

His demands make my pussy clench in response. When I sit up to flip over, I notice my juices are all over his neck and chest. Like...there's a lot.

He must notice the shock in my face because he looks down at himself and smiles.

"I think somebody likes it when she rides my face. Sexiest thing ever."

"I didn't think I could ever produce that much."

He takes his hand and rubs it all over himself. "I could bath in your juices. No amount is ever too much. One day, I'm gonna make you squirt. That's a promise. Now flip over and put my dick back in that sexy mouth of yours."

He doesn't have to ask me again. Sucking on him is becoming one of my favorite activities.

I flip over and place my hands next to his hips. His dick is directly in my face, and I waste no time starting where I left off. No need to build up to anything. We're both on the verge of losing it.

I feel his hands on my cheeks as he spreads me open. I think I hear him sigh before his mouth closes in over my clit again. This time, one of his fingers finds my back entrance again and begins to finger it.

I moan all over his dick. It provides such a foreign feeling but such a good feeling. Maybe it's the idea of it being taboo, or it just really is that pleasurable, I'm not sure.

We both get to our breaking point within minutes. He's moaning all over my pussy, and I can't hold myself back as I lick and suck.

"I'm coming," he says, the words barely audible.

The second his hot, wet cum starts pumping into my mouth, it's enough to throw me over the edge.

I fall onto his body after we both have come down from our releases. My head lies on his thigh while he is probably still all up in my business.

I don't care. I'm so damn relaxed and exhausted. I could easily fall asleep like this.

Eventually, he has to get up and go clean himself off. I made that much of a mess on him. I feel slightly embarrassed by it. When he returns, he jumps back into bed and pulls the covers over us.

We look at each other in the moonlight. That weird energy passes between us again, like we're speaking without actually using any words. It's like this cosmic connection that I don't understand.

Somehow, I know that we're both thinking the same thing.

I love you.

But I don't dare say those words out loud yet. There's a stigma around saying them too quickly, and it's only been four weeks.

Nevertheless, the words are there in my mind all the time.

"What are you thinking?" he whispers, tucking my hair behind my ear.

"You first. What are you thinking?"

"I asked first."

"Yeah, and I replied. You go first."

He laughs softly, then wraps his arms around me. "You're a pain in my ass sometimes."

"Right back at ya."

I suppose neither of us is ready to take the plunge and say the words first.

It's okay. I'm content here in his arms. The rest will come later.

Chapter Twenty

Marcus

I glance down at my clock, dreading that my Sunday family dinner starts soon. That means I have to say goodbye to Lexi.

We've been snuggled up on the couch watching football. She insisted that we watch Chicago's game and only click to Cleveland's to check the score. She had to sit through Cleveland the last two Sundays, so it's my turn to feel the pain.

Another reason I know I'm crazy about this woman, I agreed to it.

I wrap my arms around her tighter. I wish she could come with me.

The thought makes me think maybe she can. I'm serious about her, and it seems like an excellent first step to show that to her.

"What do you think about coming with me tonight?"

She turns her head away from the television to look at me.

"To your parents' house?"

"Yeah. I'd love for them to meet you. And it's not like you won't know anyone there. You know my entire family aside from my parents."

"Wow. I wasn't expecting that," she replies.

I tense up. "Um, yeah. Is it too soon?"

"No, no. I'm sorry. I'm just surprised. I mean, if you want me to meet them, I would love to."

My body floods with relief. I lean in and give her a gentle kiss. "Good. They're gonna love you."

Just like I do.

We both push off the couch and get ourselves ready for dinner. I find myself leaning over her in the bathroom to reach for my toothbrush while she puts on her mascara. It's an oddly domestic thing.

But I realize in this moment how much I like it. I want more of it.

"You ready?" I ask her after I grab my jacket and pull it over my shoulders.

"Ready." She follows me to the door. "You sure about this? Your brothers won't think it's weird?"

If they do, that shit is on them. If I want to bring my girlfriend to meet my parents, that's my right.

"They'll be fine. No time like the present to begin bringing you around them outside of work."

She smiles. "Ok."

It only takes about ten minutes to get to my parents' house. They still live in the house I grew up in, in a little neighborhood in Cleveland called Little Italy. The streets are lined with Italian restaurants and bakeries. It still has cobblestone roads.

I have many memories of growing up here.

Lexi oohs and ahhs over all of it, asking questions about what it was like growing up here.

"Are your parents like, *Italian* Italian parents?" she asks.

I chuckle at how adorable she is. "They aren't from Italy themselves, but their parents were. So, they grew up speaking Italian and English. I'd say they're about as Italian as an Italian American person can get."

"Oh my gosh. I'm about to eat some amazing food tonight, aren't I?"

"Now, that is a definite yes. Hope you brought your appetite, babe," I tell her as I pull into the driveway.

I cut the engine and get out of the car, walking over to her side first. I scan the driveway, noticing everybody is already here.

As soon as I open the front door, we're hit with the smell of Ma's cooking.

Lexi's chest expands on a large inhale. "Oh, it smells like heaven in here.'"

I love how much she appreciates good food like I do. You don't grow up Italian and not see food as more than just something to give your body energy. It's something that brings people together. It's art. It's a way of expressing yourself.

"Uncle Marc," Sienna says as she runs into my arms.

I wrap her up in a tight embrace. "My little SiSi."

"Who is this?" she asks blatantly, no filter.

"This is my girlfriend, Lexi."

"You finally have a girlfriend!" she exclaims.

Lexi chuckles next to me, a look of amusement on her face.

"Gee, thanks for making me look good in front of my girl."

I lead Lexi into the kitchen, where all the women seem to be hanging out.

Silence falls upon the room. Alexis looks so excited that she might spontaneously combust right here.

"Ma. I hope it's okay that I brought my girlfriend Lexi tonight."

Ma smiles happily at Lexi, but Lexi swats my stomach.

"You didn't ask if it was okay for me to come?" she asks in horror.

"What? No. Of course, it's ok. Right, Ma?"

Ma chuckles and opens her arms out wide. "Of course, it is. I'm so happy to meet you."

Lexi steps into Ma's arms. Watching them embrace makes my entire body fill with pride.

"Oh my gosh." Alexis jumps in and squeezes Lexi. "When Gabe told me, I was so excited. You guys are so cute together."

Mia winks at me as she comes over and leans in. "You just made Ma's night." She looks over again at the two. "Scratch that. You made her year."

"Only because she probably never saw the day coming."

Mia laughs. "True. I'm happy for you."

"Thanks, sis. It's nice that you all know each other already. Makes the entire thing feel a bit easier."

Savannah, Alexis, and Ma are already chatting away with Lexi. Based on Lexi's smiles and laughs, she seems okay.

"I'm gonna go say hi to the guys," I announce.

Apparently, I announce to no one as they ignore me and keep talking.

Mia cracks up. "They don't give a shit about your whereabouts, bro. Get out of here."

Feeling a little butt hurt, I leave the kitchen and walk into the family room where the guys are. The early evening Sunday games have started.

The guys and I are all on the same fantasy football team. None of my big players are in this game, though, so I have less skin in the game.

"If he would stop running the damn ball. I need to get some major yards from him," Luke yells to nobody in particular.

"He can get 350 yards today. That's not enough to beat me this week," Gabe says with a smirk.

Before things escalate, I decide to step in.

"What's up, brothas? Talking about how I'm gonna be the league winner this year?"

"Living in a fantasy world again?" Gabe fires back.

I laugh as I take a seat next to Pa.

"What's all the commotion in the kitchen about?" Pa asks curiously.

"Oh, that? I brought my girlfriend Lexi with me."

I try to remain blasé about it as I wait for their responses.

"Oh, yeah?" Pa says. "Your mother must be having a heartache in there."

I smile. "It was definitely a surprise."

Luke looks confused. "So, you're, like, really serious about this."

I can't help but crack up at his question. "Yes, you tool. I told you the other day that I was."

"I know. I just didn't know you were *this* serious about it."

"Well, you better believe it. I'm completely serious about this."

Mia comes in with Lexi on her arm.

"Look who I found, boys," she says while they sit together on the empty loveseat.

"Pa, this is Lexi. Lexi, meet my father, Joe."

Pa stands up and shakes Lexi's hand. "Pleasure to meet you," Pa tells her.

"Nice to meet you, too."

"I appreciate you putting up with this one over here." Pa motions in my direction. "All my boys are a little rough around the edges."

I smile as I swipe away nothing particular on my jeans. It seems to be Pa's standard line when one of his sons brings a woman home. It's like he can't believe any of us can get someone to stand us for longer than a day. I think he just likes to cut through any tension and make a joke.

Lexi chuckles. "Marcus is quite the gentleman. You've done a great job with him."

Pa seems to bask in the pride of her praise. I know he's proud of all of his kids. He says it all the time.

We get called into the kitchen for dinner. I walk in with my arm around Lexi and grab two seats for us. Gabe, Alexis, Sienna, and Luke sit across from us while Savannah and Mia sit on our side. Ma and Pa are on each end, and little Joey is in his highchair by Ma.

The table is filled with a couple of bottles of wine to be paired with Ma's chicken piccata and lemon garlic parmesan pasta.

"This all looks and smells so incredible, Patricia. Thank you so much," Lexi says.

"It's what I love to do most: feed the ones I love."

As everybody gets their food plated, I run my hand up and down Lexi's back in soothing strokes. Her and Mia are laughing about something Mia just whispered. I imagine days like this in the future. Lexi and me showing up for Sunday dinners, living together, creating a life of our own.

It all feels so natural.

"Lexi, tell us about yourself. Where did you grow up?" Pa asks.

"A suburb twenty minutes outside of Chicago."

"Oh, I just love visiting Chicago. The boys always bring me to the best Italian restaurants when we go there," Ma says.

Lexi smiles. "They are known for some great Italian food there. Although, I must say your cooking is incredible. You could open up your own restaurant."

"I think you're gonna have to marry this one," Pa jokes.

The idea isn't scary. In fact, it makes my entire body feel all warm and tingly.

I find myself absent-mindedly playing with her hair and squeezing her neck. I don't realize I'm doing it until I see Ma staring at my arm and smiling.

"What about your family?" Ma asks.

I want to step in and tell her she doesn't have to answer that. Tonight is supposed to be fun, and I don't want her to get sad talking about it, but I'm too late.

"It's just me and my mother. Always has been. I don't have any siblings, and my dad left when I was really young."

Lexi is a champ and seems willing to share her life with my parents. It's all fine until we get to her mom's current diagnosis. That's when I feel the need to step in and change the subject. I felt her body tense as soon as it came up.

I've been around her enough to know how much she thinks about her mom and worries about her. She calls her daily on the phone and then calls her mom's nurses separately to get an update.

"You know if you two got married," Sienna says casually. "I could be the flower girl."

Lexi looks at me with wide eyes. I have to chuckle at her reaction.

"You would make a beautiful flower girl, SiSi," I tell her.

She smiles adoringly up at me. Complimenting her instead of directly acknowledging her questions always works.

"So, who exactly initiated this?" Luke asks as he points between the two of us with his fork.

Savannah gives him a death stare. "Lucas Giannelli."

"What? It's a legit question. Come on, Marcus asked way more inappropriate questions to us."

The table erupts with laughter. They aren't wrong. I like to see how uncomfortable I can make my brothers. It's always a good time.

"I can see that," Lexi says as she looks over at me and smiles.

I shrug. "I was curious."

"Sooo," Luke continues.

"Me," we both say at the same time.

"What?" Lexi asks. "That is a total lie. It was me."

"I don't know," Gabe says. "Lexi, you're the quiet, inno-cent one. Marcus is the crazy one. I'm gonna say it had to be him."

Lexi looks at me, and I just smile. "Uhh, seriously. You're wrong."

"I kissed you first at the party."

"That was nothing. You kissed me with the pretense that it was for our act. I was the one who did it for real."

"Ooooh, if that's true, I'm going with Lexi," Alexis says.

"Hold on. What am I missing here?" Ma steps in. "What act?"

My head falls to my hand as I shake my head.

Here we go.

"Thanks, babe," I say, directed at Lexi.

"Sorry," she says with cringy face.

I sigh. "It was nothing. We just had to pretend to date for a weekend."

"Why on earth would you have to do that?" Ma asks.

"Cuz apparently, I had...kissed... with our largest client's daughters' friend and never called her back, so I was a man whore who made the company look bad."

"Now use your imagination with the word *kissed*," Luke says.

I scowl at him and mouth *fuck you*. He just smiles proudly. I know what he'll tell me. It's nothing I wouldn't do to him. And the truth is, he's right. But still, *fuck him* right now.

"You're telling me a client threatened not to do business with you because of Marcus's personal life based on one woman?" Pa's hand hits the table.

Gabe and Luke nod their heads.

"He sounds like a real piece of work. Probably has a small dick," Pa says.

Lexi chokes on her wine as some dribbles down her chin.

As she chokes, I hit her back.

"You, okay?" I ask.

"Yeah," she says, grabbing her napkin and cleaning herself up. "I like you, Joe."

"I only speak the truth. There's no way a man that worries about something so stupid is packing downstairs."

"Gabriel and Lucas Giannelli," Ma says. "Are you telling me that you made your brother stoop that low and pretend to be with someone all to impress that snake? You two should be ashamed of yourselves."

"What about Mia?" Gabe whines.

I love when Ma steps in, and you see twelve-year-old Gabe come out. Our parents are the only ones who can make the grown-ass man shake in his boots.

"Don't worry about Mia. I know it was one of the two of you who thought of that."

"I think what you guys are missing here is that it was that plan that brought these two together?" Luke says as he points to me and Lexi.

The table falls silent. That's not a lie. It was. When Gabe and Luke realize nobody has a comeback for that, they high-five each other.

"Oh my gosh. I love being a part of this," Lexi whispers to me after Sienna asks another random question and changes the subject. "Your brothers are so different at your parents' house. It's hilarious to see them like this."

"They aren't as suave as they try to be at the office."

The rest of the night is casual as everybody intermingles.

When we return to my place, Lexi starts to take off her jacket and walk into the house, but I grab her and bring our mouths together.

Tonight was perfect. The feeling of leaving Sunday night dinner with someone was foreign, but I felt more complete than I ever had before.

I kiss her slowly and lazily. I cup her face and move it to the side so I have better access to slide my tongue inside.

She lets out a soft moan, and it's my undoing.

I pick her up and walk her straight to my bedroom. I lay her on my bed and turn on the lamp on my nightstand. She looks perfect as she lies patiently waiting for me.

Looking into her eyes, I reach behind me and pull my shirt over my head. I love watching her squirm as she watches me. The more clothes I get rid of, the more impatient she seems.

Once I rid myself of my boxers, I reach for her jeans and slowly pull them down her slender legs.

I climb onto the bed and kneel in front of her so I can maneuver her top off her. We never stop looking into the other's eyes the entire time. Once we are both naked, I still feel no need to rush this moment together.

I glide my fingers down her body, starting from her neck all the way down to her thigh. Her breaths and the way she moves her body under my touch tell me how affected she is.

My fingers sweep back up her body, then trace gently around her breasts, never touching her nipples. I continue this all over her body, watching her break out in goose-bumps.

When I'm ready, I lean down and softly take a nipple into my mouth. I suck on it gently, then move to the other.

Kissing my way back up her neck, I find her lips again, then move in between her legs.

When I bring my fingers down to her pussy, she is already soaked. I should've known. My girl gets riled up quickly for me.

I grab my dick and line it up at her entrance. Soaking it with her arousal, then giving her clit a couple of circles and taps with it. Then, I sink it into her just about an inch.

I cage her in between my arms, lying on my elbows so I can be right there with her, and then I sink all the way.

I don't know what it is about this time, but it feels different.

We look into each other's eyes as I make slow but steady movements in and out of her pussy. Her hands grip my arms as I continue.

"You're not saying anything dirty. You normally like to talk while you fuck," she whispers.

"I don't think we're fucking right now," I whisper.

She understands what I'm saying. I'm not fucking her, not by a long shot. I'm making love to her right now.

I didn't know you could express yourself this way, but I feel like with each glide inside of her, I'm telling her how I feel.

Her hands grip my arms harder as I move my eyes from hers down to her jaw, which is now falling slack. Her pussy is starting to grip me a bit harder.

Knowing she's about to come, watching her facial reactions, it's my own undoing. We crash at the exact same time, gazing into one another's eyes.

I don't know how long we lay like this together. I don't want to break the moment.

Eventually, I pull out and climb off her to get cleaned up.

She pulls one of my T-shirts out of my drawer to sleep in while I just throw on a pair of my boxers.

Her head rests on my chest as we lay in the dark in complete silence. I think about what just happened. I didn't know it could be like that, but with Lexi, everything is different.

For the first time in my life, I feel like everything is heading in the right direction. I don't think anything can ruin this for me, for us.

Chapter Twenty-One

Lexi

"So, you, like, met his family and everything?" Grace asks.

Chaos erupts in the background as her kids' laughs and screams echo through the phone. She just ignores it like nothing is happening.

I'm always impressed when moms can ignore the noise and carry on with any conversation.

"I did."

It's been almost a week since I went to his parent's house and since I had the most intimate sex of my life. The way he refused to look away from me, it was like his eyes were trying to speak for him. I was so worried I would spill the words *I love you* to him. No one wants those first words to come out in the middle of sex, but what was happening between the two of us in that moment was so much more than just sex.

"Well..." she draws out. "How did it go?"

"It went really well. Obviously, I know his siblings already, but hanging out with them in such a personal environment was different. It was cool to see the softer side of them. And his parents are amazing. Very supportive and loving."

"Did it feel rushed to meet everybody already?"

"Not at all." I think about it more before continuing. "Honestly, it felt really natural. Him and I...we are just so in sync."

I'm sure it seems sudden to many people. But love doesn't have a timeline. There are no measures or rules to define it. I think I always knew when I found the one, it would happen quickly. Maybe it's why I knew so early on in past relationships that it wasn't worth pursuing any further.

Could this be it? It certainly feels like it.

"I'm surprised you two aren't together on a Saturday night."

"He has a dinner with his siblings and a client."

"Ah, I see. How is your mom doing?" Grace asks.

"I just talked to the nurse this morning. She's having some more episodes with the staff. When she doesn't recognize them, she can get really defensive and refuse to do what they ask."

"Sounds like your mom. She never was a woman to put up with any crap."

I laugh, even though I feel like crying. I've learned that sometimes, in these situations, it helps to find the humor in it, or you'll go crazy. Plus, Grace is right. That totally sounds like my mom.

"Tell me about it. The stories the staff tell me are horrifying, but so mom at the same time."

After we got off the phone, I decided to make myself some dinner and watch a movie. I've been craving Italian ever since eating at his parents' house last weekend. His mom's food was incredible.

If it wasn't massively high in calories, I'd eat that shit every night.

Tonight, I'm making myself a lasagna. I saw this recipe that has me using three kinds of cheese instead of just ricotta. This one has ricotta, mascarpone, and grated pecorino romano. It also told me to add some Italian-seasoned breadcrumbs to the cheese. I'm really excited to try it.

After I prepare the lasagna and place it in the oven, I open a bottle of wine.

Marcus insisted I try it. He said it's one of his favorite Chianti's. Once I pour a glass, I settle down on my couch and scroll through the movies.

A documentary on baseball comes up. It makes me think of Marcus.

Knowing he suffered a career-ending injury breaks my heart. He doesn't seem to talk about it much.

I click on it, wanting to learn more about this world of his that means so much to him.

I watch in fascination as it starts to go over the origins of baseball. There seems to be controversy over which country created it, England or America.

The way I look at it is that even if England started it, America made it what it is today.

Part way through, I pause to take my lasagna out of the oven and cut a piece for myself. I planned on having salad on the side to get my greens in, but I honestly couldn't care less about vegetables right now.

I just want to overindulge in the pasta, cheese, and sauce concoction.

I decide to say screw the salad and sit on the couch with my wine and lasagna, then press play.

There are fascinating facts that I learn as it continues. I keep thinking of Marcus, wondering how much of this he knows.

The urge to talk to him gets the better of me. I should leave him alone and let him be tonight.

Me: Did you know that there are 108 double stitches in every major league baseball?

His reply is almost instant.

Marcus: Very odd question, but yes, babe. I knew that.

Huh, that's kind of surprising to me. I would think one wouldn't care about the number of stitches in a baseball.

Me: Did you know the New York Yankees were the first team to wear numbers? Also, their numbers corresponded to their batting order at first.

I put my plate down and pick up my wine glass as I get cozier on the couch. There's no way he's going to have known that. Who knows that fact?

My phone pings with a notification.

Marcus: Did you know that the longest MLB game in history lasted 8 hours and 6 minutes?

Holy Shit. An eight-hour game? Who the hell would stay around for that? There couldn't have been many fans left in the stadium.

There aren't enough hotdogs and ice cream in the world to make me stay and watch a game that long.

Me: Nice try. I know you're trying to distract me from the fact that you clearly didn't know my fact.

He ignores my text again.

Marcus: Did you know that the record for the fastest baseball pitch by a woman is 69 mph? (wink face)

I roll my eyes at the text but find myself smiling as I type.

Me: Now you're just making shit up. Nice way to try and steer this convo to sex instead of my knowledge of baseball over you.

Ha. Take that. Trying to distract me isn't going to work.

Marcus: Look it up, babe.

Look it up?

'He can't be serious,' I think even as I type it into the search engine.

What the hell? It's true.

What a crappy coincidence for women everywhere. Of course, Marcus knows that stat.

I mean, all it will take is one more mph.

Thinking about sixty-nine has me recalling doing it with Marcus the other night.

My thighs squeeze together as I remember. I wasn't a fan of it before. I was never able to enjoy the man's tongue on me while working to try and get him off.

With Marcus, it was a totally different experience. For starters, I love pleasuring him. It only turns me on more. Also, his oral skills are top-notch.

Marcus: Now that I'm thinking about 69...

Seems like we're both thinking about the same thing. Though, I don't plan on admitting it right now.

Me: Get your mind out of the gutter and focus.

Marcus: Hey, you were the one who texted me.

Me: Yeah, with innocent baseball facts. You turned it dirty. I hope you have an uncomfortable boner right now in front of your family.

Not really. But he's fun to mess with.

Marcus: I definitely have a semi thinking of you sucking my cock. But good thing I'm seated at the table, and no one can see.

I laugh out loud, thinking about him getting uncomfortable at the table as he tries to think his way out of being hard.

Feeling a bit mischievous, I lie back on the couch and lift my shirt to show my bra. I push my breasts up where one of them has a nipple just popping out and take a picture of myself as I bite my lower lip and look into the camera.

I hit send, then get back to watching my documentary.

Marcus: Fuck, you look delicious in that photo. But that's some cruel shit. You're playing with fire. You haven't seen me angry in the bedroom, baby.

Wetness pools in my underwear. That happens a lot where Marcus is concerned.

The idea of him being angry in the bedroom sparks a new wave of excitement. I've never experienced it before, but I have a feeling it could be hot.

This adventurous side of me is new but fun to explore. Who knew there was such a wild woman behind the shy, apprehensive one I've shown the world my whole life?

Me: Maybe I want to see you angry there...

Marcus: I'm coming over tonight. You better be awake.

I sit up straight, shocked to see his text. He never comes to my place. Let's be honest; his house is incredible. My apartment is just blah compared to his.

Me: When are you coming?

Marcus: No more questions. You better be ready and waiting...

I take the last sip of my wine and look around my apartment. I generally keep it clean, so there isn't much to do. Maybe get some dishes in the dishwasher and put some clothes away in my room.

After I get my stuff in order, I freshen up in the bathroom and then change out of my cotton underwear into some black lace. I pair it with a black tank top and pajama shorts, deciding to skip the bra.

Call me crazy, but I want to look sexy when my man gets all macho with me.

I decide to have another glass of wine while I wait. I only get about halfway through before there's a sudden knock on my door.

I put my glass down and walk over to the door, butterflies in my stomach.

I open the door, and he stands there with his arms crossed at his chest. I open the door further for him to come in. He walks past me.

When I close the door and turn around, I try to lean in for a kiss, but he backs away.

"No," he says as he shakes his head back and forth. "That's not how this is going to go tonight."

He starts to advance on me. "Do you know what could have happened if someone leaned over an inch and looked at my phone tonight?"

I swallow. "What?"

"They could have seen your picture. They would have seen your breasts. Which are *mine*. You don't get to send me those pictures without my permission."

Wow. He's never talked to me so dominantly before. I should be pissed off, but my body is too busy getting hot.

His eyes study mine; then, I see a crack in his facade. A small smirk emerges, and he leans in to whisper, "You know this is part of the act, right? You can do whatever you want. I would never tell you what to do."

I suppress the laugh that wants to erupt. Only Marcus would stop and make sure I was comfortable before continuing this little game.

I nod my head for him so he knows I'm aware.

As soon as I do, his stern face is back.

"What do you think I should do to punish you?" he asks as his fingers come out and gently caress my neck.

His touch lights up my body, making every nerve ending feel ten times more sensitive.

My chest rises and falls in a heavy rhythm.

"Whatever you want."

Probably not the smartest thing to say, but I haven't the slightest clue how to respond.

His eyebrow raises. "Good answer. Now bring me to your room."

I step in front of him and let him follow me through the kitchen, down the hallway, and into the first room on the right.

Before I get more than a couple steps in, he stops me.

"Stop right there, baby." I stop and wait. He comes up behind me and brings his mouth to my ear. "Turn around."

When I turn, something has changed in his demeanor. His eyes are darker, more intense.

"Unbuckle my belt."

I look down to unbuckle.

"Ah, ah, ah." He stops me. "I want your eyes on mine while you do it."

I listen to his command and look at him while I reach down for his belt. I misjudge the distance between my hand and his belt the first time, my hand falling through the air.

We both struggle to hide our smiles. It reminds me that all of this is for fun.

My second attempt is a bit more successful. I use both hands to get his belt unbuckled, and then I unzip his pants.

He gives me a playful sigh. "I never told you to do anything but unbuckle my belt. That's one slap to the ass for you."

My thighs squeeze together in anticipation.

"Now, push my pants down to the ground."

I do it, making sure not to break eye contact with him.

"Good girl. Now reach into my boxers and pull my dick out."

Wow. Those words send a current directly to my pussy. I reach into his boxers and grab his already hard dick into my hands, then pull it out of his boxers.

"Stroke it."

I glide my hand up his length, and he breaks our eye contact when his head falls back. He groans his appreciation.

After a couple of strokes, he lifts his head.

"Stop."

I stop.

"Take everything but your panties off for me."

When I'm in nothing but my black lace underwear, he motions for me over to the bed.

"Put your hands on the mattress and stick those luscious cheeks out for me."

His warm hands start on my hips and run up my back.

"Do you know what I would've done if someone saw your picture tonight?" he growls.

He actually sounds angry about it, not just pretend.

"No," I answer.

His hands come back down on my hips and squeeze. It's hard enough to make me wonder if it'll bruise tomorrow.

"I would have flipped out. Probably caused a scene at the restaurant. Do you know why?"

He softly strokes my right cheek.

"Why?"

"Because you're mine. Nobody else gets to see you like that. I've never felt this...territorial before. It's new for me, babe."

Before I can even register his admission, a loud noise echoes throughout the room, followed by a sting on my ass.

His slap was fast but accurate. Just hard enough to leave a mark. He rubs soothing strokes on my cheek.

"Did you like that?" he leans forward and whispers in my ear.

I nod my head quickly, not wanting him to doubt for a second that I didn't like it.

He pulls back and hits me with another one, this one a bit harder. An unintentional shriek falls from my lips.

"Your ass looks incredible with my handprint on it. Do you want another one?"

I nod again, and his hand comes down again.

"Oh, God!" I shout.

He rubs a couple of soothing circles on my cheek, then slowly drags his hand between my thighs. I feel his fingers slip through my folds. At this point, I'm dripping down my legs.

He groans. "Fuck, baby. You really liked that."

He isn't wrong. There was something oddly satisfying about having him get rough but then instantly sweet with his circles around my cheek.

"I can't wait any longer. I need to feel your pussy around my dick."

He lines himself up and pushes inside of me.

It's so crazy how we can go from making love to just plain fucking. I don't think I'll ever tire of this man.

He doesn't ease into it. His thrusts are hard and punishing. His fingers back to my hips, where they are digging into me.

"Fuck. What are you doing to me?" he says under his breath.

I don't know, Marcus. The same thing you're doing to me. Making me addicted to every little thing about you.

Next thing I know, his hands are in front of me on the bed, and his body is slouched over mine. He begins to fuck me in short but powerful thrusts.

It's demanding and rough. He keeps cussing and whispering dirty things in my ear.

It's so intense. I can't take it any longer. My body gives into the pleasure. My orgasm comes quickly and erupts more powerfully than ever before.

I scream through the pleasure as wave after wave passes by. He fucks me through the entire thing until I feel him tense up and release inside of me.

He begins to pepper my body with gentle kisses. It makes me smile, and my heart flutter.

Can life get any better than this?

Chapter Twenty-Two

Marcus

I walk into the boardroom five minutes early. The trip to the breakroom for my coffee didn't eat up as much time as I had thought.

To my surprise, Lexi is already there with her laptop in front of her.

She's typing away, not having the slightest clue that I'm in the room. Not until I pull out the chair across from her.

"Oh, hey," she smiles.

"Hey, yourself. You're looking awfully cute right today."

She chuckles but gets back to typing. "Thanks."

"How was your weekend?" I ask.

She looks up and smiles. "Meh, kinda boring."

She props her chin up on her hand with a challenging look.

"Oh, really? You didn't spend some amazing time with your incredible boyfriend who blows your mind in the bedroom?"

Her face doesn't change at all. "Like I said, meh."

I reach for the nearest pen and toss it at her. "You're such a liar."

Her head falls back as she lets out a laugh.

Luke and Mia walk into the room mid-conversation. They stop when they see us waiting.

"Oh, hey, guys. How are you doing this morning?" Mia asks.

While Lexi and Mia engage in small talk, Gabe and Savannah walk in.

Gabe sits at the head of the table. Nothing has been said verbally, but he generally takes the lead at these meetings. Maybe it's because he's the oldest sibling, and our roles growing up have transferred over to work.

I can't say it's never bothered me. As much as I love my family, it's hard to escape those childhood dynamics.

"Okay," Gabe starts. "I was looking over our client list. Sales are up, and clients keep rolling in. Thanks to Lexi, our software update is working well. It's streamlined the ordering process and has taken less time away from us so we can focus on our clients."

I look over at Lexi and wink. That's my girl.

"Nice work, Lexi," Savannah jumps in. "It really has been amazing to see it come to life. So much talk about how we wanted to improve the process but to see it play out so well is great."

Lexi smiles but shrugs her shoulders. "It was nothing. You guys came up with the plans. I just executed it."

Leave it to Lexi to be so modest. She should take the compliment. She is incredible at her job, and we're lucky to have her.

"Are we going to move forward with what we discussed?" Luke cuts in.

My ears turn up, not aware of a discussion we've had recently.

"Yeah, I think it'll definitely drive up sales."

"What did we discuss?" I ask.

"Luke and I were talking about a discount program. Something to incentivize our current clients to purchase all their wine through us."

Huh, interesting.

I remember bringing something like that up a year ago, and they all nixed it. Now, not only are they all for it, but they discussed it and decided to move forward with it without talking to me.

My muscles tense, and my jaw clenches.

Sometimes, I wish they took me more seriously. I want to bring it up, to tell them how angry it makes me. I'm just worried if I do, they'll see it as me being...me: Marcus, the crazy sibling who gets irrationally angry.

What I want them to see is: Marcus, the grown adult who is standing up for himself. I just don't think it would be received like that.

So, I do what I've generally done for years since working with them—I don't say anything.

Lexi looks at me strangely. Her eyebrows are drawn in like she's trying to figure something out.

The meeting carries on, but I stay stuck in my head. I just want it to be over so I can go back to my office and blast some music in my headphones.

That's my go-to to help me deal with the rage inside me when something like this happens at work.

When the meeting is finally over, I stand up and walk out. Sometimes, I feel like I did as a kid—blind to everybody. I often wonder if that's why I took to being such a big personality.

I march into my office and promptly close the door.

As soon as I take a seat, I reach for my headphones. I put them on and play my punk rock playlist. Simple Plan has always been a good band to help ease these feelings.

The noise drowns everything out, specifically my thoughts. I must not have heard the knock on my door because the next thing I know, I see a figure standing in front of me.

If it were Lexi, which it is, I would be massively annoyed. But if anything, her presence has a soothing effect on me.

I pull my headphones off.

"Hey," I say.

"What happened in there?" she asks, arms crossed,

She leans against the side of my desk.

"What do you mean?"

"I mean the fact that your brothers made a big decision on sales for your company, and it seemed like you had no idea. It clearly bothered you."

It's almost creepy how in-tuned she is with me. How did she catch onto that?

"It's no big deal," I lie.

That just seems to piss her off more. "Cut the shit. Why didn't you say anything? I know it bothered you. It's still bothering you."

"I don't know. I just don't see the point in saying any-thing."

"Why?" she pushes.

"Because!" I scream. "Because they won't listen to me any-way."

"Then *make* them listen."

"You don't understand. If I get defensive or angry, they will just think it's typical Marcus acting like the younger sibling."

"Well...then tell them that. Tell them that you're a grown-ass adult and demand they shed the sibling bullshit and treat you like an equal person at this company."

I look up at her, completely floored that she stands up for me so strongly. Part of me thought that maybe this shit was all in my head. That I was just a jealous younger brother. Lexi is making me see that maybe my feelings are valid.

Seeing this woman standing in front of me—fighting for me. It's everything.

I stand up from my chair, grab her face, and smash my lips down onto hers. I'm so overcome with emotion. No one has ever gotten me like she does. I put everything into the kiss—hoping to express what she means to me.

When I pull away, I can't help but just stare at her in awe.

"What was that for?" she breathes out.

This is it. I need to just say it.

"I love you, Lexi," I whisper as my thumbs rub gently on her cheeks.

Her eyes begin to well up with tears as she bites her bottom lip.

"You do?"

I nod. "So fucking much."

A single tear runs down her cheek, but I catch it with my thumb and wipe it away.

"I love you, too."

I smile at her. "Really?"

She nods her head. "Of course. I just didn't want to say anything because it seems so soon."

"I know, it does. I didn't know it was possible for it to happen so quickly, but love doesn't always make sense."

I kiss her again, but this time it's different. This time, we both know exactly how the other one feels. This time, I'm kissing the woman who loves me.

I lean into it and bring her closer to me. She makes me feel whole—complete in a way I never knew possible.

When I pull away, I lean my forehead down onto hers.

"How do you do it?" I ask.

"Do what?"

"Know what I'm feeling before I've said it out loud."

She sighs. "I get you. I'm connected to you in a way I've never experienced before."

"I feel it, too."

"I know you do."

"This...us...it feels big."

"It is," she whispers.

***

"What do you think of this one?" I ask Lexi as we walk through the furniture store.

My basement remodel just got finished, leaving the final task of decorating. I wanted to get it done before football season began, but other things popped up, like wanting to spend all my time with Lex.

We've moved past spending all our time in the bedroom phase and are now doing things like shopping or running errands together.

"It's nice. I like the brown leather idea for a couch in the basement. Easy clean-up for all the beer spills when you're screaming at your team when they're losing."

"Oooh," I say as I laugh. "Nice dig there."

She smiles. "It's just too easy sometimes."

"I agree, though, with the stains. I think I want this one."

I find the salesperson who gives me a form to fill out with all my information for delivery. As I fill it out, my brain starts to wander.

After this, I want to go to the grocery store to pick up some things I'm out of and get something to cook for dinner. Plus, we need to stop at Lexi's apartment so she can get some clothes to wear tomorrow.

I wish she could just live with me. We spend all our time together.

We've only been together for six weeks, so I won't rush it. We only just said I love you to each other this week.

I hand the form back to the salesperson and give him my credit card.

When it's all paid for, we get in the car and drive to the grocery store.

"What are you in the mood for tonight?" she asks me as we walk down an aisle.

She looks over at me, and I wiggle my eyebrows at her. When she puts it like that...

"Oh, geez." She swats my chest with her hand. "Get your mind out of the gutter."

I laugh but do my best to stay focused on the mission at hand instead of how her ass looks in her jeans. I may have walked a bit slower than her a few times just to get another view.

She's wearing a brown leather jacket and brown-heeled boots. Paired with the jeans, it's a killer combination.

She told me she's starting to order more clothes online now. I'm happy if she's happy. If this outfit is her style, then I'm one lucky son of a bitch.

We are in the dairy aisle as we pick out some heavy whipping cream for the fettuccine alfredo that we're making.

I spot whipped cream in a can, and my brain pictures spraying it all over her body and licking her clean.

"You know what I've always wondered," I say as I point to the can. "Who thought of making a separate bottle strictly for sex? Have you ever seen them before?"

She shakes her head. "No, I haven't."

"They actually have them, and it tastes awful. I just don't know what's wrong with buying a regular can and using it."

She opens the door and grabs a can.

"What's that for?" I ask as she starts to walk away.

She stops and turns around. "Obviously, you've done it before and are picturing it right now with whomever you did it with. Now, we need to make another memory for you to have when you look at it."

"Are you jealous?" I ask as I walk closer.

She shakes her head. "No. Of course not."

We walk in silence for a minute. I don't speak. I just watch as she walks tensely.

"Ugh, fine. I'm jealous," she finally admits.

I wrap an arm around her shoulder. "I know you are. I think it's cute."

"Cute? You like me being jealous?"

"Yeah, I do. You're not the only one. If I even think about you being with an ex, I want to punch a hole in the wall."

"You do?" She sounds surprised as she turns to me.

"Of course. I love you. Why would I like to think of another man's hands on you? Now, on to more important topics. When are we using the whipped cream?"

She laughs. "Tonight. If you're lucky."

"Is there anything I can do to help persuade you in that direction?"

"You can talk to your siblings about what happened in the meeting this week."

"Ugh. Such a boner killer."

Though, I have thought more about it since our talk in my office. I don't know if I would necessarily go back and rehash anything, but maybe next time, I'll try to speak up.

She helps me unload the groceries when we return to my house.

"Do you want a glass of wine while I cook?" I suggest.

"Yeah, I'll get it, though, babe."

I let her mosey over to my wine selection while I start getting everything ready for dinner.

I put a little Dean Martin on. It's something Ma and Pa have always had on in the background, especially while cooking in the kitchen. Now, I find his music to be a must-have when I'm cooking Italian.

He was from Ohio, a point of pride we Italians in Ohio hold onto.

I start to sing *On An Evening In Roma* to myself as I dance around the kitchen. The times Pa would twirl and dunk Ma while Dean's music played in the background are forever etched in my brain.

Lexi comes in, holding two glasses of wine. I grab them out of her hand and place them on the counter.

"What're you doing?" she asks.

"This," I reply as I take her into my arms and dance.

I take the lead, moving forward and backward in circles in the kitchen while singing to her. She laughs as my moves get more daring, twirling her a couple of times and then bringing her back into my arms.

"*Though there's grinning and mandolining in sunny Italy. The beginning has just begun when the sun goes down,*" I sing.

"What's happening right now?" she laughs.

"I'm just serenading Mia Bella while cooking. You have a problem with that?"

I twirl her again, then take her by surprise when I dip her. She screams and laughs at the same time.

"You are wild."

"What? You don't like it?" I tease.

"I love it."

The song switches to *You're Nobody 'Til Somebody Loves You*. It's a slower song, so I grab her hand and wrap an arm around her waist. She rests her head on my chest as we sway back and forth together.

The lyrics make me think about all the years I've been single. How I never realized the little meaning they held compared to what it feels like is happening right now.

When the song ends, we pull apart from each other. I softly kiss her lips.

"Thanks for the dance," I say, then bow. "Now, I shall get back to cooking."

She takes a seat at the island with her wine, smiling. I love knowing I'm the reason it's there.

We drink our wine, laughing and talking while I continue to cook.

It feels like nothing can bring me down in life.

Then her phone rings and everything changes.

Chapter Twenty-Three

Lexi

My phone rings while Marcus is busy cooking. I want to ignore it. Whatever it is, it can wait.

Then, I steal a glance at the screen and see that it's the assisted living center.

My stomach sinks. They never call me at this hour on a weekend.

"Hello?" I answer hesitantly.

"Lexi Miller?"

"Yes, this is Lexi."

Marcus turns his head around while standing by the stove.

"Hi, Miss Miller. This is Greta from Nothing but Care. I'm calling because your mother seems to have taken a spill. She is currently on the way to the hospital."

"Oh my God. Is she okay?" I ask as my heart begins to race.

"She was awake and conscious when she left. That's all that I can confirm."

"How did this happen?" I ask.

"What I can gather is that she was having an episode—she didn't recognize her caretakers. When they kept trying to calm her down, she got agitated and tried to run away."

I can't believe it. I hate everything about this damn disease. I can't imagine the fear of not knowing what's going on, not recognizing anyone, not knowing who you are or where you are supposed to be, but just knowing that you don't feel safe.

"Ok," I say, my voice cracking as I try to hold in my tears. "Can you please tell me what hospital?"

That gets Marcus' attention. He drops his spoon and walks over to me.

I nod my head as I gather the information. When I hang up, tears instantly start running down my face.

"What happened?"

"My mom. She fell. She's on her way to the hospital."

"Is she okay?"

"All they could tell me was that she was conscious when getting into the ambulance. Oh, God," I jump off the seat. "I need to get back. She's alone and confused right now. She needs to be around someone she might recognize. Someone who can talk to her and calm her down."

I start pacing around the kitchen, unsure what to do first. Do I drive or fly? It's a five-and-a-half-hour drive. That's probably the fastest way to get there.

"I'm gonna drive there."

I bolt across the room to grab my purse and keys.

"Woah, woah, woah. Babe." Marcus follows me and puts his hands on my shoulder. "You can't drive like this. It's late, and you're upset."

"Well, I have to get to her as soon as possible. I can't wait to book a flight. I probably wouldn't get there until tomorrow."

As I put my shoes on, he pulls his phone out.

"Don't you dare walk out that door yet. Let me make a call and see what I can do."

I try to tell him I can't wait, but he holds his finger up.

"Hi, Martha. Are there any pilots on standby that could get me to Chicago tonight?"

My eyes open wide. He can't seriously be considering having me take the company's jet. That'll cost a fortune.

"Perfect. We can be there in thirty minutes. Thank you so much for accommodating this."

He puts his phone in his back pocket and then grabs his jacket.

"I can't take the jet." I stand in shock as he moves to put his shoes on.

"Why not?"

"It's too much money."

He looks up at me with confusion. "Sweetheart, your mom is in the hospital. If it were my mom, I would be willing to pay anything to get to her. Don't think about the money. Now, get your shoes on. Let's go."

I don't have time to argue. This feels a little extreme, but it will get me to my mom faster. A plane ride from Cleveland to Chicago is about an hour. If we really do hop on in and go, I'll be there in an hour and a half, compared to five hours.

He insisted on driving me, which was a great idea because now that I know how I'm getting there, and things have settled down, the tears have returned.

His hand rests on my leg. "It'll be okay. My Ma took a spill a couple of years ago. It was scary. She needed surgery but healed up just fine. I know it's different with your mom's mental state, but in terms of her body, she can come out of this."

I know his words are meant to reassure me, but they don't. I doubt that I'll feel better until I can see her.

Marcus manages to get us to the private airport within twenty minutes. Since it's already dark out, hardly any other cars are in the parking lot. As soon as we get inside, the pilot greets us.

"Hello, Mr. Giannelli. We have the jet ready to go. The crew is just doing a quick maintenance check. We should be taking off in ten minutes."

Marcus shakes his hand. "I appreciate the quick response and apologize for the last-minute request."

"Not a problem, Sir. Is it both of you flying tonight?"

"It is," Marcus replies.

"Wonderful. Follow me, and we will walk out to the jet."

Marcus takes my hand and follows the pilot.

"Marcus, you don't need to come."

He wraps an arm around me, instantly making my body feel more secure and safe. "Of course, I'm coming. I can't let you do this alone."

I want to cry. When have I ever had someone there to support me like this? Never.

My friends are incredible and would absolutely come if I asked, but they have lives. I can't expect a mom of two to drop everything with her family to come and sit with me. Chloe doesn't even live in the same state.

But here Marcus is, completely selfless and putting off his life to come with me.

As soon as we get on the plane, Marcus leads me to the back, where we take our seats next to each other. Being the gentleman he is, he lets me take the window seat.

"There isn't a stewardess tonight, but I can get you anything you want," he tells me.

I grab his hand and lean my head on his shoulder. "I just want to be near you."

He places a soft kiss on my forehead. It always makes me feel precious and adored when he does that.

The plane takes off, and we ascend into the air. After about fifteen minutes, the seat belt lights go off. Marcus unbuckles his belt and gets up. I rest my eyes while he's gone, trying to focus on the sound of the engines to keep my mind off of my mom.

He comes back holding a coffee cup.

"I made you some tea. I thought it might help calm your nerves."

He takes a seat and hands it to me.

"Thank you," I whisper.

"How are you feeling?" he asks as I take a small sip.

I try to think about all the emotions swarming me right now and focus on the strongest one. "Guilty."

"Why do you feel guilty?"

"Cuz I'm not there with her. She doesn't have anybody else but me, and I moved to another state while she needs me the most."

"You were just trying to follow your dreams."

"I guess. Still, it doesn't mean I should've taken a job so far from her."

He takes my hand, and we sit silently the rest of the way. The tea was soothing to my body, but it did nothing to calm my racing thoughts.

We hop in a car service when we get to Chicago. The hospital is another twenty-minute drive. I have already called the hospital to check on her. They said she is currently sedated while they run some tests.

That allows me to relax in the car. At least I know that she isn't awake and still freaking out.

I love how Marcus isn't pushing to talk or distract me. I'm not in the mood to be distracted. It's comforting enough to just have him here with me.

We get to the hospital and find her room on the third floor. She's already been admitted. When we get to the room, I walk in and see her fragile-looking body.

Why is it so hard to see a loved one in a hospital bed? It's such a reminder of how impermanent life is.

I take a seat next to her and hold her hand. Marcus leans against the windowsill behind me, letting me have my moment.

A doctor walks in, holding a stack of papers and a folder.

"Hello. I'm Dr. Lee. Are you Elaine's daughter?"

"I am. My name is Lexi."

"Nice to meet you, Lexi. I was just looking over your mother's x-rays. She has suffered a pretty significant crack to her hip. I believe the best course of action is immediate surgery, followed by an extensive outpatient physical therapy program."

A broken hip? How could she have fallen so hard? I'm in shock that the injury is this significant. I was thinking a broken arm or something.

"How long is the recovery process for this?" I ask.

"Full recovery is different for everybody. It depends on how mobile they are and their dedication to physical therapy. It can take anywhere from four months to a year. Now, what we are going to have an issue with is your mother's mental state. Some people with her disease can be very reluctant or flat-out refuse to participate in the physical therapy. If that's the case, she may never fully recover."

"What?" I cry. "What does that even mean?"

"If she doesn't do the physical therapy, she may need assistance with a walker or cane. Worst possible outcome with no physical therapy would be a wheelchair."

"But if she does do the therapy," Marcus chimes in behind me, "she could make a full recovery."

"Absolutely. It's just hard to know how she will react to therapy. You will have to take it one day at a time."

"When is she going to have the surgery?" I ask.

I feel Marcus's hand on my shoulder.

"Tomorrow morning."

He answers my questions as my brain struggles to think of everything I want to know.

"Will she wake up tonight?" I ask.

"We have her on some heavy sleeping and pain medications to keep her comfortable. It's preferable that she get a full night's rest before the surgery. Her body will handle the surgery better if it's well rested."

"Ok. So, I can just sleep here, I guess." I point to the chair in the corner of the room.

"You can. You are always more than welcome.," the doctor says. "But she will be sleeping the rest of the night. It would be good for you to get a good night's rest, too. You can be here first thing in the morning before she wakes up."

With that, he leaves us alone in the room. I look over at Mom, so fragile looking in her hospital gown.

Life was supposed to get better for her. I was looking forward to giving her grandkids, letting her retire and live the second half of her life a hell of a lot better than her first.

"It's not fair," I whisper.

His hand finds its way back to my shoulder. "No, it's not. I'm sorry this is happening, babe. I think you should come to the hotel with me. Like the doctor said, you both need a good night's sleep tonight."

I turn my head to look up at him. "You don't think that makes me a horrible daughter? I don't want her to wake up and be alone."

"Babe, you're an amazing daughter. You taking care of yourself and getting sleep is so that you *can* be there for her tomorrow."

I guess that's true. She'll be in pain and immobile tomorrow. I need to be ready to do what I can to make her more comfortable and support her.

I stand up and kiss her on the forehead.

"Goodnight, Ma. I'll see you tomorrow."

When he leads me out, holding my hand, I realize how much better my life is with him in it. I can't imagine doing this without him. His support is everything to me.

Chapter Twenty-Four

Marcus

The bathroom door opens as Lexi steps out in a towel. I just made her eat dinner and then told her to take a long, hot shower.

Hopefully, it will all help her relax enough to get a good night's sleep.

"How was the shower?" I ask her.

"It was good."

She starts to sort through the bag on the desk.

"I can't believe you paid someone to buy us clothes. You're either really lazy or have too much money."

I laugh. "Probably both. Plus, I love you and didn't want you to have to worry about such trivial shit right now."

She steps into her pajamas and throws on a top. She crawls into bed and falls into my arms, one leg wrapped over mine.

I squeeze her into me, wishing that, somehow, I could transfer some of my strength to her.

"Thank you," she whispers. "For everything. I..." she pauses, choking up when she starts to talk again. "I don't know what I would have done without you."

"Don't mention it, babe. I'm just happy to be here with you. Thanks for letting me come along."

"Of course. Why wouldn't I let you?"

I look up at the ceiling, trying to figure out how to articulate my insecurities. "I don't know. I was worried that maybe I was overstepping by wanting to come. I thought maybe we weren't there yet. This is a pretty intimate thing."

"You've put your finger in my ass. I think we're intimate enough."

I begin to crack up. "Oh my God. Lexi. I'm talkin' emotionally intimate, that's being physically intimate."

"I beg to differ. Letting someone do that to you takes a lot of trust. Trust is emotional intimacy."

I shake my head. "Whatever you say."

We fall into silence for a bit. I start to twirl her hair around my finger.

"We are totally there, though, by the way," she says.

"Where?"

"At the level of emotional intimacy where I wouldn't think twice about having you here with me."

I smile up at the ceiling. "Good."

***

"How are you doing?" I ask as I watch Lexi pace over the same tiles in the waiting room for what feels like the hundredth time.

"I'm fine," she lies. "I think maybe I could use another cup of coffee."

Shit, that is the last thing she needs. She's already had two, and she is completely wired right now. I watch her bite her thumbnail and continue her pacing. I'd be surprised if there is even a nail left for her to bite.

"No problem. I'll be right back." I get up and head to the cafeteria. I'm not going to tell her, but I'm getting decaf.

There is no way her body can handle another ounce of caffeine.

When we got here this morning, her mom was just waking up. She was in relatively good spirits and recognized Lexi. I was worried about how Lexi would take it if her mom was agitated and didn't recognize her.

With all the commotion, nurses going in and out, Lexi only got around to introducing for a second. There was no discussion of who I am to her daughter.

From what I've heard, Elaine isn't the biggest fan of men. It seems I've got my work cut out for me.

I just hope she doesn't hate me.

When I get back to the waiting room, Lexi is still pacing. She spots me, and I see her shoulders momentarily relax.

"Here you go," I say as I hand her the cup.

Her hand trembles as she grabs the cup and looks up at me. "Maybe I shouldn't have this."

"Way ahead of you. It's decaf," I say, then wink.

"Have I told you that I loved you yet?" she smiles and then takes a sip of coffee.

"You have, but I don't think I'll ever tire of hearing it."

I let her drink her coffee while I take a seat. I pull my phone out and text my family, letting them know I won't be home for Sunday dinner tonight.

Mia: You're in Chicago? Why?

Me: Lexi's mom fell yesterday. She's having surgery right now. I took the jet out here with her last night as soon as we found out.

Ma: Oh, that poor girl. Please tell her we are thinking and praying for her. Keep us updated.

Me: Thanks, Ma.

Gabe: Sorry to hear that. We are all thinking of her. Tell her not to worry about work this week. We don't want her to split her focus.

Me: Appreciate that. I'll let her know.

I put my phone in my back pocket to focus on Lexi, and the doctor comes out and heads toward her.

I stand from my chair and walk over to her.

"Lexi, Marcus," the doctor says as he addresses us. I'm honestly surprised with all he has to focus on, like surgery and saving lives, that he has enough space in his brain to remember our names.

He turns to focus on Lexi. "Surgery went well. Your mother is on her way to the recovery room. She'll likely remain asleep for another hour or so."

Lexi sighs. "Thank you so much. When can I see her?"

"The nurse will be out shortly to tell you her floor and room number. You can head straight there. The nurses will help your mom in the following days with her recovery. I'll be in and out to check on how she is progressing. Then we will set up a physical therapy and recovery plan for her."

"Ok. Thank you again, doctor."

"My pleasure."

After he walks away, Lexi turns to me, and I see her tension begin to fade away. She walks into my arms.

"I'm so relieved," she whispers into my chest.

"Me too. Surgery was the first hurdle. She made it through that."

I feel her head shake up and down on my chest.

"What if she doesn't do her physical therapy?"

"One day at a time, remember? We can't play the *what if* game. That's just asking to drive yourself crazy."

"Ok."

I haven't told her yet, but I've already made some calls to find the best physical therapist in the city and the best mental health therapist who works solely with dementia patients.

Insurance won't cover the best of the best, and I want her mom to have that.

I want her to have the peace of mind that her mom is receiving the best care out there.

The nurse comes out to let us know where Elaine is. I walk hand in hand with Lexi to find the elevator and get to the wing of the hospital where the recovery patients are.

For the first time since we've arrived, I feel like Lexi is breathing a bit easier.

We walk into the room and see Elaine hooked up to machines and resting peacefully.

"You go ahead and sit with her," I tell her. "I'm going to go grab us some lunch."

Even though we need to eat, I'm mainly using this as an excuse to give Lexi time alone with her mom. I think it should just be her there when she wakes up.

So, I take my time in the cafeteria, perusing the menu options. Hospital cafeteria food has come a long way since I remember. I can recall being in them a lot when my grandparents were in the hospital, and the options were gross.

Or maybe as a kid, anything but chicken nuggets and fries wasn't good enough for me.

Either way, I occupy myself until I feel like it's been enough time, then grab some turkey sandwiches. Before returning to the room, I stop in the gift shop and get Elaine a bouquet of flowers.

When I get back, I hear voices before I round the corner to turn into the room.

"That man, the handsome fella, he's your boyfriend?" I hear her mom's soft voice.

I tense, waiting for a shit storm to ensue.

"He is. I love him," her beautiful voice echoes in the room.

"How long have you two been seeing each other?"

"Over a month, maybe closer to two now. I haven't done the math."

"You haven't said anything. We talk on the phone all the time."

Silence falls between the two. I'm surprised Elaine is as cognizant as she is. They said sometimes injuries or significant events can make them temporarily more lucid.

"I know, Mom. I didn't know how to tell you, I guess."

"Why not?" Elaine asks.

"Because...because you're always telling me to stay away from men, that they are evil, especially the good-looking ones."

"I'm just trying to look out for you. I don't want you to go through the same thing that I did."

Lexi sighs. "I know that, Mom. I know you were just trying to look out for me, but I'm happy. He means a lot to me, so if you could just give him a chance."

"I suppose I could do that. I'm no fool. I know I'm sick. Something's wrong with me. I do want someone who will be there to take good care of you. I suppose it never occurred to me that I'd be gone one day and that you might need someone by your side. I'm sorry, Lexi. I never meant to transfer my issues onto you."

"Thanks, Mom. I really appreciate you saying that." I hear Lexi's voice break. "He's amazing. I've never felt so loved and supported before. Thanks for listening to me, for being understanding. I'm so happy we've finally had this conversation."

It sounds like Lexi is crying.

I fear that if I don't walk in now, something could be said that will unravel the progress they just made. I'm not sure if it's the right move. I know I'm good at making bad decisions, but my gut tells me to step in and let Lexi end this conversation where it is now.

"Knock, knock," I say as I tap on the door. I walk in, holding the bags of food up as I enter. "I come baring gifts."

I place them on the table by the hospital bed and pull out the flowers I was hiding behind my back.

"These are for you." I hold the flowers up for Elaine. "I'll just put them over here on the nightstand. Maybe we can put them in a cup of water for you."

"Aw, that's so sweet of you." Lexi smiles.

"Thank you. That was very kind of you. Although, I should tell you, I'm not impressed by flowers. Treat my daughter right; that's what will impress me."

I chuckle. "Of course. I love her. I don't mistreat those that I love. You can ask my Ma."

"You're close with your mother?" Elaine asks, sounding surprised.

"Oh, Patricia Giannelli? She and I are two peas in a pod. I tell her everything."

She looks skeptically at me. "My ex-husband treated his mother very poorly. That should've been my first warning sign."

"I agree. You can always tell how a man will treat his wife by how he treats his mother. Ma used to tell me and my brothers that all the time."

"Sounds like a wise woman," Elaine says.

"Very wise."

"I still don't trust you yet," she replies.

I smile. "Fair enough. I'll tell you what: I'll work to earn your trust. If I do something stupid like break your daughter's heart, which I won't, I give you the permission to personally have me whacked."

"Oh, geez," Lexi shakes her head. "That's the Italian in him speaking, Ma."

"Although I have no interest in going to jail, I appreciate your intention," Elaine responds, trying to hide a smile that's forming.

I'll treasure this moment. I did a lot of research on dementia last night, long after Lexi went to bed. I know this could be short-lived. Tomorrow, she could opt to hate me or not ever remember me.

But I'll know that for the five minutes that her mother was herself, I slipped in through the cracks of her armor and got her to like me.

Chapter Twenty-Five

Lexi

The nurses have been flooding in and out of the room, checking on Mom. She has been asleep for several hours now.

Marcus and I have taken turns in the room while the other goes to get a snack, coffee, or just to stretch their legs.

The conversation I had with her earlier has been on constant repeat. I've never had it with her before, never had the courage to. But knowing that she was somehow acting like her old self and Marcus was here, it felt like the conversation had to be done.

I can't get over how amazing Marcus is with her. He didn't seem the least bit intimidated or mad that my mother was flat-out telling him she didn't trust him. Compared to my experience with his mother, the welcoming hug and sweet disposition, I would have thought he would be a bit frustrated by how he was being treated.

But that's just how Marcus is. He doesn't judge people by their shortcomings. He understands their past and chooses to be nice regardless of what is thrown at him. If there were more people like him in this world, we would be better off.

At one point, I return to the room, and Marcus and my mother are playing cards.

"Rummy," my mom exclaims as she puts down the last of her cards.

"Awww, man," Marcus grumbles as he slams down his cards. "I'm normally better at this game. You're just getting lucky."

I smile as I watch from outside the door, hoping they don't see me.

"No such thing as luck in rummy. It's not about the cards you get, but what you decide to do with them."

"That's what lucky people say."

Mom laughs, a genuine fit of laughter.

"And that's what sore losers say," Mom responds.

"Touché," Marcus replies. "Nice game, Elaine."

I walk in, and the two people I love most in the world smile back at me. It fills my heart.

After dinner, when it's time to go to bed, Marcus and my mom convince me that I should stay in the hotel again. Mom said I will just disrupt her sleep by being in the room.

I don't know if that's true, but the nurse stepped in and told me people sleeping in the rooms with the patients sometimes leads to the family member eventually becoming drained.

She told me to save my energy for when Mom gets released.

That sparked a new concern.

What am I going to do about her recovery? Will they have physical therapists that come to the assisted living center?

I knew this particular assisted living center prided itself on letting the residents have some form of independence. There's a possibility she will need to transfer somewhere else that provides more hands-on assistance.

It starts to dawn on me that this next year will be impossible to get through if I live in Cleveland.

"You seem awfully quiet," Marcus says while we sit in the car, bringing us to our hotel.

"I'm just tired," I lie.

I don't know if I'm ready to bring to fruition the thought that's been on my mind.

"We'll get back to the hotel and get a good night's sleep."

"Don't you need to get back to work tomorrow?" I ask.

"Don't worry about work. I'll head back when I feel like I have to."

I close my eyes and rest my head on his shoulder. It feels like it's been ages since he and I were just coworkers. It's incredible how one silly little weekend could change the course of our lives so drastically.

When we get back to the hotel, it's much of the same as last night. He insists I take a shower first.

When I get in, I crank the heat up to high in an effort to work out the tension in my muscles. It's not easy to have so much cortisol running through your body continuously for days. My body feels like it could use a massage and a full day of rest. For now, it will have to settle for a hot shower.

After Marcus showers, we eat dinner in bed and watch a rerun of one of our favorite shows.

The show's familiarity gives me some sense of calm amid this storm.

I don't have much appetite, but I manage to get down most of my steak.

When it's time to settle into bed, I lie in his arms and listen to the steady rhythm of his heart.

The more I've thought about it, the more I feel like coming back home to Chicago is inevitable. I just can't let my mom slip away alone in a nursing home. I know she's not always with it, but there are still good days every week.

Soon, she will slip into a permanent life of memory loss.

"You're quiet again. I can feel that something is weighing on you. Talk to me, Lex."

I take a deep breath. He's right, I should talk to him about it. No good can come from keeping it bottled up and hidden from him.

"I've been thinking about moving back to Chicago."

There, I said it. It's out in the open, but the shift in the room is palpable. His body has gone from warm and snuggly to tense and cold.

"Have you?"

I nod my head. "This is going to be a long recovery for her. I can't leave her alone for it. Not while there is still some of my mom left in her brain right now."

"That makes sense."

"Plus, I doubt her current facility will be able to accommodate her level of care. I'll have to help her get settled in a new place. It's just too much to do from another state."

I start to cry. Oh, gosh, we just started dating. There's no way he wants to commit to a long-distance relationship so soon.

Plus, I have to move back home for good. If I do it, I can't just leave when my mom's condition worsens. That would be horrible.

No, this move back will have to be permanent. And Marcus's life is back in Cleveland: his siblings, their company, his parents.

"Hey," he nudges me with his arm. "Don't cry, baby."

"What does this mean for us?" I ask through thick, heavy tears.

"One day at a time."

I look up at him through my tears. Nothing about any of this is fair. Just when I found someone who I love and who loves me. Just when my life was starting to turn around, and I was feeling truly happy for the first time in my life.

He takes my face in his hands and brings me to him. Our lips close down on each other. It feels raw. We are standing at the precipice of heartbreak, not sure what life has in store for us.

But right now, all I want is to feel his lips on mine, to savor the feeling of his body against mine.

When his tongue slips inside of my mouth, everything else feels like it's miles away. I don't know how he does it. His hands move my head to the side to deepen the kiss even further.

I feel weightless. That's what he does to me. He takes all the stress that is holding me down and removes it, if only for a moment.

We strip each other's clothes off, and he lays me down on the bed. I open my legs for him.

When he sinks into me, we both sigh in relief. This is exactly what I need. He rests his head on my shoulder and freezes for a second.

"I love you so much, Lex," he whispers.

"I love you, too."

He starts to slide out of me, and it feels like a sudden loss, just to feel complete again when he pushes back in. That's the rhythm I feel like he creates, loss filled by fulfillment...over and over again.

He takes me all the way to the edge, then slows down.

"Wait for me. I want to come with you," he tells me.

He leans down and kisses me. His tongue feels like it's working in sync with his thrusts. It's enough to drive me wild and send me right over the edge. I moan into his mouth as the spasms begin to clench around him. His release follows, and we come together, just like he wanted.

He lifts his head and looks down at me while he works to catch his breath. I don't know what he's thinking, but I can tell he has a lot of thoughts swirling around his head.

This has been a big day for both of us.

I can't think about what would happen if I lost him. The ache would be too much to bear. If I keep thinking about it, I won't be able to sleep.

So, for now, I'm just going to put everything aside and pretend it's not happening, and maybe I'll luck out and fall asleep.

Chapter Twenty-Six

Marcus

I walk into my apartment, but nothing feels the same. Everything feels dull and lifeless.

This past week has been draining and confusing as fuck.

Elaine is doing well and will be released from the hospital in a couple of days. Lexi is working on finding a new facility to accommodate the new level of care that her mother now needs.

Meanwhile, I have to get back to work. I have deadlines that I'm running the risk of not hitting, which is unlike me, but I just couldn't leave Lexi.

I throw my keys on the counter and grab a beer. It's nine on Thursday evening, but I can't think about doing anything until I just chill with a cold beer for a minute.

It's been three days since she told me she's considering moving back to Chicago. Every day since I've wanted to ask her what her plans are, but I know it's wrong.

I need to be there for her through this time, not worry about myself.

I've been thinking about what would happen if she did move. A long-distance relationship isn't ideal when you haven't been together for very long, but it's doable. We're not talking about living across the country from each other. We'd be two states away, five-hour drive, one-hour plane ride. Plus, we have a private jet we can use.

Although, it won't be available all the time. Business trips will always take priority over my personal life. It also feels wrong to ask the company to rack up so much of that cost when it's not business-related.

I want to figure out a way to make it work for her to still live here, but in the end, something tells me she will move, and I need to be ready for that.

***

"Hey, man," Gabe walks into my office. "Good to have you back."

I drop my pen and lean back in my chair. My head falls back as I open my eyes wide to ease them from straining at the computer for so long.

"Thanks."

"How's Lexi holdin' up?" He takes a seat across from me.

"She's hanging in there. Today's a bit rough. Her mom has slipped back into her dementia. She's a bit irritable and confused."

"Shit, I feel for her. I was a wreck when Ma fell a couple of years ago and needed surgery. To think of adding dementia on top of that."

"Ya," I laugh sarcastically. "It's a lot for her to deal with on her own. We all at least had each other."

The four of us were able to take turns helping Ma out, plus she had Pa. Lexi has nobody but me. The thought makes me irrationally angry at the world.

How can someone so sweet be dealt such a shitty hand in life?

"I didn't even think of that. It must be tough not to have someone else to go through it with you. It's a good thing you went with her."

"Yeah, that was an easy decision."

He looks at me thoughtfully. "It's weird to see you like this."

"Like what?" I ask.

He shrugs. "I don't know. All in love and everything."

I laugh softly. "I'm sure it is. Considering it's the first time and all."

"Well, it's nice to see. You seem happy, you know, despite the current circumstances."

"Thanks. I am happy."

I want to talk to him and tell him what's keeping me up at night. This happiness I've finally found is on the verge of being taken away from me. Even if we stay together, it will be different—harder.

But I also know I can't divulge that information to her current employer without her permission. It would be a serious break in trust.

"Well, I should get back to work. Keep us updated on everything."

"Sure. Hey, by the way," I say. "Thanks for being cool with her focusing on her mom and missing work."

"Don't mention it. We'll figure it out."

On the way home, I get my phone out and call Lexi.

"Hey, you," she answers right away.

The tension I've felt in my body all damn day finally starts to fade away. It's incredible that just hearing her voice can have such a direct effect on my body.

"Hey, babe."

"Are you just getting off work?"

I lean my neck to the right to stretch it, and it cracks. Damn, I'm pent-up.

"Yeah, I'm on my way home. How are you?"

"I'm alright. Just got word that she will be released tomorrow."

"That's good news. It means her recovery is exactly where they hoped it would be."

I know none of this sounds like good news, but you have to take the victories where you can.

"Yeah," she says unenthusiastically. "She was able to take a couple more steps today with the walker but got really angry and almost fell again."

Shit. That doesn't sound good. I hate that I'm not there to take care of her.

"Well, a couple more steps are a couple more steps," I say, trying to look on the bright side.

"I guess so."

She sounds so defeated.

"I'm sorry I'm not there."

"Marcus, I told you not to worry about that. We both can't take off work this long. I'm surprised you guys haven't fired me."

"FMLA includes taking care of a loved one. You can get up to twelve weeks for that, and it's not even been two yet. How about you give yourself a break?"

"Yeah, but that only counts for companies with fifty or more employees. You guys could fire me if you wanted."

"Geez, are you trying to point out that we're not a big enough company for that? That hurts."

I hear a laugh on her end, and it feels like a victory.

"It must be the awesome IT Director who has streamlined your software for you."

I smile. "Of course, she's smart...and super-hot."

She chuckles and then exhales. "I miss you."

"I miss you too, babe. What are your plans for dinner?"

"I was just gonna grab something down at the cafeteria. I'll probably stay with Mom until visiting hours are over at seven."

"Remember what the nurses have been saying," I remind her.

"I know, I know. Don't burn myself out."

"Are you listening to their advice?" I ask.

"I'm going back to the hotel at night."

I'm worried about her. She has so much guilt from her mom having this disease and living so far away that she doesn't seem to realize what she's doing to herself.

"You're deflecting," I point out.

"And you're annoying," she fires back.

I laugh. "Nothing I haven't heard before."

"What are your plans for dinner?" she asks.

"I was just gonna order in and relax. Wanna have dinner together?"

"What do you mean?"

"We can video chat."

"I'll be in the cafeteria."

"Good. Looks like I will be able to keep you company."

She pauses. "People will think I'm crazy."

I smile to myself. "Who cares what people think? If this is the only way I can share a meal with you, I'll take it."

"Ok. It's a date. What time?"

"You tell me. I'll be ready whenever you are."

Chapter Twenty-Seven

Lexi

Two Weeks Later

I walk into the office for the second time since I've been back.

Things were getting crazy, and system errors needed my attention.

I'm here, but my brain isn't. It's all I can do to focus enough to get the task at hand done.

My mom has been at the new nursing home for a couple of weeks now. Grace was a huge help. She would come to visit with me and keep me company. I was spending my nights at her house.

But I knew I needed to get back to my life, if only for a moment, to regroup and figure out what I would do.

It only took two days of being back to know I couldn't stay here.

Grace has gone to see Mom for me, but that shouldn't fall on her.

I hardly slept last night, thinking about how I would break the news to Marcus. Then it dawned on me—he will never break up with me or tell me he can't do the long distance. His heart is too big.

He's so focused on my emotional well-being. Every day, every night—he calls, texts, sends flowers or desserts to me.

I need to be the one to do it. I need to let him off the hook.

He's young, gorgeous, funny, smart, generous, kind. He deserves a life where he can run his business and see his girlfriend regularly. And I know he wants to be a dad.

How could we make that happen when there is no future in sight with us in the same state?

It's the last thing I want to do. I cried myself to sleep last night when I realized it was the best way to make sure I didn't drag him down with me.

Now, I just have to get enough courage to tell him.

When my computer fires up, I find myself staring at it but not really seeing anything. It's like I'm paralyzed.

I can't believe I was so close to finding happiness, and it got ripped away from me again. Maybe I just need to accept that some people just don't get their happily ever after.

My mom sure as hell didn't. I should've listened to her.

A knock on my door pulls me from my thoughts.

"Hey, you," Alexis appears at the door.

"Alexis, hi. What're you doing at the office?" I ask, surprised to see her here.

"I was worried about you. I came with some pick-me-ups." She walks into my office and places a coffee cup on my desk. "It's October, pumpkin spice season has begun. I also brought a chocolate-chip pumpkin muffin." She places a bag down with the muffin.

I look down at the coffee and bag, completely shocked.

My eyes suddenly start to water at the incredibly sweet gesture. I won't just be losing the love of my life. I'll be losing these friends that I've made.

"That's so sweet of you. Thank you."

I reach for the coffee first and take a sip. If there is anything in this world that could offer a temporary lift, it's pumpkin spice anything.

"How are you holding up?" she asks as she takes a seat with her own coffee in hand.

"Terrible."

She smiles. "I appreciate you being honest. I know it must be hard to be away from her. How is she doing?"

"I just talked to the nurse this morning. She has physical therapy at two today. We will see how it goes. She was willing to do about ten minutes of it yesterday before they said she was on the verge of getting angry. It's a balance between pushing her and not triggering an episode."

"How're you handling it?"

Another wave of tears threatens to come. I blink rapidly to try and keep them away. "It's...hard."

"If you ever need to talk about it, I'm here for you. I didn't exactly have an easy upbringing or many people here for me when I was new to the city. I know Marcus is a good guy, but sometimes you just need another woman to confide in."

She's right. The benefits you get from the comfort of your significant other are not the same ones you get from a girlfriend. Unfortunately, the thing weighing heaviest on me right now is something that I can't confide in with her.

She would probably feel obligated to her brother-in-law to tell him what's coming, and I want to be the one to have the conversation with him.

"That's so sweet of you. I'll tell you what..." I lift the coffee, "Pumpkin anything is its own kind of therapy."

She smiles. "I knew I liked you."

We share a laugh and talk about lighter topics for a couple of minutes. She's easy to talk to, and it does momentarily take my mind off of my problems.

"Anyway, I don't want to bother you. I'm sure you have a lot to catch up on. Remember what I said: I'm here if you need me."

"Thanks, Alexis."

Hours later, I somehow managed to get through the day without breaking down. Marcus stopped in once, but we're both trying to play catch up, so he only stayed for a minute.

On my way out, I popped into his office to say bye, agreeing to go to his place for dinner tonight.

Now, here I am, sitting in my car, trying to get the courage to go inside. Once I do, I know what needs to be done.

Just get out of the car and get it over with, Lexi.

When I get to his front door, I let myself in. It's something I've grown accustomed to doing lately.

I call his name, but there's no response. I can't find him anywhere until I come across him in the library, sitting in his chair.

He looks so peaceful.

When he looks over and sees me, he smiles.

"Hey, beautiful."

I walk in and sit on the armrest of his chair.

"What're you reading?" I ask.

He closes the book, and I see the cover. *'Everything You Need to Know About Dementia.'*

My heart nearly bursts out of my chest.

He looks slightly shy, getting caught reading the book. "I just don't know much about the disease. I wanted to understand it more, you know, so I could maybe be of more help."

Tears are already running down my face. Until the day I die, nothing anyone will do or say will be this sweet and thoughtful.

"I'm moving back to Chicago," I blurt out as the tears fall faster.

It feels like the world stops turning as I sit here waiting for him to respond. When he finally looks up at me, I see the sadness in his eyes.

"I understand."

"You do?" I ask.

"Of course. You need to be there for your mom like she's been there for you all of your life. I know there are things she's said, and advice she has given that may not be accurate or even appropriate, but she's loved you no matter what. You need to be there for her."

"I do," I cry.

I wipe the tears from my cheeks.

"When are you going back?" he asks.

I take a deep breath. "I'm going to give the company my two-week notice. Then I'll be gone."

He raises his eyebrows at me. "You know you don't have to do that. You don't have to give us two weeks. Let me talk to the group about you working from Chicago."

"I can't ask you guys to do that. It's not fair. Your company hired me to work in Cleveland."

"That doesn't matter. We can still work with you if you are in Chicago. It's 2023. People are working remotely everywhere."

"It's...not just that. I've been thinking about what happens to us when I leave."

He grabs my hand. "We can figure that out, too. Plane rides or driving, we can make it work."

I smile to myself. I knew he would make it sound so simple, like it would be a piece of cake for him.

"You're so sweet," I tell him.

I can see that he senses something is coming by how he slowly drops my hand.

"I just can't do that to you. You don't need to worry about me and my life. I'll be so busy working when I find a new job and caring for my mom. I won't have all that time to travel and see you very often. Even if I do, I won't get to you until Friday night, and I'd have to leave Sunday afternoon. We'd only have a day and a half together."

"What are you saying?" he asks, his voice a bit shaky.

My tears, which were beginning to settle, are back. I take a deep breath to summon the courage to go on.

"I'm saying you're too much of a catch to waste your thirties waiting for a weekend with me here and there. If it was short-term, I can see us waiting it out, but it's not. Are you willing to do the next five-ten years long-distance with me? My mom may be suffering from dementia, but she isn't going anywhere anytime soon."

"I...." he pauses. "I don't know what to say."

"I know. I'm so sorry. I love you so much. I hate this."

"But I mean, what if we just see how it went for a while?"

My hands ache to reach out to him, but I resist the urge.

"I'm scared. I'm scared that if I do that, I'll never let you go. I don't doubt our connection. I know we could do just fine long-distance. But do you see an opportunity in the next decade where we would live in the same place?"

It's like everything is finally clicking in for him. His shoulders fall. "No, I don't. My life is here, my company is here."

"And I have to do this for my mom."

"I guess you're right. I don't want to take away the opportunity for you to settle down and get married. If I can't be there for you, you deserve someone who can."

Crap. It makes it so much worse when he's so kind. I wish he would stand up and scream at me. Tell me I'm breaking his heart and to get out of his home, out of his life.

At least then, I could tell myself he never really loved me.

We both sit in silence as we take in the words just spoken.

"So, what now?" I whisper.

He sighs. "Well, I don't want you waiting two weeks to get to your mom. You go ahead and take the week to figure everything out. Don't worry about us."

"But I can't do that," I begin to speak, but he cuts me off.

"It's non-negotiable. You worry about yourself. We will figure it out. Okay?"

I nod my head. "Okay. Thank you." I look around the room, taking in the memories that I have in here. "I guess I should go."

He nods his head and stands up from the chair. We both walk to the front door in silence.

As soon as we get there, I turn around, but before I speak, his hands are on me, and his lips come crashing down on mine.

The kiss takes me by surprise, but I give everything over to him and let it happen. It's passionate, it's eager, it's sad...it's everything we're feeling put into one last desperate kiss.

When he pulls away, I'm shaking.

"Never forget what we have. I know I never will," he whispers.

"Never," I cry.

I walk out the door. With each step that I take, I feel my heart breaking. By the time I get to my car and drive to my apartment, my entire body feels hollow and numb.

Chapter Twenty-Eight

Marcus

The second she walks out the door, I feel a pain in my chest that I've never felt before.

I don't know how long I'm stuck in place after she leaves, not having the slightest clue what to do.

Next thing I know, I'm in my kitchen, popping open a bottle of wine. It's all I can think of to dull this ache that has taken residence in my chest.

I'm sure breaking up is the right thing to do. When she put it into perspective for me, I didn't have any good response to come back with.

Where will I be for the next decade of my life?

Here, of course.

I can't ask my siblings to uproot their entire lives and move our company to Chicago. Though, if I thought they would, I'd probably fucking ask.

Anything to have her back in my arms.

I return to the only room in the house with the slightest chance of calming me down...the library.

But when I walk in, I picture our sexual encounter on the ladder, the nights she spent reading out loud where I fell asleep on her chest.

She's everywhere. Not just in my mind or my heart, but memories marked everywhere I look.

I know I can't escape them, so despite the memories flooding in, I sit in my chair and take a big gulp of wine.

Suddenly, it dawns on me that I don't even know if I'm supposed to tell the gang that she won't be coming in anymore.

I pull out my phone to text her.

Me: Should I tell my siblings tonight?

She answers instantly.

Lexi: If you don't mind, I'd like to come in tomorrow and do it face-to-face.

Me: Yeah. No problem.

We sound so formal with each other. Just the other night, I was inside of her, telling her how much I loved her. Now, I'm talking to her like I would a client.

It's crazy how quickly a relationship can change. How I would do anything to make her happy, protect her at all costs, and now I'm expected to be indifferent to her.

***

I reach into my desk drawer and pull out my bottle of ibuprofen. My head is killing me. One look at the lights on my screen, and the throbbing gets persistently worse.

It's my own damn fault. I'm the one who finished the entire bottle of wine last night.

It was only meant to be a glass or two to calm me down. But after two glasses, I still felt miserable. So, I did the only thing I could think of: I drank more.

This morning is even worse. I can't explain the pain I felt when I woke up and realized it wasn't all just a bad dream.

Being with her was like learning to breathe deeply for the first time. Now, each breath feels like it takes effort, and even then, it still doesn't feel like enough.

If this is the shit my brother felt when his ex-wife abandoned him and my niece, then I'm the shittiest brother ever. I should have been by his side every night to help him through it.

It's only ten in the morning, but I can't seem to sit still. I don't know if Lexi has told them yet. I don't know anything because it's not for me to know anymore.

There's a light knock on my open door.

"Hey."

I look up and see my three siblings walking in, closing the door behind them.

"We heard the news," Mia says softly. "How are you holding up?"

"I've been better. Where is Lexi?"

"She's packing up her office," Luke answers. "We told her she could leave immediately if she felt more comfortable getting to her mom sooner. Her friend called her last night and said she visited, and her mom wasn't doing so well. Was in pain and refused to walk."

Fuck. Lexi must be worrying herself sick right now. This is exactly what the doctors were warning her about. Her mom needs to get up and move to do her therapy, or she won't recover.

I want to walk out of my office and wrap my arms around her. I want to kiss her. I want to be her *person* in this.

"Are you going to go with her to help her settle in?" Gabe asks.

"What? Why would I do that?" I bark out quickly.

"Becaaaause you're her boyfriend. You love her," he responds.

She didn't tell them the part where we broke up? I guess that makes sense. She's a professional. She came in to give her notice, not air out our personal life to my family.

"I'm not her boyfriend anymore. We broke up."

"What?" Luke asks.

"You broke up with her?" Gabe seconds Luke's sound of shock. "I thought you loved her."

"I do." I can't believe this is their reaction.

Not how are you? Not asking what happened. Just *assuming* I was the one to end it. It's the typical assumption of my life.

Marcus, the one who makes poor decisions. The young and immature one. Will I ever outgrow those labels put on me from childhood?

"Seriously, man. I knew you rushed into this too soon. The moment things get tough, you end it. That's not how relationships work, that's not how love works," Luke says.

It's my final straw. I'm hurting right now, more than I ever have, and their words just add to it.

"That's enough!" I shout as I stand from my chair. "I've had it with you guys assuming the worst of me. For your information, Lexi broke up with me. You would know that if you didn't assume that everything bad in my life is my damn fault. When will you guys wake up and realize I'm not a child anymore? I'm so sick of this treatment. It's all the time. I can't even be treated equally in this business. It's always you two consulting each other and leaving me out. Like the other week, that little marketing sales idea you claim was yours. I brought that shit up a year ago, and you slammed it down. Now, all of a sudden, it's your idea. And the worst part is, you didn't even pitch it to me to get my opinion. You two decided on your own. Then, it was the fucking incident with William. Instead of telling him he's way off base about me, you make me jump through hoops to prove I'm not a total fuckup."

I stop to take a breath, winded from speaking the truth for the first time in all these years. Nobody says anything to me, not a word.

Are they waiting for me to apologize for my outburst? Probably.

It will be another immature thing that Marcus said at work, and I'm so damn over it.

"You know what, screw this. I'm outta here," I say,

I grab my briefcase and storm out. I don't give them a chance to further piss me off.

I get in my car and speed off, not sure where the hell I'm going or what I want to do. I just know I can't do this anymore. I can't sit back and watch the love of my life walk away while simultaneously being told it's my fault...by my family.

With nowhere else to go, I wind up at home on a Tuesday afternoon, drinking my feelings.

Each of my siblings has called me a dozen times, but I hit ignore every time.

There's nothing else that needs to be said at the moment. I just need to be alone.

I see Lexi's name light up on my phone in between all my other calls. I stare at it for a second, not sure if I want to answer. I'm worried just hearing her voice will make me fall further into this dark pit of despair.

But I'm too weak. It's still Lexi. I can't ignore her.

"Hello," I answer.

"Hi," she whispers.

Silence.

It feels like I've used up all of my energy to stand up for myself today. I don't have it in me to start the conversation. She's the one who called me.

"I heard what you said to your siblings."

Shit, I didn't think about the fact that she was right there on the other side of the door.

"Yeah," is all I can get out. I don't know what to say about it.

"I'm proud of you."

"You are?"

She sighs. "Of course. Look, I know they love you and think they're doing or saying what's best, but they're wrong. As an outsider, it's obvious that they haven't shed the image of the youngster you once were that they needed to keep in line. You said what needed to be said. So, yes, I'm proud of you."

Her unwavering support just makes this whole thing so much harder.

"Thanks. It was long overdue."

"It was."

Everything in me wants to scream at her to give us a chance. We can make it work somehow, but I'm too exhausted. Also, my ego is screaming at me that she ended things.

It's telling me that it shouldn't have been so easy for her to say goodbye.

"Well..." she says awkwardly. I realize I've been thinking instead of talking. "I'll let you go. I just wanted to tell you what you did was a good thing. Don't regret it or apologize to them."

"Thanks, Lexi."

"Bye, Marcus," she says, her voice breaking at the end.

"Bye."

I click off the phone with her and pour myself another glass.

Chapter Twenty-Nine

Lexi

As soon as I close the door to my apartment, I fall to the ground and cry.

Listening to him defend himself like that, all I wanted to do was tell him how proud I was. All the call did was break my heart. He was so distant, so cold. *I hated it.*

I don't want to hurt him. I don't want to hurt myself. I've never felt so damn lost and confused in my life.

If this is the right decision, why is it so painful?

I should feel relieved. I can just focus on getting ready to pack up and head home. Gabe even insisted on giving me a couple of months' salary so I didn't feel pressured to find work the second I got home.

Everything is set up and made easy for me, but the relief isn't there. It's pushed far down, overshadowed by the pain of losing the love of my life.

This afternoon, I scheduled the movers to pick my stuff up on Saturday. I really only have three more days here. Three days to pack up the life I started.

My phone beeps in my pocket. I pull it out to see who's texting me.

Grace: I found a small two-bedroom home. You can rent it for a month, fully furnished. The couple will be in Europe for the month. The storage unit for all your stuff is already booked and ready.

She is a lifesaver. I don't know what I would do without her. The ray of light in this whole mess is that I get to see her all the time again.

Me: I hate that you have to help so much...but thank you!! I'll make it up to you. Free babysitting so you can have date nights.

Grace: I see my husband all the time. We can make him watch the kids so the two of us can go out!

I smile at my screen.

Me: I won't say no to that :)

The only way I will get through this week is if I stay busy. If I keep my brain occupied, I might have a fighting shot at getting out of here with a piece of my heart still working. Because right now, the feelings swarming me, they could easily take me down like a tsunami.

I still have broken-down boxes in my closet from when I moved in. And possibly from copious amounts of online shopping.

I'm a sucker for ordering everything online, but that's not something I need to acknowledge right now. At least it has provided me with the materials to make this move.

Over the next couple of hours, I throw myself into packing mode. Starting in the kitchen, I pack up all my utensils and dishes. I know I will sleep like hell tonight, so I push myself until I'm utterly exhausted. The entire kitchen is completely packed up, boxes labeled and taped up.

After a long, hot shower, all I can do is hope that it's enough to allow me to get some rest tonight.

Yet, three hours later, I'm lying awake in my bed. As soon as I close my eyes, I picture him. I crave his arms, his touch, his voice in my ear whispering goodnight.

I didn't know an ache for someone could be so fierce, so deep that you feel it down into your bones. My body physically aches from the pain of knowing I will never see him again.

My pillowcase is soaked with my tears. I pick it up and throw it across the room.

The sadness is turning to anger. This is how my mother became bitter. When life hands you one too many shitty cards, how can you not become bitter?

I grab the other pillow and lie my head down, but sleep still doesn't come.

***

"Are you all packed up yet?" my friend Chloe asks as I walk around my room searching for the packing tape.

I sigh. "Mostly. Just down to odds and ends."

"That's awesome that Grace found you a temporary place to stay."

"Yeah," I reply dimly.

I grab my suitcase packed with clothes and toiletries. I've packed all my luggage to go with me to the house I'm staying at. Everything else will go into storage.

My apartment is spotless. I got on my hands and knees to scrub every inch of this place. There is no way they will need a cleaner to come in.

It was all I could think to do to keep from running back to Marcus and begging him to take me back.

The last three days, I've been living in this stupid fantasy world where he decides I am an idiot and comes back for me. He takes me in his arms and tells me nothing can keep us apart, even long distance.

"What time do the movers come tomorrow?"

"They get here at eight. Getting my stuff in the truck shouldn't take them longer than an hour. I should be on the road by nine."

"And Grace will meet you at the storage unit?" she asks.

"Uh, yeah. I guess."

"Lexi. I'm worried about you. I've known you for a long time. You've never sounded like this before."

It's the same thing I've heard from Grace. I don't know what to tell them. I figure honesty is the best route.

"I've never felt this way before."

"Oh, Lexi. I wish there were something I could do. Are you sure you don't want to give the relationship a go from afar?"

That's the question I've been playing in my head over and over. It's not like I don't want to. It's all I want. But I also don't want to be the person that drags him down.

"Even if I did, once I laid it all out for him, he understood. He didn't fight the break-up or tell me to screw the logistics and the unknowns, that he wants to be with me."

"Well, even so, don't not go to him because you're too proud to take back what you said."

"I'm just trying to do the right thing for both of us. He shouldn't hold off on his life, on finding a wife and starting a family, because I have to move away. This is for the best."

"You don't sound so sure about that."

"I'm not sure about anything anymore."

"Just think about it tonight. It's your last chance before you leave. Don't let your ego or pride or fear...any of that shit...don't let it get in the way."

"Ok. I'm pretty much done packing, so all I have is time to think about it tonight anyway."

I look around the nearly empty bedroom. There's one thing I need tonight that will make me feel better.

I walk into the kitchen, where my box of Italian pastries from Corbo's sits on the counter. I open it up and pull out a coconut square.

My first bite must be half of the coconut square, but I don't feel bad about it. It's too damn delicious to care.

"What's that noise?" Chloe asks.

I realize I might've been moaning over my dessert. "Sorry, I'm eating my feelings right now."

She laughs. "A great way to temporarily forget your troubles."

"It's the best way."

"Well, you go ahead and eat your feelings. Call me tomorrow on your drive."

"I will. Thanks for everything. I love you."

"Love you, too."

Now, it's just me and my food to keep my thoughts company tonight in this lonely, empty apartment.

I try envisioning what it would be like to do long-distance with Marcus. I can picture weekends together in Chicago, walking hand-in-hand as we window shop or enjoy lunch on the water. Or curled up together in front of his fireplace on cold winter nights. Reading in his library while cuddling together on my favorite chair.

Then I think about him wanting to settle down and get married. Me telling him I can't leave my mom. Us fighting, him eventually resenting me. The thought makes me feel sick to my stomach. I couldn't bear it if he ever hated me.

I walk back to the kitchen counter and grab another dessert. Why does this feel like an impossible decision? It feels like the choice is either break each other's hearts today—or in the future.

Chapter Thirty

Marcus

"When are you coming back to work?" Mia asks as I flip through the channels on my television.

I take a deep breath as I try to keep my composure. "I don't know. Monday."

"I miss you over here. I know it's only been a couple of days, but still."

It'd be a lie to tell her I miss her. The only one on my mind right now is Lexi. I miss Lexi. I haven't showered since Tuesday when I last spoke to her. It's now Friday.

I've never felt this before. I don't want to do anything. All I have the motivation to do is eat, drink, go to the bathroom, and watch television.

"I guess you aren't ready to talk about it yet?" Mia says.

"No, I'm not."

"Are you coming to Ma and Pa's on Sunday?"

"It depends. I'll see how I feel."

"Well, call me if you need anything. Remember, we all love you."

"Thanks. Love you, too."

The childish part of me wants to pass on telling her I love her, but I can't do that. I may be depressed about Lexi and angry at my family, but I still love them. Especially Mia, she's always had my back. She sometimes seems caught in the middle of having my back or being tough on me like my brothers, but her heart is pure.

I look down at my watch. It's only noon. She's at work right now.

I told them I needed the rest of the week to myself.

Not that anything has helped. I wish somebody warned me that love could lift you up, but it could also crush you.

I need to get out of here, so I head to the only place I can think that might help me: Ma and Pa's.

Since I'm showing up unannounced, I knock on the door.

Ma opens it. "What in heavens are you doing here? Is everything alright?"

I shrug my shoulders as I stare at the ground. If I look up at her, I know I run the risk of letting a tear break free.

"Get in here," she demands, pulling me by the sleeve.

The door closes behind me, and I kick off my shoes. We go into the family room, where Pa is reading the paper.

It's such a nostalgic feeling. It's like time has stood still in this house. The age of technology hasn't infiltrated it, and there is something so calming about that.

"What are you doing here?" Pa peeks over the paper.

I sigh. Walking into the room, I take a seat on the couch diagonal from him. "Just took some time off work. I needed to clear my head."

"What's going on?" Ma takes a seat next to Pa.

I can tell she is antsy to get my response. Ma is normally calm and collected, unless she thinks something is wrong with one of her kids.

I shrug. "Lexi moves back to Chicago tomorrow. She needs to be with her mom."

"Oh, that poor girl. It must be so hard to take all that on," Ma says sympathetically.

"Yeah, it's definitely taken a toll on her."

"It's a good thing she has you now," Pa says.

I blow out a breath and let out a small, bitter laugh. "Not really. We broke up."

"You what? Why?" Ma asks.

"It was her idea. I don't know, I didn't want to, but once she brought it up, I didn't really have any good argument against her concerns."

"What are her concerns?" says Ma.

"That she'll hold me back from starting a family. She doesn't see a time in the next decade where she won't be held down in Chicago, and my company is here."

Ma and Pa do a sideways glance at each other.

"Those are valid concerns. I imagine you do want to start a family," Pa says.

I nod my head. "Of course I do."

"How do you feel about it all?" he continues.

I pause. It's almost impossible to articulate. I've been asking myself that question for days. What I feel is complete and utter despair. What I think changes at any given minute of the day.

"I don't know. That's why I'm here."

"I think you do know. You just aren't ready to admit it," Ma says.

"No, really. I'm so confused. What am I supposed to do?"

My leg is bouncing uncontrollably. I can't sit still. The nervous energy coursing through me needs an outlet, but I've had no motivation to go for a run to release it.

"I heard about your fight with your brothers," Ma says.

I release a frustrated breath. "Of course, they told you."

She ignores my comment. "It's about time you stood up to them."

"What?" I ask because I'm not sure I heard her right.

"I was waiting for you to do it. Those boys love you like crazy—too much sometimes. Even when you were little, they would follow you around to make sure you were safe. They would do anything to console you if you fell and bumped your head. As you grew up and started acting out, like all boys do, they made it their mission to try and protect you from yourself. They made the same mistakes. They didn't want you to have to learn the hard way like them."

Her words are making my head spin.

"Trust me, those boys are no saints. Anything you can think of to get into trouble, one of them did it. But what they haven't realized is that it's not their job to protect you. It's their job to support you. It was only going to change when you demanded it to."

I don't know how to respond. Her words are so shocking that I can only stare at her. That fact that she saw what I've felt all of these years is enough to make me want to hug her.

"Why didn't you ever say anything?" I finally respond.

She smiles kindly at me. "You needed to see it for yourself and have the confidence to speak up. It's not like I haven't told the boys to go easy on you over the years, but you know them, always thinking I worry too much."

"Lexi gave me the confidence."

The words are so staggering that I'm overcome with emotion. She got me on a level unlike anything I have ever, or likely will ever, experience again. The realization is damn depressing.

"What should I do next?" I finally ask.

"You know what you should do," Pa tells me.

"What?"

"You should go for a walk," he says.

I try to understand his advice. "Go for...a walk?"

"Sure. If my thoughts are ever muddled and confusing, or I have an important decision to make, I've found that going for a walk helps clear my head."

"That's it...your big advice for me. Go for a walk."

I almost can't believe the words I'm hearing.

"Well, you got any other ideas, smarty pants?" he fires back.

"No."

"Okay, then. If you don't have any ideas, let's not go criticizing the people who *do* have ideas."

That shuts me up. He's right about one thing: I don't have any ideas right now. I feel like my life is at a crossroads. I'm at this point where a major decision needs to be made. I just don't know what that decision is. Or do I? Clearly, Ma and Pa think I need to make this decision on my own, and they think I already know what it is.

"Alright. A walk it is," I say as I stand.

"Your father is right. A walk always clears my head. You should make it an outdoor walk, though. The fresh air is part of what helps clear the mind."

"Got it," I reply. "I guess I'll get right on that."

They walk me to the door, where Ma gives me a huge hug, and Pa shakes my hand.

"Don't worry, you'll figure it out. Trust yourself," Ma says as her parting words.

Trust myself.

Sometimes that's hard to do. After years of people doubting my decisions, it starts to mess with you. You begin to wonder if you're capable of ever making the right decision.

With nothing else to lose, I get in my car and head to my favorite park. It's cold outside, but maybe the chill will also breathe some life back into me.

Chapter Thirty-One

Lexi

"Everything in here, boxes and furniture are good to go on the truck," I tell the mover.

"Sounds good. We'll get to work right now."

I hold my disposable cup of coffee that I picked up this morning. Everything is packed away, but there is no way I can survive this morning without getting some caffeine in me.

My car is already packed with my suitcases and bags. All there is to do is lock up once the movers are done.

Last night, I really tried to consider what Chloe told me to. Should I go back to Marcus? The fact still remains: I can't give him what he deserves. If I feel like this now after weeks with him, what will it feel like after years when we are at a crossroads and have to end it?

I'd *never* survive it.

If I thought I could come back to Cleveland eventually, even five years from now, it wouldn't even be a question in my mind. I just don't see that happening. I can't predict when my mom will pass, nor do I want to put myself in a position where I get to be with the man that I love when she does pass. That would feel too much like waiting for it to happen.

The tears threaten to come while standing here watching the movers, so I grab my coat and walk outside. The cold fall weather is feeling more and more like winter.

The wind whips through the streets, causing an instant chill throughout my body.

I walk around the complex grounds as I drink my coffee. I know it might sound ridiculous, but when I'm having intense thoughts and don't want to think about them, I count my steps.

I've heard that's a bit of an OCD tendency. Whatever you want to call it, it helps me.

Somewhere around six hundred steps, I realize my coffee is gone. I always take slow steps, so it's probably been twenty minutes. I don't know if I've ever counted for that long. It's a testament to how messed up I am in the head right now.

I walk back to the front of the building and see the guys carrying my dresser. The truck is already halfway full. Somehow, in the six hundred steps that make me sound like I need some serious mental help, they've managed to accomplish a lot.

The guy I spoke with earlier sees me. "We will probably be done in the next twenty minutes."

"Wow. You guys work fast."

He smiles. "That's what they pay us to do."

I give them another ten minutes before I walk back upstairs. The sight is eerie. Everything is almost gone—the life I built here, gone in an instant.

As I walk around the place, the heaviness I felt in my chest last night is magnetized by a hundred.

This is it. I know I decided to leave everything behind, including the man I love, but what if I'm wrong?

What if it's not the right decision? What if something happens in the next couple of years that opens up an opportunity for us to be together, and we won't have the chance because I gave up on us?

The thought is enough to paralyze me right where I stand.

My mind starts racing. Should I call him? Should I go to him? Will he even listen?

"Ma'am," the mover interrupts my minor freakout. "We are all set."

He holds a clipboard in front of me. "I just need you to sign this."

I don't even read the contents of the paper. I sign it and hand it back to him.

"The truck is scheduled to arrive at the storage unit in approximately six hours."

"Thank you."

He walks out of the apartment, leaving me alone in the family room. I guess there's nothing I can do now. I have to hit the road so I can beat the truck there.

I pull out my keys, take the apartment key off, and place it on the island.

I open the front door with shaky hands, trying to hold in the tears.

"Marcus," I breathe when I see him standing in front of me.

"Hi," he gives me a small smile.

"What are you doing here?"

My heart is about to beat out of my chest. I notice the strap on his shoulder holding up a bag.

He takes a deep breath. "I'm coming with you."

"You're what? What do you mean?"

I don't think I heard him correctly. I think maybe I was right downstairs about the mental issues because now I think I'm hallucinating.

"I'm coming with you to Chicago."

He stands there with his hands in his pockets, waiting for me to figure out how to speak again.

"I, I mean, I still don't...." I stutter.

He smiles and then takes a step closer to me. "I'm moving to Chicago."

"What? How? Marcus, this doesn't make any sense."

He shrugs. "It makes perfect sense to me. I was on another walk this morning. My parents insisted a walk was the only way to clear my head. You know what's messed up?"

Another step towards me. For some reason, I take a step back. It's like I'm too afraid to accept this as reality because if it's not, I don't know if I can recover.

"What?"

"The walk worked. I was walking around this morning, ready to let you walk out of my life forever, when it dawned on me. Why would I let the best thing that has ever happened to me get away? I have more than enough money saved away for us to settle down in Chicago and figure out our next steps. When I thought about going back to work without you there, it felt wrong. Everything in my life was dark and almost impossible to picture without you. You are my happiness. Where you go, I go."

I can't believe what he's saying. He's willing to give everything up for me. My eyes are blurred from my tears, but I can still make out the man standing in front of me.

"What about your company?" I ask.

"I'm out."

"What?" I almost scream.

"I just called my siblings and let them know. We can work the logistics out later."

"Wait. You're not leaving because of the other day, right? People have disagreements on how to run a company all the time, that's no reason to leave. They love you."

"I know they do, and I love them. But not as much as I love you."

His hand grabs mine as his thumb rubs comforting circles around my knuckles.

"I can't believe you would do that for me," I whisper.

"Baby, it's just as much for me, if not more. Don't make me out to be some kind of hero. I'm a mess without you, and I don't want to live in a world where I don't get to see your face every day."

I wrap my arms around his neck. When his arms engulf me, everything feels right again.

"Is this really happening?" I ask.

His laughter vibrates along my body. "It is if you'll let it."

I let go of him.

"Of course. It feels too good to be true." I notice the bag on his shoulder again. "What's in the bag?"

He smiles and shrugs. "Nothing. It's empty. I wanted to make some grand gesture, and I thought a bag would help for dramatic effect. I only just came to this conclusion an hour or so ago. All I had in my trunk was an empty gym bag."

A laugh erupts from deep in my belly. Damn, it feels good to feel like this again.

"You're insane, but I love it."

"Come here. I haven't tasted these lips in days, but it feels like a damn eternity."

He pulls me back into his arms and slams his lips onto mine. We both groan instantly. It's like coming home. Every single part of my body comes alive when his lips are on me.

I'm not sure how long we kiss, but neither of us seems in a rush to break apart.

He eventually pulls away but leaves his hands on my cheeks.

"What time are you leaving?" he asks.

I cringe. "Right now."

His eyes open wide. "Right now? You mean I was seconds away from missing you?"

I smile up at him. "You made it. That's all that matters. But I really do have to get going so I can meet the truck at the storage unit."

"Okay. I'll come with you."

"Don't you have like...stuff to work out?"

The number of things he needs to get in order to move must be a mile long. I want to question this, ask him if he's sure again, but I don't want to make him think I don't want this.

"I have a ton of shit to work out," he laughs. "But right now, I want to help you get settled in. I can come back gradually and get it all figured out."

As we walk out of the apartment, the realization of his moving away hits me.

"Oh my God," I gasp as I stop in my tracks.

"What?" he asks concerned.

"Your parents are going to hate me. You're gonna be so far away from them."

He laughs loudly. "My parents don't hate you."

"They already know?"

"Of course. They were the first ones I called. They fully support my decision. Ma says she thinks it's the right one."

"She actually said that?" I ask.

He grabs my hand and leads me toward the front of the building.

"She said if I love you, I need to take care of you. And if taking care of you means moving to Chicago, then that's what I'm going to do."

I chew on my bottom lip as I try to hide the smile that wants to break free. I don't know how I got so lucky. Marcus is so much more than I could have ever dreamed of.

"Good. I wouldn't be able to live with myself if they blamed me."

He wraps an arm around me. "No way, babe. They can tell what we have. Can you follow me back to my place? It's only ten minutes away. I can drop my car off and throw some things in a suitcase."

I glance down at my watch. It'll be tight, but it's doable. Plus, Grace will be there with her husband to help. They set it all up for me and have the keys. I could always count on them to open the unit for the guys.

"Yeah, we have time. We have to make it fast, though."

"This will be the only situation where my speed will impress the hell out of you," he says with a wink.

Chapter Thirty-Two

Marcus

I look over at Lexi as she takes a nap. It's difficult to tear my eyes away from her. I just want to take it all in, to keep reminding myself that she's mine.

Neither of us has slept well since last weekend. She insisted on driving, but when I saw her yawning, exhaustion taking over her eyes, I told her I could take over.

This morning has been complete chaos. Yet when I made the decision, when it all came to me, I just *knew* it was the right answer. Everything inside of me settled, and the world became clear again.

The answer was right there all along. So damn obvious yet so hard to find.

When I told my siblings, to say they were shocked is an understatement. But I didn't leave room for their opinions or concerns. I told them I am in love with her, this decision has nothing to do with them, and that I've never been more sure of anything in my life.

I can tell how much my brothers were itching to ask questions, but they held back.

It might take time, but they will see. None of this is because of what I said last week.

The truth is, I love working with them. Just because I decided to put up some boundaries doesn't mean the majority of the time we didn't work well together. We all feed off each other's ideas and congratulate one another on victories.

If I sit around and think about it for too long, the reality of never working with them again is gonna hit hard. Although, I know I need to process that and face it, right now is not the time.

I just need to focus on getting Lexi settled in.

After that, I can deal with my own emotions.

When Lexi wakes up, we're only about half an hour from the address she gave me.

"Morning," I smile as she stretches with a lazy grin on her face.

"Mmmm, mornin'."

She looks at the clock and then sits up straighter.

"Oh my gosh! I can't believe I slept that long. You should have woken me up."

"Why would I do that? You needed your rest."

She looks at me like I'm crazy. "Because you're tired too. You said it yourself. I was going to take over and let you take a nap, too."

I chuckle. "I can handle it. All the traveling around the world the last couple of years has made me an expert at adjusting to time zones and fighting through exhaustion."

"Doesn't mean you should do it if you have the option not to."

I steal a glance at her. "I'll never wake you up and ask you to drive. That's just not gonna happen. So, you better get over it now."

"You're kinda stubborn. You know that?" she asks.

"I've heard that before," I say with a smile.

I listen to the navigation as it guides me through the town. This is going to be my new home. It's so wild to think about.

"You said you have friends meeting us here?" I ask as I pull into the parking lot.

"Yeah, Grace and her husband Matt. I've known Grace since I was a kid."

I pull into the row of storage units. It's obvious which one is hers based on the truck currently sitting in front of it.

I park the car on the other side. When we get out, the truck is already opened, and the guys are unloading it.

I see a couple get out of their car. It must be her friends. They walk our way, the woman picking up the pace and running towards Lexi.

"Yay! You're here," her friend says as she wraps her arms around Lexi.

Lexi reciprocates the gesture. "Thank you so much for being here to open the unit."

"No problem. You are only about five minutes behind the truck. They just got here."

Her friend notices me and looks at me curiously.

"Uh, who is this?" she asks Lexi, her eyes never leaving me.

"Oh, um, this is Marcus."

I'm guessing by her using my name that she's already talked about me. The way her friend's eyes light up confirms it.

"I wasn't expecting you to be here," she says, then offers me her hand. "I'm Grace." She motions to her husband standing next to her. "This is my husband, Matt. Matt, this is Marcus. He's Lexi's...."

"Boyfriend," I finish for her.

I shake both of their hands.

"So, when did this happen?" Grace asks.

Matt shakes his head. "Babe, a bit of a personal question while we're standing here in forty-degree weather.

I laugh. I can tell I'm going to like this guy already.

"Nice to meet you," Matt says to me. "I hear you're the guy who's gonna make Lexi squirt one day."

I don't even register the look of horror on the women's faces.

"Fuck yeah, I am. I told her I'd figure it out." I look to Lexi, who can't seem to believe this conversation is happening. "I see you've been talking about me."

I wink, and her jaw falls further to the ground.

"Matt, what in the actual fuck!" Grace says. "And you said my question was too personal."

Matt just smiles. "If you figure it out, let me know. I'll try it out on Grace."

"I like this dude," I say with a smile.

"Oh. My. God. There's two of them," Grace says to Lexi.

Lexi shakes her head. "I can't believe that's the first thing you two talk about when meeting."

I shrug my shoulders and put my arms around her. "Clearly, it's important to you, too, if you told them about it."

Lexi puts her finger up. "Correction. I told *Grace* about it, and she clearly has a big mouth."

Grace cringes. "Sorry. I'm a mom of two. I don't have a lot else to talk about. Your life is my source of entertainment. Speaking of...what's going on here."

She points between the two of us.

"I'm moving here."

"What?" Grace asks. "You are?"

"I am."

"When did this happen?"

"This morning," Lexi responds. "It's all kind of last minute."

"Wow. Well, you two need to come over for dinner soon. It'll be like a little welcoming party," Grace says.

"Totally. When we get settled in," "Lexi tells her.

We talk for a few more minutes, then have to say goodbye since it's too cold to stand out here and chit-chat. It's still early in the season, and our bodies have not adjusted to this kind of weather yet.

The movers get everything into the unit and pull away. I tell Lexi to get warm in the car while I close up the unit. Once it's locked, I jog back to the car.

"Ok. Where to now?" I ask. "I haven't even asked if we have a place to live yet."

She laughs. "This is insane. You're insane. Yes, we have a temporary place to live. I rented a fully furnished two-bed-room home for a bit while the couple is on a European vacation."

"Perfect. We can settle in and then start finding a home we want to buy."

She shakes her head but gives me the address to punch into my phone.

"Are you sure we should buy right away?" she asks as we pull out of the parking lot.

"Of course. I never care to throw my money away on rent when it could be well spent in a long-term investment."

"But neither of us even have a job, and you don't know how long it will take to sell your home in Cleveland."

I find her worry over money adorable. Not only am I a good saver, but I'm also a good investor. We can do just fine for years without a job.

"Money isn't a concern. My house will sell when it sells. Don't worry about any of it."

"I don't want to make you pay for all of this stuff," she says as she fidgets in her seat.

"We're a team now. You're not *making* me do anything."

When we arrive at the address, I'm surprised the home we are staying in is in such good shape. It's the smallest house in the neighborhood by far, but we don't need a ton of space.

It's in a quaint little area with trees that remind me of home in Shaker Heights. The large branches hang over the street like they're creating a little tunnel along the road.

I pull into the driveway.

"It's cute," she says.

"Home sweet home, baby."

She turns to me in the car. "This is so wild. Are you sure this is what you want?"

It seems like words are not getting through to her. I lean in slowly and decide to show her the reason why I'm here.

I kiss her slowly and passionately, putting everything I have into it. My lips move against hers and start to get more demanding. I want her to know what I can do to her.

I feel her entire body melt into me as I take charge. It takes everything in me to pull away, but when I do, I see her droopy eyes and notice her chest moving up and down rapidly.

"Does that answer your question?"

"Yes," she breathes heavily.

"Good. Now, let's unload our things."

It takes us about an hour to get all our suitcases in and unpacked in the master bedroom.

The house is updated inside with nice furniture. It's a cozy little place for us to spend our first month living together.

I worked up a bit of a sweat carrying everything in. I need a shower. I walk over to Lexi, who's currently moving around her clothes in the dresser.

I wrap my arms around her. Putting my chin on her neck, I whisper in her. "I'm going to take a shower. You want to join me?"

"Of course," she says as she leans her head back.

I take her hand and lead her into the bathroom. We already unpacked her bathroom bag, which has just enough towels for us right now. We'll need to stop and get some more. Though I know she wasn't anticipating another person living with her when she was packing up.

We walk into the bathroom and undress in front of each other in silence. I can't tear my eyes away as she slowly reveals each beautiful part of her body. When I pull down my boxers, my dick springs free, showing just how happy he is to finally be near her again.

I grip it while I lean in and turn on the shower, letting the water get warm.

She bites her lip as she watches me run my hand along my length.

"I could watch you do that for hours," she whispers.

"Does it make you wet?" I ask her as I continue.

She nods her head.

"Give me a taste. Stick your pretty little fingers in that wet pussy, and let me get a lick of them."

Her eyes grow darker from my demand. I love that she is always right with me, just as turned on as I am.

I watch as she sinks two fingers into her folders, and she rubs back and forth.

"Fuck, baby," I growl. "I can hear your wetness from here. Now, bring those fingers over here to me."

She saunters over to me while her fingers still play between her folds. Her eyes never leave my hand as it still moves along my shaft. When she is directly in front of me, she brings her fingers up to my mouth. I open for them as she gently places them on my tongue.

I close my lips around her fingers and suck. I groan as soon as I get a taste of the pussy I've been missing all week. I feel her other hand stop mine as it moves down my dick and push it away. She replaces my hand with hers. We both stand outside of the shower, me sucking on her fingers, her hand sliding over my dick.

I pop off her fingers.

"I think the water is warm," I whisper, then open the door.

I let her step in first, then I walk in, close the door, and fuck her pussy like it's the last day I'll ever have the chance to.

Chapter Thirty-Three

Gabe

I can barely get the sandwich down that sits on my desk in front of me. I've been sick to my stomach since Marcus abruptly called us yesterday and announced that he was leaving the company and moving.

I've been running through everything I may have said over his lifetime that would make him feel like he didn't want to be around anymore.

I get he loves Lexi, but moving there, instead of just doing long distance first, feels more about getting away from us.

I know I've been harsh over the years, but I'm only trying to make sure he doesn't make the same mistakes that I've made. From the moment Ma came home from the hospital with him, it felt like my responsibility as the oldest to protect him. Luke and I are too close in age for me to have had that instinct when he was born. But I felt it fiercely when Marcus came along.

I feel the same with Mia. They are the two that I worry most about.

It was a powerful sense of loyalty I felt when I held him for the first time. When he cried, I would follow Ma around, worried sick.

If he was scared of the dark when he was younger, I let him slide into my bed with me. I wanted to chase all his monsters away for him.

"You ready to go?" Alexis walks into the room. "The kids are already in the car waiting."

"Yeah. I'm ready."

I help her into her coat before we get into the car. The ride is mostly quiet, as I'm not much in the mood for small talk. I haven't been since Marcus blew up at me.

"It's not your fault, honey," Alexis says, pulling me from my thoughts.

"What do you mean?"

She sighs. "Marcus. He loves Lexi. His leaving has nothing to do with you."

I wish I agreed, but I can't stop this nagging feeling that I'm responsible for all this. I'm the oldest sibling. I'm supposed to know what to do and how to keep the family together.

"If I wasn't so hard on him or was willing to see past the role I thought I had to protect him."

"Did you sometimes treat him like your baby brother and not your business partner? Yes. I'm not going to pretend with you. But it was all from a place of love. He knows that. But you can't look at this as something you could have stopped. I'm a woman, trust me. He just wants to be with the woman *he* loves."

"Maybe," I sigh.

As soon as we get to my parents' house, Alexis finds Ma and Savannah in the kitchen. I go straight for the guys watching football, typical Sunday routine, but there's one difference...Marcus isn't here.

Suddenly, realizing he'll rarely be at family dinners on Sundays hits me hard.

I back out of the room and find myself storming into the bathroom. Closing the door, I pace around in circles and try to catch my breath. Tears spring to my eyes.

I'll never be able to make it through this dinner. I'm just imagining his empty chair at the dinner table. I know this may seem like an overreaction, and it probably shows the unhealthy relationship I've had with him since he was born. Marcus is not my child; he is my brother. I need to get that straight.

There's a knock on the door. I open the door to see Luke standing there.

"Are you having a hard time with it, too?" he asks.

"I think it's just, I don't know, I feel like we pushed him away," I start as I continue to pace.

"He wasn't wrong. We do treat him differently. Always have."

"I know." I hang my head in shame. "The reasons for it don't even matter. There's no excuse."

"It's crazy how you can grow up but still look at each other like you did when you were ten," he says.

A sarcastic laugh falls from my mouth. "Yeah. I don't know. Maybe he needed to spread his wings away from us. Maybe this is all how it's supposed to happen. Maybe we held him back."

"But he's so good at what he does. I just wish he didn't have to give that up."

An idea pops into my head. "Maybe he doesn't."

Luke gives me a curious look. "What do you mean?"

I pat him on the shoulder. "Let's talk more about it at dinner. I've learned my lesson about having big discussions without all members of the company present. Mia needs to be a part of it."

We walk out of the bathroom and go sit down with Pa. No talking is needed while watching the game, giving me time to think about my idea.

I don't know why it didn't occur to me sooner. It's so obvious.

When Ma calls us in for dinner, I'm excited to share it with Mia and Luke.

I carry Joey over to the highchair and strap him in. He's clapping his hands with excitement. At two, he already knows to be excited about Grandma's cooking. Smart child I have here.

When I sit with Joey on my right and Alexis on my left, I notice Luke watching me closely.

He's ready to hear what I have to say. I feel bad making him wait, but I'm trying to be more aware of how my actions make other siblings feel.

Luke and I are closest in age, so he's always been the one I bounced my ideas off of first. It was never meant to isolate anybody.

"I guess we need to address the elephant in the room," Ma says after everybody has plated their food. "I know tensions are high, and emotions are all over the place with Marcus gone. But I just wanted to say that you are all family. We love each of you and are proud. Marcus's decision was the right one. He loves Lexi, and we should all be happy for him that he found the woman he loves enough to make such a significant change."

"Thanks, Ma," Mia says sincerely.

"I've been thinking about everything," I start as I twirl a piece of lemon garlic spaghetti onto my fork. "Lexi and Marcus are both a part of our success at our company, right?"

Luke and Mia nod their heads in agreement.

"Well, what if we just have them open a Chicago office? We can keep Lexi on as the IT Director and hire someone to work under her here in Cleveland. We have plenty of clients in Chicago, and one of them is our largest. Marcus can run the office. We know we needed to expand our workforce and get some people in under us to do a lot of the contract work while we go out and bring in the clients. We also know that getting some employees underneath us to trust enough one day to help with sales is something we need to implement sooner rather than later."

No one answers immediately. Instead, everyone seems to think about my suggestion. Mia speaks first.

"I think that's an excellent idea. Keeping both of them on board is a win for the company. It's 2023, there's no reason we can't do Zoom meetings and work around the distance between us. If we're going to be a top wine distributor, we need to think like it."

True. Our goal to move from a million-dollar revenue company to a billion dollar will only happen with expansion.

Lexi has been streamlining our systems to get us in that direction, but a larger sales team will be what makes the difference.

Marcus leading the way on training would actually be perfect. His personality is perfect for it. Everybody instantly loves him. He has that kind of warmth.

Now that I know Mia's on board, I look over at Luke. He shrugs his shoulders.

"I'm just mad I didn't think of the idea first," he says. "Seems so damn obvious."

"It is a great idea," Ma says. "When are you going to tell him?"

"I'd like it to be sooner rather than later. What if we flew there in a couple of days? We can scope out some offices to temporarily rent. Short-term leases until we have an idea of what we want, and we can surprise him there."

"I'll look into office space," Savannah offers. "I'm sure I can have a nice list for you by tomorrow evening."

"Perfect. Thank you," I respond. "Maybe we can fly out on Tuesday then."

Mia and Luke agree. Now, I just hope that Marcus doesn't hate me and accepts the offer.

Chapter Thirty-Four

Lexi

The morning sun sneaks in through a gap in the curtains.

I stretch my arms over my head and look to my right. Marcus is sleeping soundly, his mouth halfway open. I smile to myself as I look at him.

Despite him trying to put on a brave face, I know the last couple of days have been hard on him.

He's texted with his family here and there, but nothing really significant. At one point, he will have to acknowledge his feelings about leaving his home.

Even if he is ready to do this, it's okay to feel sad for what he is leaving behind.

He has an entire family unit back there that loves him unconditionally. Sure, they have some issues, like most families do, but I know he will miss them.

I'm not going to force him to deal with it if he's not ready.

I just hope that he doesn't regret moving here down the road. I don't want to be the reason for any unhappiness he has in life.

He begins to stir in his sleep. One eye pops open, and he looks over at me.

He groans. "Why are you watching me like a psycho?"

I laugh. "I can't help it. You look so sweet and innocent when you sleep."

"Sweet and innocent. Are you saying I'm not those things when I'm awake?" he says with both eyes closed.

I shrug despite the fact that he can't see me. "No. It's just extra cute when you're asleep."

He doesn't say anything, so I'm thrown off guard when the comforter flies up, and his arms wrap around my body. He throws me down on the sheets and rolls on top of me.

"Cute...sweet...innocent..." he draws out. "These are not words that people normally use to describe me."

"Well," I smile. "I think they should. You're cute. Especially when your mouth hangs open when you sleep. I can almost picture younger Marcus when I look at you."

His hand grips the side of my stomach and squeezes.

"Maybe I don't want that to be how you describe me when we're in bed together."

I try to contain the laughter as he continues to tickle my side.

"Stop!" I barely get out.

"Only if you promise to only ever describe me with words like sexy and skilled in the bedroom."

I want to refuse, but I also desperately need him to stop tickling me. I decide to cross my fingers when I respond.

"Fine! Fine!" I breathe heavily.

He stops, and I can finally breathe again. His smile spreads across his face effortlessly.

"Good. I was gonna have to," he begins but stops abruptly. I see his eyes zero in on my fingers, which I now realize are still crossed. "Did you cross your fingers when you said that?"

"Uhhh, noo," I lie with them still crossed.

He gasps. "You little shit."

His hand comes back to my side, and my laugh continues.

"Okay, okay." I hold my hands up to show I'm not crossing any fingers. "I promise."

"I don't know if I can trust you anymore. You're sneaky."

He kisses my neck.

"But..." Another kiss. "You're beautiful."

Kiss.

"I think..."

Kiss

"I can forgive you."

I close my eyes and focus on the feelings his lips on my body evoke.

After he spends an adequate amount of time worshipping my body, making me come twice before sliding into me, we get cleaned up in the shower.

"What are the plans for today?" he asks after he takes a sip of coffee.

We're sitting on the couch together after enjoying a nice breakfast of eggs, bacon, and toast.

"Hmmm. Well, I wanted to stop by and see my mom. Since she had such a good day yesterday, I figured we could bring her a little treat."

"Of course. What kind of treat are you thinking?"

"Picking up her favorite dessert. A slice of atomic cake."

He looks at me strangely. "Atomic cake? I've never heard of it."

I smile over my cup of coffee. "You've got a lot to learn about Chicago. I'll just have to introduce you to the famous dessert today."

"I look forward to it. We should pick up some flowers for her too. Her room could use it."

He has been so incredible with my mom. It's only been a couple of days, and he is so concerned with how to make her comfortable and happy. He's patient with her remarks and makes her laugh more often than I've seen anyone do before.

"I forgot to ask what the realtor said about your home yesterday."

"Ah. I need to stop by the post office today. I'm going to mail her a copy of my key. Ma is going to straighten it up, and then she is going to go in with a photographer to take pictures. It should be on the market in the next week."

"Did she tell you how long it should take?"

I know he says not to worry, but it would be nice if he could get it sold sooner rather than later.

"With the pictures I sent her that I had in my phone, she thinks it'll have multiple offers the day it goes on the market. It's a seller's market right now and a highly sought-after neighborhood."

"Are you gonna miss your house?" I ask.

He laughs. "You keep thinking this decision is gonna end up with me filled with regret. The only thing that I would have ever regretted was not doing what I needed to keep us together. Trust me. I'm happy. I'm excited to be here with you."

"Sorry. I'm going to stop asking."

"Good. Now, let's get our day started. I need to start exploring my new neighborhood. We should go out to eat tonight."

We grab our jackets and get into my car.

"Sure. Are you thinking fancy restaurant or more casual?" I ask.

"Let's go for casual."

"Alright. I haven't lived here for over a year. We may need to do some research."

"On it. I'll look some things up this afternoon."

The afternoon goes by quickly. From the errands we ran to the time we spent at the bakery. Marcus loved the atomic cake, but I don't think I've met someone who doesn't.

Mom was in heaven with her slice of the cake. She had another good day today and recognized Marcus right away.

I took him to the local grocery store, where we stocked up on everything we needed. I quickly learned that his taste in food is expensive. He went for thirty-dollar blocks of cheese, sausage that I didn't know could get that expensive, and all the finest wine.

We're gonna have to have a serious talk about my inability to say no to good food. If he wants me to fit in my clothes, I can't live in a kitchen full of these foods all the time.

When we take a break to relax for a bit, I think about when I should start looking for work. It keeps running through my head. I know he wants to take some time to settle in with each other, but I don't have a thick bank account like him, and I don't want to use his money.

It's one thing for him to say he wants to put the down payment on a house; it's something else entirely to use his money for my everyday living costs.

I have a great resume, and everybody needs an IT person, so work generally isn't hard to come by in my field.

The job will likely be in the city, which is okay. I love downtown Chicago. Having lunch on the steps by the river, watching the boats pass by. I always loved it when I would catch the Wednesday or Saturday morning bridge lifts along the river. Watching all the sailboats with the backdrop of the city is a sight worth seeing.

I'm excited to be able to show Marcus these things, too. He finds the fun in every situation, and there's plenty of fun to be had in Chicago.

Chapter Thirty-Five

Marcus

"We should probably get both," I tell Lexi as she is debating between two bottles of wine.

She looks over at me with her insanely adorable face, trying to give me a look of annoyance.

"That's your answer for everything. How about we make a decision and act like two people who don't have jobs."

I smile. "You're right. Let's pretend like we have no money."

I'll go along with it if it makes her feel better. She wants to pretend like my money isn't hers, but she'll get used to it.

"What about this one?" I pick up a five-dollar bottle of wine.

"I mean..." She looks between the fifty-dollar bottle and the five. "We should probably get the cheaper one."

I gasp at her decision. "Absolutely not. Who are you? Did you learn nothing about wine while you worked with me?"

She starts to crack up, bending over to catch her breath.

"Sucker," she finally quips.

"Ooh, you're hilarious," I reply sarcastically, then put the bottle on the shelf and walk away.

She follows behind me. "Aww, can't take a joke, huh?"

I may be a little butt-hurt that she got me, but I'm not going to admit it. Instead, I change the subject to which dessert to get. If there's one thing her brain can get stuck on, it's sugar.

In the bakery section, I spot my Ma's favorite, tiramisu.

I just talked to her last night. She's kept up with me in the four days I've been here. My siblings haven't said anything. Ma even asked for my new address to send us something. I think she's really trying to make us feel loved from afar.

I know my siblings are hurt and confused by my departure, but I guess I was hoping they would be equally supportive of the life change.

This is a huge step for me, and I just wish they were here for me.

I guess I can't expect to leave the company we built together like this and then expect them to be over it within a week.

But I did tell them I'm willing to phase myself out of it. I don't want to leave anyone high and dry.

I just need to get settled here first, and then I can go back and dot my i's and cross my t's.

When we return to the house, a strange car is parked in the driveway.

"I wonder who that is. Maybe they are here for the owners of the home," Lexi says.

When I pull up next to the car, I look over to see Mia in the backseat. Luke and Gabe are in the front.

I'm too stunned for words. I don't know what they're doing here. How did they know where I live? Why didn't they call first?

Lexi and I get out of the car. They follow suit, meeting us at the front of our cars.

Mia comes in for a hug.

"Hi," I say as we hug, then shake my brother's hands. "What are you doing here?"

"It's freezing out here, "Lexi steps in. "Let's all go inside first."

We walk inside the house, and Lexi leads everyone to sit in the family room. Without knowing what they're doing here, my body feels tense.

"So," I say as we all sit in silence. "What brings you to Chicago?"

"There's a lot we have to work through. The three of us didn't like how everything was left between us," Gabe says. "But first, I wanted to apologize for everything. I've thought long and hard about what you said to me, and you're right."

I'm caught off guard. This isn't how I saw this conversation going.

He continues. "I've been insensitive to you. I've spent so long looking at you as someone I need to protect that I was blinded to the fact that you grew up and don't need my protection anymore. You need my support. I'm so sorry I carried that older brother role over to our business. It had no place for it, and it doesn't reflect at all how talented I believe you are."

I have to adjust myself in my seat. Everything he has said hits me straight in the gut. It's everything I've wanted to hear him say, and I'm trying my best not to get emotional.

"I second that," Luke says. "I guess I always look up to Gabe, and instead of breaking away from the pattern, I followed it. It doesn't make it right, but I hope you know how much I love you. I support whatever decisions you make, and I'm so proud of the man you've become."

A lone tear falls down my cheek. I turn my head and try to wipe it inconspicuously before anybody notices.

"And I always knew these two were fools and always believed in you," Mia says. It lightens the mood a bit. "But I'm sorry I never stood up or said anything."

"Way to be humble about it all," Luke replies.

Mia shrugs. "I'm not going down with you."

"I appreciate what you guys just said. It really means a lot," I say. "And you guys didn't have to fly here to make your apology. A phone call really would have been enough."

"Well, that's not the main reason we're here," Gabe states.

"It's not?" I ask. I wonder if they have some business meeting I don't know about and decided to kill two birds.

It hurts a little. Thinking they flew all the way out here for me seemed like an incredible grand gesture to show how much they love me.

"No, we also had some news for both of you," Luke replies.

"What's that?" Lexi asks.

"We've been thinking about your decision to leave the company, Marcus, and it just doesn't feel right." Gabe seems nervous, which is unlike him. "The truth is, you're a huge reason for the success of our company. We love that you came here to be with Lexi, and we're completely supportive of it. Instead of losing both of you, since Lexi has been so valuable to us, we thought you two should open up a Chicago office."

I thought his apology was surprising. This is another level of shock.

"You know we need to expand. Chicago would open up a whole new level of talent that we could hire to train and expand our sales staff. You would be the perfect person to take that on."

"You would trust me to run an office entirely on my own?" I ask.

"Of course. We would also love it if Lexi could continue her role as IT Director. Lexi, you could hire someone underneath you to be our staff member in Cleveland. It may take some trips back to our office to get them trained, but after that, I'd think it would be easily managed from here."

"I don't know what to say," Lexi whispers.

I look over at her, and there are tears in her eyes.

"What do you think?" she asks me.

"You guys aren't doing this out of sympathy or anything?" I ask.

"Marcus!" Lexi hits me. "You know that's not true."

My siblings laugh.

I raise my hands. "I'm sorry. I just don't even know what to say. Of course, I would love to open a Chicago branch. That sounds like a dream."

"Good," Luke smiles. "Just one thing."

"What's that?" I ask.

"You still have to come home and visit... a lot," he says. "I have a baby on the way, and he or she better know it's Uncle Marcus."

"Yeah, and SiSi won't know what to do if she doesn't get her Uncle Marcus's attention," Gabe adds.

It is ridiculous that they even think I wouldn't be home to still be a part of their kids' lives.

"You don't have to worry about that. Lexi and I plan to make it back as often as we can. Right, babe?"

"Of course. I love how close you guys are. I would never want that to change just because we moved."

"Well," Gabe starts. "It looks like we have a deal."

I can't contain my smile. "Deal."

Mia claps her hands excitedly. "Now, do we get to tell them the best part?"

Luke nods at her.

"Savannah found the greatest office downtown for you guys. It's a one-year lease that you can re-sign if you would like. It's small but gives you the room to grow if necessary. There are eight offices, conference rooms, and a nice-sized kitchen. It's also right on the main section of the Chicago River."

Lexi nearly jumps off her seat. "Are you serious? I was thinking the other day about how much I would love to work by the river again."

"It seems like your wish came true. Do you guys want to go check it out?" Gabe asks.

"Right now?" I reply.

"Why not," he says with a shrug. "We could check out the office and then grab some dinner downtown."

"I'm down," Lexi says.

"Our hotel is down there anyway," Mia says. "Why don't we all get cleaned up and meet at the office in a couple of hours?"

We agree to meet there at around four. My siblings hop in their rental car, leaving Lexi and me at the house.

As soon as I shut the door, I turn to Lexi.

"Can you believe it?" she asks with her hands over her mouth.

I shake my head. "Honestly, no. I really didn't see that coming at all."

"It makes sense, though, right? Your largest client is here, and it's a great location for an office. The location alone can put the company on the map for tons of buyers."

"It makes perfect sense. It's just...last week, I went off on them because I thought they didn't value me or my opinion. Today, they are apologizing and trusting me to take on something this significant in our company."

"I don't think they didn't ever value you. You heard them. They always thought they were protecting you. It might just take some time for you to adjust to this."

She's right. She's always right. Everything that has happened in my life since we started seeing each other has been long overdue.

"You're right. All of this, it's because of you."

"What? Not at all. This is all your hard work that they're recognizing."

I grab her hand and pull her to me, wrapping my arms around her waist.

"No, it's you. I would've never stood up for myself if I didn't have your encouragement to do so. You came into my life and opened my eyes to so much. I owe all of this to you. Thank you."

Her face softens as her eyes meet mine. "You're welcome. You did the same for me."

"I didn't do a damn thing," I whisper. "You were always perfect."

"Not true."

She leans in for a kiss. When I woke up this morning, I thought my siblings weren't being supportive. Little did I know, they were about to give me the best gift I'd ever receive from them. It's not the new office or them letting me take on this role; it's the trust they showed that they have in me.

It means the world to me. Because at the end of the day, it's always been the four of us against the world, and I can't imagine a life without them.

Chapter Thirty-Six

Lexi

"How about we pick back up tomorrow morning? I don't want to overload you with too much at once," I tell Roger.

After interviewing him in Cleveland a week ago, I decided to extend the offer to him for the position.

I look out the window as the sun sets over the Chicago River, the reflection of the buildings running along the water.

It's been three weeks since we got the surprise visit from Marcus's siblings, and it's been like a dream ever since.

Marcus and I hit the ground running, setting up the office with the needed equipment. The printer was just installed this morning, which I think was the last thing on our checklist for now.

It's been an adjustment for Marcus. He's still trying to wrap his brain around the fact that they flew out here and handed him his own branch of the company, no questions asked.

I know he feels this immense pressure to exceed their expectations, so I've had to try and calm him down a couple of times.

Luckily, I know his weak spot. I have an array of different shades of lipstick in my desk drawer. When I put one on and meander into his office, his eyes turn darker than the midnight sky.

He pushes away from his desk and makes room for me to get on my knees.

I love how much it provides a release of stress for him.

Speak of the devil. He appears at my doorway—dressed to kill in his perfectly tailored grey suit, leaning against the doorframe.

A grin spreads across his face.

"Have I told you how breathtaking you look with that sunset and view right behind you?" he says.

"Only every day," I reply.

He takes a couple of steps inside. "I can't help it. I have to say it every time."

"You seem to be in an awfully good mood right now."

I lock my computer and stand up. Meeting him in the middle of the room, he takes me in his arms and gives me a soft kiss on the lips.

"I am. I have a surprise for you."

"A surprise? Oooh, what is it?"

He chuckles. "You have to wait and see."

"Ugh, fine. What do you want to do for dinner?"

I grab my purse, and we head out of my office, stopping to lock my door first. He holds my hand as we walk to the elevator.

We're on the thirty-second floor. The ride down to the lobby is fast. Marcus leads me to his car. We took a trip to Cleveland last weekend so he could pack some more things from his house and drive his car back.

His house was sold on the day it was put on the market. We have to go back this weekend to pack everything up. We're going to need another storage unit for his belongings as well.

I've been trying not to panic, but we only have a week left on our current lease. Marcus keeps telling me to chill out, that we can move to a hotel for a while if we need to.

I just don't want to be living out of a hotel for too long. It's such a waste of money, especially with the cost of a room in the city.

The other night, we went over to Grace and Matt's for dinner. Their daughters Layla and Addy were two balls of energy. I thought Marcus was only good with his niece and nephew because they were his family.

I found out he's just good with kids in general. He sat with the girls and let them play dress up with him. He made them burst out in a fit of laughter.

I couldn't help but picture him with our kids. It made me realize how ready I am to start my own family soon. Marcus and I have a lot to do to settle into our new lives; he hasn't even proposed to me, but I could see it all so clearly.

He's it for me. I'll always look back on my time in Cleveland as a pivotal point of my life. It's where I grew, learned to be myself, but most importantly, it's where we fell in love.

Marcus is strangely quiet as he takes us out of the city, winding through back roads.

I try not to ask any questions since I don't want to spoil whatever my surprise might be.

As we continue through the neighborhoods, I notice the houses getting bigger and bigger. Until we suddenly pull into the driveway of a home I've never been to before.

It's huge with a gorgeous white stone exterior. The landscaping is impeccable and gives off a chic European vibe.

"Where are we?" I ask.

He gets out of the car and walks over to my side to open my door. He leads us to the front door, where he types in a code on the lockbox.

"Marcus?" I ask wearily. "Did you buy this house?"

He smiles as he opens the front door. "Of course not." We walk into a foyer I could have only ever dreamed of owning. The dark wooden floors expand beyond the entrance, while the two side entryway stairs make the room feel massive. "I need your permission first before I put in an offer."

"Marcus, this place is too much. I could never help with the payment," I start, but he puts a finger on my lips.

"Babe, stop it. This house would be a present to us from me. It could be the perfect start to our new life out here. Please, just try not to worry about the cost and picture yourself living here. Can you do that for me?"

I nod my head.

"Good. Let's start over here."

He takes me straight to the kitchen.

"Holy. Shit. It's huge."

"Thanks, babe, but I'm trying to show you the kitchen."

I give him the stink eye. "Ha, ha. Hilarious. Seriously, this kitchen is insane."

"I know. I fell in love with it the second I saw it."

I look at him and think I could say the same about you. The first day I walked into the office and met him, I was a bit speechless by how handsome he was. I think I always knew deep down that I felt something different towards him that I hadn't experienced before.

We walk through the backyard, which is big and has a playground set already installed. Is this something that we are going to skate over or acknowledge?

"I like the playground. It'll be perfect for when the kids visit with Gabe and Luke. Plus," he shrugs, "you never know what'll happen with us a few years down the line."

He looks shy as he says it.

I smile up at him. "It's perfect."

As he takes me around the rest of the house, each room is just as beautiful as the last, from the intricate molding to the beautiful hardwood floors.

When we get to the master bathroom, he gets a bit distracted, telling me all the places he wants to have his way with me.

I have to remind him we don't own this place, and what if they're weirdos with cameras everywhere? I don't want to be caught having sex.

He gets to one final room on the first floor. It has two large dark wooden French doors. I don't know what could possibly be on the other side, but he stops and turns around before we go in.

"What's wrong?" I ask.

"Nothing. I just wanted to tell you first that this is the room that has completely sold me on this place. It's not what the room is today, but what it could be."

I raise my eyebrows. "Ok."

He pushes the doors open behind him and then backs into the room.

The room is a large two-story office. The walls are all painted a dark gray. It's decorated beautifully right now, but I lose my breath when I see the floor-to-ceiling bay windows in the front of the room.

I gasp when it occurs to me. "A library."

He smiles. "I knew you'd get it instantly."

"It would be an incredible library. Just like the one you have in your house."

He nods his head as he looks around the room. "Only this time, we would design it together. A little bit of both of us would be incorporated into it."

My eyes begin to water. It sounds absolutely perfect. The nights we've spent together in his library have been some of the best. It was the perfect place to relieve stress in our lives. Well, minus the bedroom. However, we did that in the library, too.

Even thinking about the time on the ladder makes me blush.

"Do you like it?" he asks, staring intently at me.

I nod my head as the tears begin to spill down my cheeks. "I love it. It's amazing."

He takes my face in his hands gently. Wiping away the tears like he has done before.

"You will need to pick out the lounge chair," he says. "I need a good place to rest my head on you and listen to your voice while you read. And it could be a great place for bedtime stories one day."

"Oh God," I laugh as more tears come. "It would be a wonderful place for that."

"So, me saying things like that don't freak you out?"

"I'm looking at a home for us to buy together. I think it's safe to say we're getting a bit serious."

"True. I'm sorry this is all out of order from how it normally progresses."

I laugh. "I don't care. Nothing about us has been normal from the beginning."

He smiles. "You mean people don't pretend to date first like we did before they fall in love?"

"Not that I know of, but I love our story."

"Me too." He leans in for a kiss. "You're the most important thing in my life. I promise I will do whatever I can to make you happy. Our time together in Cleveland will always be where we fell in love, but this new chapter here is where we make our dreams come true."

"My dreams have already come true. They did the moment I met you."

His lips crash back down on mine. I bask in the euphoria that his lips provide.

I can't believe this man is mine. Who knew the disheveled girl I once was would evolve so much into the woman I am today?

The truth is, I owe so much of who I am to everyone who's ever crossed paths with me. Each piece is a part of me, and I cherish each one, even the painful ones. Because each painful memory was a lesson that turned me into the woman that this man fell in love with. And who can regret that?

THE END

Epilogue

Marcus

Three Months Later

That's a wrap. Thank God!

I push away from my desk and stretch my arms over my head. I have to fly to Italy tonight to meet a potential client this week. Lexi has been working too hard lately, and I want to surprise her with a trip.

I already squared everything away with the rest of the gang.

She has no idea she is coming with me tonight.

I did promise her I'd bring her to Italy with me one of these days.

Her mom is finally starting to turn a corner with her physical therapy. She is walking with a cane now.

The night I admitted that I've been secretly paying the bills was interesting. She was upset for a while, until I distracted her by going down on her for an hour.

She eventually gave in. It's what's best for her mom, and we are seeing the results. I think once I pointed out how good her mom was doing, she knew what the right thing to do was.

We've had a great time putting together the Chicago office. She already has the Cleveland IT employee trained, and he's working out great.

We've spent our lunch breaks exploring the city and finding the best places to eat. I really can't imagine a better life.

It all got me thinking.

We're already living together. We're not getting any younger. Her mom still has some of her memory left.

We should get married.

I have the ring tucked safely away in my jacket pocket. I plan to propose when we are in Italy.

My family already knows and are one-hundred percent on board. Everybody is anxiously waiting for pictures.

"Hey," Lexi says, strolling into my office.

She walks around my desk and plops into my lap, wrapping her arms around my neck. Her lips meet mine with a quick and gentle kiss.

"I wanted to say goodbye before you head out. What time do you have to leave?"

I look down at my watch. "Right now."

She gives a little pouty face. "I'm gonna miss you."

I smirk at her. "What if I told you I had a surprise for you?"

"Oooh, what is it? Sex on your desk before you leave?" she says with a smile.

Yeah, we're the only two people in the office. We've fucked on every damn surface of this place. It's been quite an eventful three months.

A deep laugh escapes. "I could do that too. First, why don't you go take a look in my closet."

Her eyebrow raises in suspicion. "You want me to go open your closet? Is something going to pop out at me?"

"Just go, babe."

She climbs off of my lap. "Ugh, fine."

I watch her with a grin on my face as she walks over to the corner of my office. She opens the door, and pauses while she looks up and down. The moment she notices, she turns to me.

"What's my suitcase doing in here with yours?" she asks.

"Well," I stand and meet her at the closet. "I'm glad you asked. You see, I remember telling you that I was going to steel you away on my next trip to Italy. So, that's exactly what I'm doing."

Her eyes open wide in shock. "What? You want me to go to Italy with you?"

I shake my head. "No. I don't want you to. You *are* coming with me. I have it all worked out. Roger is ready to take everything over while you're gone. You can bring your laptop in case of emergencies, but you know he's solid and can handle it. Grace is going to visit your mom. There's nothing for you to worry about."

"But..." she starts, "I don't know a thing about sales. What if I screw it up?"

I chuckle at her concern and wrap my arms around her waist. "You don't have to try to sell anything. Just maybe don't tell them that they're wine sucks and you should be good. You're just there to observe and see how this side of the business works. The rest of the time, we get to explore wherever you'd like."

"Are you serious?" Her eyes light up with excitement.

"Of course, I'm serious."

She engulfs me in a tight hug. "Thank you. Thank you. Thank you."

I can't help but laugh at her enthusiasm. "No problem." I glance down at our luggage. "Now, let's grab our stuff and get out of here. Our plane takes off in an hour."

"Oh my gosh. Let me go pack up my things."

She takes off running in her heels, leaving me behind to shake my head and smile.

This is another thing I love about her. She's adventurous. Some girls would freak out and need to know what I packed for them or if I packed the right outfits and make-up.

Lexi is okay with giving up control and just enjoying the moment. It makes surprising her so much fun.

I grab our luggage and wait for her by the elevator. Within minutes, she comes running towards me, completely out of breath.

"You don't have to run," I say with a smile. "We're only thirty minutes from the airport. Plus, the plane can't take off without us."

"I'm excited! I can't believe I'm going to Italy! You spoil me too much."

I lean down and kiss her. "That's not possible."

We ride the elevator down to the car that's waiting for us. Once I load the luggage, we hop into the backseat.

I can't wait to get a ring on her finger this weekend. I want everybody to know she's taken.

One day, when our kids are older, we will have quite the story to tell them about how we fell in love. It may not have been at first sight, but the moment my lips touched hers, she owned my heart.

Follow the Author

To have access to a Bonus Scene with Marcus and Lexi–
visit my website and subscribe to my newsletter with *Bonus
Scene* written in the message!

www.nicolebakerauthor.com

Facebook @nicolebakerauthor

Instagram @nicolebaker_author

TikTok @authornicolebaker

Also By Nicole Baker

Made in the USA
Monee, IL
04 November 2024

69322823R00225